ANAPHASE

ANAPHASE

DNA STRAND 3

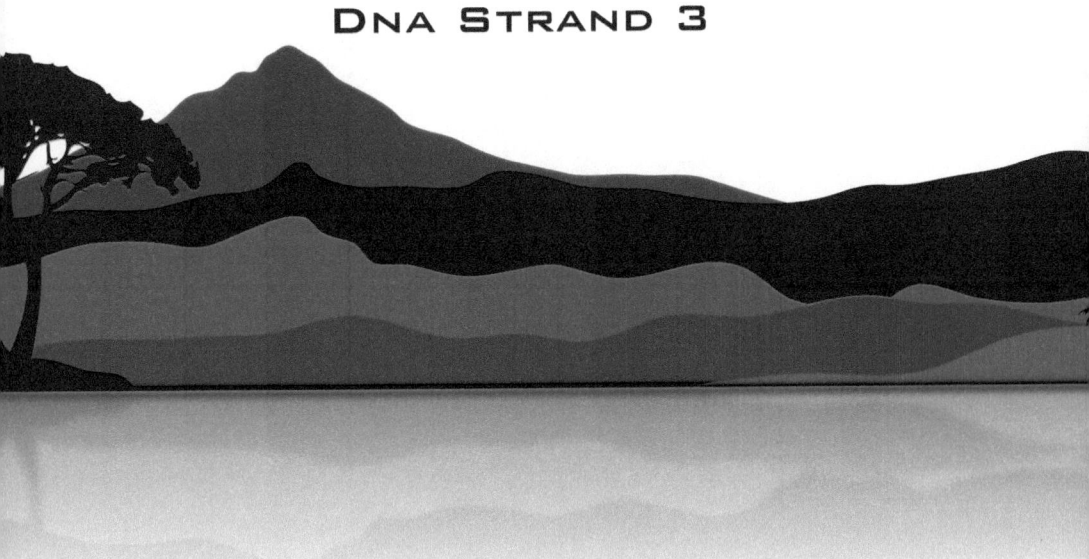

JORDANA WELLS

ANAPHASE

DNA Strand 3

Jordana Wells

Includes SWITCH - a bonus short story

Edited by Karen Robinson

Proofread by Jennifer Oberth

Formatted and Typeset by Jo Michaels

- all of INDIE Books Gone Wild

Cover Design by Robin Ludwig Design Inc.

CONTENTS

Chapter 0 - Nine .... P 1

Chapter 1 - True Love .... P 4

Chapter 2 - Tab A into Slot B .... P 12

Chapter 3 - Killing Time .... P 21

Chapter 4 - Broken Typewriter .... P 26

Chapter 5 - Seeing Red .... P 33

Chapter 6 - Fight for Life .... P 38

Chapter 7 - Black and White .... P 45

Chapter 8 - Angry at God .... P 51

Chapter 9 - The Sky and the Earth .... P 55

Chapter 10 - Stirrings .... P 61

Chapter 11 - Orion's Child .... P 65

Chapter 12 - Unwanted Opportunities.. P 70

Chapter 13 - Jason .... P 78

Chapter 14 - Boundaries .... P 85

Chapter 15 - Not My Monkey .... P 90

Chapter 16 - Veritas .... P 96

Chapter 17 - Risk of Exposure .... P 107

Chapter 18 - A Warm Winter .... P 118

Chapter 19 - A Blow to Mecca .... P 124

Chapter 20 - Dodging a Bullet .... P 131

Chapter 21 - Vigilante .... P 140

Chapter 22 - Bur .... P 146

Chapter 23 - Toe to Toe .... P 154

Chapter 24 - A Time to Kill .... P 159

Chapter 25 - Losing Ground .... P 165

CONTENTS

Chapter 26 - Adrift .... P 170

Chapter 27 - Striking Distance .... P 176

Chapter 28 - Governor's Ball .... P 183

Chapter 29 - Rendezvous .... P 186

Chapter 30 - W + T .... P 194

Chapter 31 - Scar Tissue .... P 201

Chapter 32 - Dry Run .... P 206

Chapter 33 - Doppelganger .... P 213

Chapter 34 - Good Night .... P 219

Chapter 35 - Weak Spot .... P 227

Chapter 36 - Whispers of Death .... P 232

Chapter 37 - Blind Eye .... P 240

Chapter 38 - MoSTly .... P 246

Chapter 39 - Sex Games .... P 254

Chapter 40 - Space Cadet .... P 260

Chapter 41 - Don't Let the Bedbugs Bite .... P 269

Chapter 42 - Date with Destiny .... P 276

Chapter 43 - Inside, Outside, Upside Down .... P 281

Chapter 44 - Wink .... P 288

Chapter 45 - Option One .... P 293

Chpater 46 - Apollo .... P 298

Chapter 47 - Guardrail .... P 306

Chpater 48 - Sheriff Higgins .... P 316

Chapter 49 - Freedom .... P 325

CHAPTER 0

NINE

Lucas was on my mind while I was spreading the parts of the handgun on the threadbare towel. I suppressed the guilt of letting him believe I was dead as well as the unease at the possibility he knew I had survived. Some days I definitely felt eyes on me.

Instead, I tried to remember the assassin's methods for cleaning his gear as I snatched a few minutes for myself out of sight behind a boulder. I had only a smattering of knowledge about the care of guns other than the obvious need to keep them clean, dry, and hidden from a government that would take them.

I had managed to dismantle the weapon in a way that led me to believe I could get it back together again. Lucas had used cloth, brushes, and a special fluid, but all I had were scraps of lint-free fabric and a slim metal rod I'd found on the ground. It would have to be enough.

It was a strange experience trying to remove residue created when Mauss had fired three rounds at me. Well, into me. At me? It was difficult to accurately categorize the event.

My hand went to my chest and pressed so I could feel the lumpiness of the healed ribs. There was no give. My heart beat slowly and steadily within its bony cage.

Thank you for the body armor, God. It was weak and old, and I still ended up needing composite fibers and three mangled bullets dug out of the gore and gristle, but I'm alive.

Into me, I reluctantly decided. The bullets penetrated, but not as much as suggested by the term. Mauss fired into me.

Would I ever get rid of the gun? I didn't like the reminder of that day, but he'd deactivated or damaged the biometric lock so anyone could use it. The biometric printer was also missing from the magazine. Traditional ballistics methods could prove bullets retrieved from different crimes scenes were fired from the same gun, but the bullets themselves wouldn't contain any information about who pulled the trigger.

No, it was better to keep the weapon, at least for now.

Careful not to leave fingerprints, I reassembled the weapon. Should I clean the bullets? I had never seen Lucas do that, but he had cleaned the magazine.

Nine rounds remained. Lighter and smaller than they should've been given their lethal capacity, they were nevertheless difficult for me to touch.

Bullets don't kill people.

My thumb hurt from the force of shoving the rounds back in the magazine and out of sight.

People kill people.

Scalpels don't cut people either; people cut people. People detain and lie and use and cut and shoot and—

"Ty?" Cris called out.

"Over here," I said cheerfully.

My fingers flew, wrapping the gun in the cloth and thrusting the bundle in my backpack. When my boy-friend stepped around the boulder toweling the stream water from his hair, I had one of his philosophy books open on my lap.

He teased, "For a woman who wanted to explore the whole world, I catch you sitting behind rocks reading a lot."

I smiled at him, my expression a facade of innocence and youth.

CHAPTER 1

TRUE LOVE

A week later, the late summer sun picked out the red strands in Cris's dark hair, and I itched to sink my fingers through the mass to the living heat of him beneath. It was 2127, and we'd been working our way west across the Republic of Texas with no other plan than to do what pleased us. I hoped he didn't want to go right up to the Clan Hernandez border, though. I suspected they still had a powerful reason to want me back.

Even so, my calculations suggested Cris and I could roam for another few weeks before I had to ease us on a southerly heading.

As he neared, I saw a pale strand in his hair and frowned slightly. Was that a gray hair? He was in his mid-to-late thirties, and I looked barely twenty-one. He generally didn't have a problem with our apparent age difference, teasing me that I was an old soul.

I automatically started doing the math to figure out exactly what our age difference was, but it depressed me so I gave it up yet again and focused on the easy strength of his big body instead of the signs he was aging.

"You've got to stop stealing my Kierkegaard," he said.

He was nowhere as orderly about his pack's contents as I was about mine, which is why I'd thought I could get away with appropriating his book. When he'd finally had to upend his bag to find his smallest screwdriver, he'd only needed a glance across the mess to see a book was missing. At least the man had his priorities straight.

He burst into laughter. "Oh, my God, I can't believe I said that." He swept me off my feet and whirled me around. "You read Kierkegaard."

I burrowed into his embrace. What we had couldn't last. He seemed to know it, too, never asking anything about my past and rarely mentioning the future. When we'd met and compared notes about Jason's disappearance, I'd mentioned the lab, but Cris had apparently dismissed what I'd said as a childish bid for attention. By the time he and I had crossed paths again years later, his brother, my former mentor, had safely returned from his mysterious journey, so it must've been easy for Cris to pretend the past didn't matter. I tried to, but it often felt like it clung to me like my shadow.

He set me on my feet and scooped up the flower that had fallen from my hair.

I'd forgotten about that flora. I'd found it balanced on my backpack in the morning and hadn't found the nerve to ask if he'd left it for me. The last time someone had given me flowers, he had breached the lab's security to sneak into my room while I slept. The gesture hadn't been romantic either. Those particular flowers had warned of an enemy within the walls.

The ground around my knapsack was too rocky to hold footprints, so hours ago, when Cris had taken the flower from my hand and tucked it behind my ear, I'd wanted to believe he was the one who'd left me the gift.

In case he meant to return it to my hair, I stepped away. He looked like he wanted to say something, and I failed to think up an explanation for my odd behavior.

With the flower cradled in his hand, he closed the distance between us and kissed the tip of my nose. "You look beautiful with it, but please don't pick flowers from the wild again. The pollinator insects need all the food they can get."

I struggled to find my voice. Someone *was* watching me.

I snatched the flower from his hand and was about to grind it beneath my heel when I thought better of it.

I rifled through my pack and retrieved my notebook and pencil. A photo would've been preferable, but I wasn't comfortable with using Cris's palmer for anything related to the lab.

The sprig was already limp, the cut end shriveled. The white pointed sepals surrounding the tiny, clawed petals fell off as I sketched. The flower sat in a ring of airy bracts and ferny leaves that were hopefully so distinctive that identification would be easy once I had access to a computer on the network.

Once I was satisfied I had the necessary data, I let the bloom fall to the ground to disintegrate and feed the local ecosystem.

"I didn't mean to hurt your feelings," he said, lips turning downward at the edges at the sight of the discarded flower.

"You didn't," I said. "You're right. I drew it so I can keep it forever instead of a day or two."

"What a great idea."

"Will be when I learn how to draw," I said, showing him my sketch.

His mouth twitched, but he assured me it was a wonderful likeness.

I returned my notebook and pencil to their proper places in my pack.

"Oh, and don't be so pleased I read Kierkegaard," I told him as I held out his book. "I read anything."

"Do you know how tough it is to find someone who is willing and able to read difficult material? The conversations you and I have are *amazing*. You're too good to be true."

I felt someone's presence and whirled to see a woman limp into our campsite. Because her back was to the sun, she could see us a hell of a lot better than we could see her, but she seemed to be in raggedy clothes and worn shoes.

"Got any water to spare?"

"No," I said without hesitation.

"Please. I haven't had anything to drink in three days."

Ignoring her, I loaded my pack into the Beast. With the flower man around, I wanted to sleep somewhere secure tonight even if it meant driving for hours to get to a big city hotel. If her situation were real, I ached for her, but her choice of approach suggested cunning, not desperation.

"I do have a little filter you can have," Cris said. "I made it myself, so it'll probably last longer than anything you can buy around here."

"Need the water, not a filter," she said.

I told her, "Tell the men you brought with you to show themselves."

"I'm alone."

"I can see their shadows moving."

As if surprised her crew could be so sloppy, she turned to look but stopped herself.

I dropped down so her friends couldn't get a clean shot. Since finding ammo was such a challenge, most people didn't have guns, but people had found plenty of ways to kill each other before firearms had been invented.

I pulled Cris's shotgun out of the scabbard and crouched behind the Beast, resting the barrels on the hood and putting her squarely in the sights.

Walk away, lady. You're a sloppy, petty thug who saw our books and our manners and followed us out here thinking we were easy marks, but I have no intention of making this easy. Leave before you make me show Cris what a bitch I can be.

"Press on," I told her, finger light on the trigger. "Bayness is four hours from here on foot. They'll have water."

I pointed north, but her eyes had already darted south, the direction the town actually was.

I smiled. She knew exactly where she was and where she could find water.

Her eyes narrowed, and my smile widened.

See, I proved what you are yet again. You can't win, so stop trying. I've had a belly full of killing already. Can't you see I want to be left alone? I'm not bothering anyone, so please leave while you still can.

At the back of the vehicle, Cris took out one of his clever filters. "Take it," he urged the woman. "It really does work."

I told him, "She's a local. We're keeping the filter for someone who honestly needs it."

He tossed it at her, and she caught it easily, smiling at me. "See you later."

"Not unless I see you first."

She acknowledged that with a slight dip of her head and left, her gait far less pitiful than it'd been on her way in.

Twenty minutes later, when Cris and I were well and truly clear, I stopped scanning the freeway behind us and pretended to choke him. "Stop offering thieves the means to stay healthy enough to rob us."

"Even thieves don't deserve to die from a water-borne illness."

Frankly, I was okay with them getting diarrhea.

As he drove, the Texas wind whipped my hair around, reminding me I had yet to master the French braid that would prevent anyone from being able to grab my hair in a fight. Shaving off my hair was a better solution, but it would've made me stand out and given me yet another area to slather with insanely priced sunscreen.

"So I guess you don't fall apart in an emergency," he commented.

"That reminds me," I said. "Will you show me how to use your rifle? I don't even know where the safety is."

Amused, he said, "For a woman who doesn't know what she's doing, you run a fine bluff."

"Seriously? Because I thought it was obvious I was about to wet my pants."

"It didn't show," he promised me. "And it's a shotgun, not a rifle. It doesn't have a safety."

"Ah," I said, pretending to digest that. I'd known all along how to fire his shotgun. It would've been a useless tool if I'd been ignorant. "Good to know."

"Now back to Kierkegaard..."

A few hours later, Cris perked up at the sight of a small, rundown town that had struggled to get a foothold in the scrabbly dirt on either side of the highway. When he pulled in front of the diner, I grimaced. He had a disconcerting trust, choosing to enjoy the flavorings of the local cuisine instead of questioning the meat source. Personally, I favored being able to properly gauge the risk of intestinal parasites. Well, and growing up as an American, I preferred to think of certain animals as pets, not a food supply.

"You go ahead without me," I told him, politely refusing his extended hand. "Last time I pulled a whisker out of my stew."

"You did not eat puppy meat," he promised me.

My stomach flipped over. Spying a distinctive antenna on a roof down the street, I told him, "Please, take your time. I'll be at the learning center."

According to the online databases, Love-in-a-Mist was a flower widespread in English cutting gardens, not the Texan wilderness, but it was easy to grow from seed. Its usual color was blue, but some varieties were white. Satisfied with the identification of my mystery sprig, I glanced around the room to see if anyone was getting impatient for the computer. People were waiting, but I needed to do one more search, so I signaled to the next person in line that I was almost done.

Love-in-a-Mist indeed had a specific meaning in the Victorian language of flowers: perplexity.

I sat back, frowning.

Perplexity? Whoever had left me the flower was puzzled? About what? Why I wasn't in lab custody? Why I was with Cris? Who the hell was this guy? Finley had known, and he hadn't been pleased. I'd thought the ashes in the second lab's incinerator were those of the flower man, yet here he was.

Worse yet, he showed skill at sneaking into my campsite. I could've learned that when he slit my throat. I used to sleep lightly, catching ten or fifteen minutes between periods of still watchfulness. How easy it had been to slip into complacency.

Should I tell Cris of the breach in our security? Or would it be enough to move to another area of the outlands, sleeping with Mauss's gun in the hand that wasn't wrapped in my boyfriend's?

"Ty?"

I exited the search program and scrambled to my feet. "Right here."

"You don't have to leave yet. I can get the groceries."

Touched by the thoughtfulness and aching from our short separation, I lifted up on my tiptoes and kissed him. I even tasted his toothpaste instead of mystery meat.

"No, I'll go with you. I just wanted to check the weather forecasts anyway."

Beaming at me, he laced his fingers with mine. "So let's go."

As we strolled away, I tried to enjoy the sensation of his warm fingers among mine, but all I could think was that he'd taken my gun hand.

CHAPTER 2
TAB A INTO SLOT B

A few days later, I was stargazing with Cris's high-powered binoculars when he stretched out beside me, facing me so his breath washed over my cheek.

I asked, "Want to see the Andromeda galaxy? I'll set up the tripod."

"Another time," he said. "It's time to talk about the future."

"Of what?"

"You and me." His features were flat and ominous in the moonlight. Was he dumping me? "You know there's more to life than drifting, don't you?"

"Like what?"

"I was thinking about renting a house somewhere and getting a job," he admitted. "This is the longest I've gone without having one."

I frowned. "That's not a reason to get one."

He looked sheepish. "Well, I love admiring the sunrise, discussing philosophy, and trying to get into your pants, but I don't feel like I'm making meaningful contributions to society. Even one person can make a difference."

"Of course one person can't make a difference," I murmured, my argument half-hearted because I was distracted by his mention of sex. "Hitler couldn't have accomplished anything without his supporters."

Perhaps I should've fought the attraction to someone so experienced, so potent. Even the passion of his kisses overwhelmed me sometimes. He'd been patient so far, surrendering the lead while reminding me he was there for as much or as little as I wanted, but the force of his masculinity was always there between us.

I needed to get it over with. My rebuilt body still had its hymen, so I suspected the first time wasn't going to be pleasant, but having sex would bring me one step closer to the life I wanted.

Cris was big, though. Big hands, big body, big erection. Why couldn't I have fallen for one of those mythical men with small penises? I tried to imagine riding him. There was a lot to straddle. Big hips. I could already imagine how badly the muscles in my ass were going to cramp.

I did want to make love to him, though. He was smart and ironic and sexy and fascinating. The lab had said all my body parts operated at an optimal level, so was I really postponing the event over a few minutes of discomfort?

My heart skipped a beat, giving me a moment of panic that my bodily wiring was failing. My fingers slipped to my throat and pressed against my carotid. The blood pulsed smoothly, steadily. I was all right. It was just the thought of the lab that had triggered the misfire.

I glanced at Cris from beneath my lashes. Intimacy with him meant I would have to forget about lying down on operating tables. I would have to forget about hands on me bringing pain instead of pleasure. I would have to forget the number of times I went to sleep assuming I was safe only to discover upon waking surgery had been performed without my consent. I had escaped the lab physically, and all I had to do to get my life back was to escape it mentally.

Interrupting his assertion of how one person could indeed change the world, I said, "We should have sex."

"That's the same tone you used at breakfast to tell me we should have oatmeal for the manganese. Very romantic."

"I'm not a romantic person."

"I am," he informed me. "Where are the chocolates and violins?"

I pointed at the gibbous moon. "Moonlight. That's classic romance. May we please have sex now?"

"Nice. You now sound like a little girl begging for candy. I feel like the pedophile your friend accused me of being."

"He wasn't my friend." The twist in my belly at the disloyalty to Lucas made me recant. "Well, yes, he was my friend. Sort of. I don't want to think about him. Do you have a condom?"

"Stop trying to get me into bed."

I scrubbed my cheeks with my hands, muttering, "I couldn't suck any more at this. If sex were engineering, I would've had your binary one in my binary zero by now."

He laughed and gathered me up. "One of my brothers dates dumb girls, but I'll take a genius any day of the week."

"Even Thursdays?"

"Especially Thursdays."

"What is that?" Cris asked me less than an hour later.

I colored. Why was I embarrassed? I hadn't been the first time around. Then again, my first lover had been so clueless he hadn't actually noticed anything had been in his way.

"Nothing," I lied. Why did I lie? What the hell could possibly be gained from it?

He retreated slightly and eased forward again. I fought to keep my legs wide instead of closing in an attempt to keep him out.

"Ty, have you ever had sex before?" he asked delicately.

"Of course I have," I said defiantly.

"In this particular orifice? Because that's either what I think it is, or you forgot to take something out before you let me in."

I was dying. I'd been through so much in my life, but humiliation over this one round of intimacy threatened to level me. "I'm not a virgin, but I'm intact. There, I said it. It's not a big deal. Everyone starts out a virgin."

And some of us get to be one twice. Lucky me.

"I don't like hurting women at all, let alone making them bleed."

"Fine. I'll go out and be redehymenated by someone else. Give me the keys."

"You're not going anywhere," he said firmly as he withdrew.

My legs almost snapped shut.

"You want to tell me how old you are again?" he said, looking down at the vise my legs made.

"There's nothing wrong with me," I barked. "And I'm of age."

I hoped he didn't press that point because I wasn't exactly sure how old I was anymore. Twenty? Twenty-one maybe? Older than eighteen, at any rate.

"There's nothing wrong with you," he agreed. "Just let me think a minute."

"I can tolerate you making me bleed this once, so you can withstand it as well. Let's write off this round of sex as a necessary evil and then start fresh tomorrow night."

He laughed uncertainly. "Necessary evil. Great."

"Well, let's get it over with."

"Stop talking," he suggested.

Lying between my legs, he gave me a few gentle pushes and gritted his teeth. "It's like it's made of some industrial alloy."

"Thrust, don't push," I told him, forcing my fingernails to withdraw from the muscles in his shoulders. "Put your back into it."

"Stop being such a bossy virgin. I'm trying not to hurt you."

"I'm not a virgin."

His nose twitched ominously.

"You look like a bug flew up your nostril," I said. "Or are you trying not to laugh?"

He sneezed and speared me. I cried out, my back arching.

"God, I'm so sorry," he gasped, paling. "Just hold absolutely still so I don't hurt you any more."

He sneezed again without warning.

"For the love of Christ," he said, withdrawing hurriedly. He sneezed twice more in rapid succession.

"Maybe you're allergic to me," I commented, grinning in relief that the deed was finally done. It had been painful, but the discomfort was already fading.

"Just your hymen, apparently," he said weakly. When he saw the blood, he gagged. "Oh, God. Let me go vomit behind a bush, and I'll get you some aspirin and a warm cloth to clean you up."

"Vomit? Who's being romantic now?" I teased.

He stumbled away, tugging at the condom.

16

I laced my fingers behind my head and grinned at the thought of how pissed my surgeon would've been about the loss of my virginity. He'd treated me like his own personal property, too valuable to be used the way nature intended.

Cris retched out of sight, and I laughed, loving the unpredictability of life outside the lab.

"Does this require self-soothing with new books?" I asked. "Because if that's the case, I've been traumatized, too."

As I perused the selection of books to trade at the ragged learning center the next morning, I felt my lips press together in disapproval and forced them to relax. So what if there wasn't an academic book in the tattered stack? A world of information would be at my fingertips if I were willing to get an electronic device. Granted, every keystroke would be tracked by Texas's Home Security Bureau as well as a plethora of advertisers. Some would argue it was a small price to pay for access to more books than I could read in a lifetime. But those people weren't hiding secrets like mine.

"There are other ways. You know the clones are out there."

Alarmed, I swung around to stare at the pair of women leaving the sole working computer terminal. I must've heard wrong.

As I'd browsed, I'd managed to mostly ignore their tearful frustration as they checked on a loved one's position on the organ transplant waiting list. It was a theme I knew all too well, having succumbed to kidney failure myself once. But she hadn't actually mentioned a clone, had she?

"That's just a rumor," the other said. "Don't waste my time."

The feeling of a fist squeezing my heart eased.

"Don't kid yourself. The technology is out there no matter what that stupid computer says. It's simply a matter of finding it."

"And paying for it. Even if I sold everything I have, would it even be enough for a black market organ?"

"We have to try. Or do you want Miguel to die before his tenth birthday?"

I wanted to leave, but my feet wouldn't move.

"What about the clone?" I asked in a strangled voice. "You can't be okay with killing an innocent person to get the part you need."

"No, they grow the organs in dishes, don't they?" the worried mother asked her friend.

"Of course. This eavesdropping bitch doesn't know what she's talking about." The friend turned to me. "Even if we were considering using a full clone, okay, first, they don't have souls, so it's not like they're real people. Second, that's what they're made for. Third, it would have to be a humane termination so the organs stayed intact. Fourth, you'd do it, too, if it were your kid."

Ice on my spine, I listened to the argument. We had the attention of the people around us, but no one looked like they disagreed with her. In fact, any hostility was aimed my way, not theirs. Must've been a popular little kid.

"Are you a vegetarian?" she asked me, getting so close to me I took an involuntary step backward. "The animals you eat are raised for a purpose. The ones you catch in the wild were put there by God for us to eat. Otherwise they wouldn't be edible. We should've been cloning for medical purposes a long time ago."

I bit my tongue, forcing my hands to stay flat against my thighs instead of curling into fists.

"So are you a vegetarian or not?"

I turned away.

"That's what I thought," she called out. People laughed.

I strode to Cris's vehicle and threw my unexchanged books in the back.

"Trouble?" he asked as he approached with a small bag of parts.

"Nothing more than a systemic lack of ethics. I'm becoming a vegetarian, by the way."

"Do I have to, too?"

"No, I respect your right to eat the way nature designed you to eat. You've got the teeth and digestive system of an omnivore, so feel free to omnivate."

"But you now have a cow's four stomachs?"

"Don't confuse the issue with facts and logic. I'm full of angst over killing fowl for the meat."

He fought back a smile. "So we're both eating vegetarian for the next three weeks or so and then we're probably going back to being omnivores?"

I sighed. I wanted to ask him how he felt about cloning, but it was a deal-breaker if he gave me a response like that woman's. He had a higher sense of morality and ethics than most people I'd come across, but if we were still in the courtship phase, perhaps it was more act than truth.

His eyes showing his seriousness, he brushed his lips across mine. "I feel guilty about slaughtering them, too. I've been a vegetarian on and off since I was fifteen. It'll be a challenge getting what we need to do it in the outlands, but I'm willing to try."

"Practical vegetarianism?" I offered. "When we can swing it, we do it, but if we can't get the protein we need, chickens have to die."

He choked on a horrified laugh.

"Survival versus ethics," I said, frowning, realizing I was edging closer to the woman's argument. "Rationalization is a powerful tool, isn't it?"

"Couldn't get through the day without it," he agreed, not looking the least bit proud of that. "What really happened in there?"

"I'm an evolved being in a land of cavemen."

"The same cavemen who successfully formed family units and still had enough time after all the hunting and killing to create art on their walls?"

My smile was reluctant. "Poor choice of words on my part."

"Such elegant paintings, too. I find it fascinating that there seems to be an innate need in human beings to create art."

"It's recordkeeping, not art."

He grinned. "Looks like we've found today's topic. I totally expected you to bring up bioethics after I saw how upset you were during that news report about the new biotech laws."

My jaw tightened. "Recordkeeping. Journaling. Pride over a big kill. Not art."

My eyes went to the side mirror as we drove away, and I saw the two women leaving the learning center. Impotent rage twisted my gut and brought a flush of color to my cheeks. I shifted my gaze and saw my reflection. Her reflection. The reflection of the laboratory-created being whose life had been cut short to make room for mine.

I closed my eyes.

CHAPTER 3

KILLING TIME

A few days later, Cris sat with his arms crossed over the steering wheel and his cowboy hat pushed back on his head as he regarded the muddy, turbulent creek. "So much for it being the dry season. What do you think?"

His hybrid vehicle had a snorkel, but I said, "I was taught you can't trust the depth or speed of floodwater. We could camp here tonight and see if it goes down."

"Getting low on food."

"We have plenty."

"Getting low on food I like to eat now that we're out of hot sauce," he said, sending me a sideways smile. "We could drive south for an hour and if there's no way to cross it, we'll rethink waiting it out. I really don't want to turn back."

Thirty minutes later, he hit the brakes with enough force to send me flying against my harness.

"Sorry," he said with a grimace. "But see it behind the trees? Isn't it perfect? No tracks either, so it's probably abandoned. I want to take a look."

We parked a respectful distance away and approached the house slowly, giving any inhabitants plenty of warning we were coming. Cris called out that we were friendly, and I bit back the comment it was probably what everyone said no matter their motives.

When Cris knocked on the front door, it opened a little. "Hello?" he called out. "We're interested in possibly buying your property. Is anyone here?"

I pushed through the door before he could stop me. The house had been empty for a while if the dust was any indication. The structure was intact, though. It was a solid little building built by someone who'd put considerable thought into the layout and materials used. Even on this frigid day, the house wasn't as dark and chilly as I expected. When I said as much, he indicated the large bank of windows where the sun shone through the leafless branches.

"Passive solar. Heat sink, too," he said, pointing to the stonework fireplace with a satisfied smile. He crossed the room and peered up into the chimney. "Flue's intact. I want this house. Is it too far from everywhere for you?"

"Farther's better for me," I said. I peered out the kitchen window to the concrete block boundaries and rotten trellises of a kitchen garden. "Small outbuilding out there. There's a lot to like, but let's be practical. We can set up wind and solar power with little fuss, but if that creek is only there after days of rain and there's no well, we're screwed. As it is, we're at least five kilometers from that water source. That's a hike of forty-five minutes."

"I'll build an aqueduct," he said, looking thrilled to death to put his engineering skills to good use.

I wandered the property for the rest of the day, trying to figure out its boundaries. It looked like the area had once been an enormous subdivision, but the houses had been leveled long ago, leaving nothing but cracked concrete pads with a few pipes sticking up out of the ground and a few basements filled with debris. How long had it been since people had lived in this neighborhood? Fifty years? Seventy-five? Longer? The little homestead wasn't that old, surely.

He joined me as I surveyed the area with his binoculars.

"What do you think?"

"You need to check the entirety of that aqueduct I found," I told him, pointing in the general direction without lowering the binoculars. "For the creek being that high, there should be more signs of water at our end."

"I will."

"Are you sure you want to do this? I'm happy with solitude, but you're a social man who's already craving a job. Where would you work?"

"I want meaningful occupation. Creating a homestead would suit me for a while, especially if we could donate extra vegetables to the food banks."

I made a doubtful noise. "Let's squat here for a month and see how you feel about it before we hunt down a deed."

He looked uneasy. "Someone owns this. Even walking through it made me uncomfortable."

"Okay, so we'll camp beyond the boundary where you think the plot ends. It'll give us time to examine the plants to get a feel for what'll grow and check the water quality. I'm a little concerned by the lack of wildlife, too. If there's food, water, and shelter, there should be animal signs."

Unfortunately for him, a sudden, violent storm sent us trespassing into the shelter of the house anyway. After dark, the weather eased, but he fell asleep amid his protests that we should leave. Seeing no reason to rouse him, I curled against him and went to sleep.

I woke alone. It was pitch black.

The killing time.

I knew better than to call out, to make any sound, any movement at all at first. Some nights in my dreams, I still saw the bright muzzle flash accompanied by the muffled pop of the round traveling through the silencer.

Wind pushed through the cracks of the homestead in a whine one moment and a howl the next. The reassuring bulk of my pack was against my hip, and I shifted so I could reach Mauss's gun.

Be silent. Don't rush. Get the gun and hide because it's the killing time.

A door banged open, and I rolled onto my back, weapon pointed at the sound, my finger slipping off the safety as a bitter cold gust stung my cheeks.

"Shit," Cris said under his breath, the soft glow of his palmer casting eerie green shadows. He snatched the doorknob and shut the door, struggling with the latch.

Jesus. I'd almost blown him away.

I shoved the gun back in my pack before he could see it. "You scared me," I snapped.

"I'm sorry. I had to piss and didn't think to check if the plumbing was intact while it was still light out. It's so dark out there, I almost broke my ankle. Mind if I turn on the lantern?"

"I don't care what you do as long as it involves curling around me at some point. I'm freezing."

"I've heard the best way to warm a human body is to both be naked as we curl up together," he said innocently.

Thinking the best way to banish my memories would be to create new ones with my man, I said, "I would love that."

CHAPTER 4

BROKEN TYPEWRITER

Months later, as the first sliver of the sun peeked over the horizon, I felt a piercing pleasure. Seeing that big fiery ball emerge from the darkness was never going to get old.

Sitting on the uneven rock on the east side of the house was less enjoyable. The percolating in my abdomen, well, that was already getting old.

It was possible the discomfort was a warning I was getting ready for a period. They had been light and infrequent since I'd left the lab, but still, my nose wrinkled at the thought of having one. I wasn't a fan of bloody messes, particularly when it was my own blood.

The screen door squeaked as Cris left the house. He sat beside me without touching, but I could still feel his heat. He held out a mug of dandelion root tea, but I declined. It tasted like burnt coffee to me.

"Pretty morning," he murmured.

"They all are to me."

"How are you feeling?"

I glanced at him, surprised by the question. "Good. How are you feeling?"

He smiled slightly but didn't answer. "You can tell me anything. You know that, right?"

My brow furrowed as I studied his expectant face. "I'm not a mind reader. If there's something you want to ask me, ask me."

"I did. I asked you how you felt, and you gave me a meaningless reply," he said without heat.

"Specifically, I've got a blister on my hand from double-digging the garden beds, my left ear is ringing, and I'm going to have my period so my belly's upset."

"About that," he said, gesturing to my hand cradling my abdomen. "So you're having your periods?"

"My belly feels odd, and I'm all bloaty," I said. "But that could easily be the cabbage from yesterday's lunch."

He sat by my side for a long time, sipping his tea.

The sun felt good, like its heat was penetrating me to the core. That plus the warmth radiating from Cris made me feel like I was wrapped in a blanket.

"Are you going to town this morning?" he asked.

"I can if you need me to."

He shook his head. "Don't worry. I can pick it up on my way home from work."

It, I found out that night, was a home pregnancy test.

"Your scent is different," he told me. "I thought it might be my imagination, but I can't ignore it now that you've got symptoms."

I gave him an odd smile. "Don't you think I'd know if I were pregnant?"

"I would've thought so, but humor me."

"You wear a condom," I reminded him. "Always."

"Accidents happen."

27

I shook my head. "I have periods."

"Near as I can tell, you've spotted for a day or two here and there. I looked it up, and some pregnancies come with a little spotting."

The next morning, I followed the instructions to direct my concentrated urine flow over the first stick and put five drops of blood in the well of the second stick.

He compared my results with the photos on the box. His dark eyes flicked to mine.

"Both indicate a pregnancy," he said in a neutral tone.

We stared at each other watchfully.

The awkward silence stretched until I asked, "Is this a problem?"

"You tell me."

Coward.

"I do want to have a kid at some point, but this is just…" I couldn't come up with any words. I'd been away from the lab less than two years and still struggled with letting go of that fear and pain.

"Well, on my end, even though it wasn't intentional, I honestly don't mind the idea of being a father."

His tone suggested otherwise.

"But?"

He shrugged. "The MoD encouraged my parents to have kids and stay together to raise them. Their relationship suffered a lot from the pressure. I don't know why the MoD thought it would be better for the five of us to grow up in a household where our parents fought so bitterly."

"You're saying we need to figure out what we want to be to each other over the long haul," I said with a sinking belly, feeling the weight of reality threatening to smother me. Coming up with a long-term plan wasn't exactly my specialty. I was crazy about Cris, but I'd never planned on committing to him.

"Are you going to get an abortion?" he asked me.

My hands shot over my belly protectively. Texan law required the request of only one parent for an abortion to be done, so if he didn't want a kid, it would be a scramble to get away before the cops could catch me for dodging my legal obligation.

"Are you going to make me?" I said coldly.

"No. Never."

I relaxed. Sort of. "Well, no, never right back at you."

He gave me a lopsided smile.

"I might be having a baby," I said, shocked. I dragged a kitchen chair to the bathroom and stood on it so I could see my abdomen's profile in the mirror over the sink. I pushed down my jeans and lifted my shirt.

"Ty, you couldn't have been that innocent as to what your bodily changes meant."

"I thought I was bloating," I protested. "Shouldn't I be having morning sickness?"

"That's a baby," he decided, peering at my minuscule bump.

"Perhaps it's a tumor."

"I'm pretty sure that's not a tumor. We need to see a doctor."

I covered myself and hurriedly left the room. "I don't like doctors."

"You're not in the system, are you?"

I whirled at him. "No, I'm not. I'm free, and I refuse to let some government tell me who I can and cannot make a baby with. No one's taking my freedom, my body, or my child."

"Well, long live the revolution, but I would still like to know if my baby's healthy and seated properly in your womb. I can probably learn enough to serve as your mid-wife, but I'm not going to be able to pull off an atypical birth. Like it or not, we need to see a doctor."

"A doctor won't see me if I'm not in the system," I said triumphantly. "This baby's going to be born free."

"I guess that answers my question whether you finished the book on the revolutionary Thomiss Grohout," he sighed. "Look, if I can find a doctor who won't register you, will you please—"

"No. I feel fine. The baby's fine."

"Woman, I knew you were pregnant before you did, so forgive my disbelief that you know how he's doing. My brother's girlfriend is a pediatrician. I'll tell her I want to check for STDs so she'll let me use her Big Blue for a private bioscan. No one will know you were with me."

"No records?"

"I promise."

"Well, okay," I said.

Again we were staring at each other, this time with cautiously delighted expressions. He looked like he very much wanted to hug me, but I didn't want him to ruin what I felt by overwhelming me with affection so I didn't go in for the embrace.

That night after he went to bed, I stretched out on the couch and curled my hands over my abdomen, amazed that another life was growing inside me.

So it was possible. Redemption. God had given me a child. I sent waves of appreciation and love to the Creator for the trust and faith He put in me. The lab hadn't been able to break my soul after all. My life was so beautiful.

I brushed away tears before they could drip into my ears.

"Are you okay?" he asked from the doorway, his voice deep and husky.

"As if you weren't enough of a blessing, now God gave me this," I said, flexing the hand over my bump.

He rushed toward me with a groan of relief. "When I saw you crying, I thought you—"

"Never. The more I think about it, the more amazed I am this is happening to me."

I lifted my shirt, pushed my panties down a bit, and placed his hand on the swelling.

"Hello, baby," he murmured and bent down to kiss my abdomen. "How are you tonight?"

It took me a minute or two to regain my composure. Sharing my pregnancy with someone in such a personal way changed the whole experience for me somehow.

"I talked to him while you were in the shower," I confessed in a tiny voice. "The fetus. I let the sun shine on my bare skin, too. I'm not certain when a fetus develops hearing or sight, but it was important to me that he hear my voice and see the sun. Remember when you were a kid and you'd hold a flashlight against your palm and there was a bright pink glow on the top of your hand? Or when you heard sounds with your head underwater? I don't want my child to grow in silence and darkness, you know?"

He smiled his understanding.

I said slowly, "I don't want the kid to know he was unplanned. Someone once told me that fetuses pick up on the mother's thoughts, so I'm trying to be positive and welcoming in my thoughts like this was the plan all along."

His big tanned hand smoothed over my abdomen, and his eyes were luminous as he gazed at the swelling. "I'm going to be a papa."

I wrapped my hand around the back of his neck and drew him closer. "I want you," I said huskily against his lips.

"Are you sure?"

"Very."

But by midnight, I cried again, this time locked in the bathroom with my heart clenched into a knot. How could I have forgotten I wasn't in my born body anymore? That my cloned body got pregnant at all was a miracle, but conceiving and being able to give a fetus what it needed for nine months were two different things.

And what about afterward? What if everything went right, and I ended up holding an infant in my arms? Could Cris and I actually live together day after day, year after year? How long could he go without asking me about my past? More to the point, how would I be able to protect either of them if the lab came after me?

Christ, he had fertilized a clone's egg. How horribly wrong could that go? What if people learned what my child was? What if they went after my kid the way Mauss had come after me in his attempt to keep the human race pure? What if the lab wanted my child to experiment on even more than they'd wanted me? How far would they go to get him?

I saw stars as the anxiety jacked up my heart rate and respiration. When my nose went numb, I grabbed it.

"Just stop it," I muttered. "Calm down. This is going to be okay. I'll find a way to make it work. It's just another problem with multiple solutions like any other."

I went outside and stared up at the heavens.

I trust in You, God. I promise I will eat properly and think properly and see a doctor every few days if they say that's the best way to keep the fetus happy and healthy. Thank You for entrusting me with such precious cargo.

CHAPTER 5

SEEING RED

In the finished basement of his brother Shaun's house, Cris watched me as I programmed the bioscanner. My mouth was tight with tension as memories of the lab threatened to overwhelm me. The glacial chill of the tiny built-in medical suite, the harsh lighting, and the god-awful purity of the easy-to-clean white walls and flooring were all the same. All that was missing was the glint of silver as Isidro wielded his scalpel with that peculiar smile of his that told me he had enjoyed cutting into me a little too much when I pissed him off.

Cris opened his mouth to say something, and I spared him a sharp look.

"Don't tell me everything will be all right," I said through gritted teeth. "You don't know what the future holds any more than I do, but I'll believe you for a moment and I'll hate you if you're mistaken. If you're trying to be consoling, remind me that you're here and that I don't have to be alone after reading this bioscan."

Impulsively, he reached out and squeezed my hand even as I tried to pull it away.

His expression showed hurt and confusion at my withdrawal, and I jerked my gaze away.

"It's not you. I hate places like this," I said, indicating the sterile room.

I stripped off my clothes, folding them and setting them on the chair.

"Angel, whoever told you that you had to get naked for a scan was lying to you."

"Anyone who says you can get a great scan through layers of clothes with metal and plastic fastenings has issues about your nudity or thinks you do. I'm going for the most sensitive scan this Blue is capable of. That means I'll be lying naked on the table for four long hours. I don't need you to keep me company for this part, so go ahead and watch a movie or something."

"I'll stay with you," he said.

My expression was hardly meek and mild, but I was a naked woman and he was big, clothed, and male, making me appear so much more vulnerable by comparison. Leaving me alone seemed to disturb him at an elemental level.

Then he added politely, "Unless being naked in front of me like this bothers you."

A lab full of people had known more about my body than I ever would. I also had lived under their constant surveillance for so long that any notion I had of privacy had long faded.

The machine started its scan. Through my eyelashes, I saw Cris glance at the data streaming in and then dig a novel out of his pocket.

Closing my eyes, I wondered which of my secrets the bioscanner would reveal. This bioscanner was a newer model, so would the cloning show? What would I tell him? What would he believe?

No, I couldn't think about that now. I quieted my thoughts and concentrated on keeping my breathing even.

A long while later, the bioscanner pinged and I woke up. Without so much as a stretch and a yawn, I dressed quickly. Christ, Isidro would've punished me for falling asleep on the table. I was supposed to be calm and blank when being scanned, not asleep where a slip into dreaming would jack with my physiology.

I reviewed the scan, my pulse lurching.

"Do you know how to interpret the data?" Cris asked.

"Yes, but how are we doing for time? There's a lot to go through. I need half an hour."

"I'll call them and make sure they stay away."

I alternated between studying the 3D map and the readout. Everything above the neck was still holding. What a relief. I was more than a little fond of my brain, the only original part of me that remained. Blue wasn't able to isolate any genetic anomaly or markers, either. My cloned parts were still hidden, at least from this series bioscanner.

In fact, none of my life in the lab showed on the screen. They'd been so careful not to leave scars. Even when they'd needed to crack open my skull, they separated the plates along the suture lines to minimize sign they'd been in there at all. It was like it had never happened to me. Shouldn't Hell leave its mark?

My stomach dropped out when I came across the anomaly.

Perhaps it had.

When he returned, I said in a brusque tone, "All in all, I'm very healthy. Let me erase this from Blue's memory, and we can get out of here."

He drove in silence for a few blocks, regularly glancing at my chest as if my nudity on that slab had reminded him of the three circular scars over my heart.

Finally, he said, "Seeing as we're going to be together a while, maybe it's time for a few answers. How did you get those marks on your chest? At first, I thought they were burns from a cigar, but when I touched them, I could feel how lumpy the bone was underneath. It's like someone shot you."

I gave him a strange look. "Why would someone shoot me? Well, unless it was over philosophical differences."

"Who would try to kill someone over that?"

"You don't think Descartes or Marx made people that angry?"

He paused, his big brain seemingly going into overdrive as if he were considering the question. God, I loved that about him. His education was extensive, but he'd acquired it because of a genuine hunger for knowledge, not because it was a formal hoop to jump through to get a job.

"Have I told you lately how much I love your mind?" I sighed, still awestruck by him.

"The feeling is definitely mutual," he said, squeezing my hand.

Did he notice I'd sidestepped the issue of my scars, those tangible reminders of my final showdown with Mauss?

I stared out the window as the blocks went by. I focused on the clean architecture of the city structures in an attempt to prevent the image of the red highlighted area on the bioscan to come to mind. My stomach had shriveled into a knot, and, mindful of the baby, I resisted the urge to press my hand against my gut in an attempt to ease the pain.

I said Cris's name.

"What? Are you hungry?" he asked, glancing over his shoulder as he changed lanes. "I know a good Thai place near here."

"The bioscanner marked the fetus in red," I said tonelessly, looking out the passenger window, my hands now cupping God's chance of redemption.

"Must be so any medical personnel would know to take extra precautions because you're pregnant."

"It's red because there's an anomaly," I corrected in that same flat voice, having finally stilled the horror in my mind long enough to get the words out. "I think the fetus is dying."

Cris's fingers were chilly as he placed the inexpensive gold band on the ring finger of my left hand.

"You may kiss the bride."

The touch of his lips was so fleeting that I barely felt it. I barely felt anything, really. We were engaging in an unwanted marriage to save the life of an unexpected child.

After ensuring the paperwork was finished, he rushed me out of the chapel. Did the ring on his finger feel like a manacle, too? It was worth the medical coverage I would receive as his wife, though.

I breathed deeply and kept my manner calm despite the urgency.

I trust You, God.

CHAPTER 6

FIGHT FOR LIFE

The hospital bed was old, creaking when I moved. The IV stand had a speck of rust the shape of a kidney. The doctor's voice was gravel, each word tearing my skin open like I had crashed a motorcycle and was tumbling down the freeway.

Cris's helpless gaze never left my face. His worry and grief were nearly tangible.

After telling us the counselor was on his way, the doctor left us alone.

"What do you want to do?" Cris whispered.

"Do I want to murder our dying child before she dies and rots inside me, poisoning me like I apparently poisoned her?"

He flinched. It took him several tries before he could speak. "It's a developmental issue. They said it's nothing you did."

"Do you honestly think they would tell me if it were my fault?"

He swallowed audibly. "You're five months pregnant. A miscarriage could cost you your life."

"Why can't they save her?" I demanded. "In me or out of me, she's five months along already. Why can't they save her?"

"Ty, they don't even understand how she was able to survive as long as she did."

"*Has*, not *did*. Don't use the past tense like she's already dead."

"Do you think I want this?" he said, shoving his hand through his hair. "She's my child, too. I can't lose both of you."

"So you're okay with killing her to save me?"

"Stop saying it like that. She's already dying. Even if by the grace of God she survives, she probably won't ever be able to walk or talk or see or cognate properly. What kind of life would she have with a bunch of machines breathing for her, pumping her blood, filtering the waste from her system?"

"You're making a lot of assumptions here. I'm not saying she'll be perfect, but do you need a child to be perfect to love her?"

"Of course not. But I don't know that the life she'd have would be a humane one."

"Would you actually put up a fight if the baby were a son like we assumed?"

"This has nothing to do with that."

"I'm not throwing away my child."

"No one blames you," he cried. "If we'd identified it sooner, they said there's still nothing they could've done about it. No one takes better care of herself than you do. Sometimes cells don't divide correctly."

"I'm not abandoning my child."

"Neither am I. I just don't know what we can do for her. Look, this isn't some backyard abortion. She'll be painlessly euthanized as soon as she's removed from you."

"No."

"Then tell me what to do," he begged. "Tell me how she can be made self-aware instead of being nothing more than an ill-fitting collection of human cells kept barely functioning due to a battery of machines."

"Stop being so dramatic. I can't afford to get upset," I said, smoothing my hands over my abdomen. "I don't want her to hear what you're saying either."

"Ty."

"She can hear you," I insisted.

"No," he said helplessly, "she can't. You saw the scans, and you heard them explain them."

"I don't need you to raise this child."

"I'm not going to abandon you. Or her. I do want our child, and I do believe in miracles. But we also need to be brutally honest about what her quality of life will be like if they can stop her from dying for a while longer. But the risk to your own life is your choice to make. I will support your decision."

"And I respect your right to be involved in the decision."

God help me, but I thought of the lab. Did they have the tech to save her like they'd saved me? What would be the cost of it? Me caged, her caged, Cris left with the bewildering pain of us disappearing without a trace? What would happen to him if he tried to look for us? Worse yet, what would happen to him if he found us?

But in the end, the fetus chose her own path, dying in my womb less than ten minutes later.

A bump against my hospital bed made me wake. My hands shot to my belly. "Where is my child?"

The nurse's eyes went wide. "I'm sorry?"

"My baby died in my womb not disappeared from it," I retorted. "Where is my child?"

She seemed to pretend she didn't understand me before fleeing the room.

"She was cremated," Cris said, his voice raw with emotion. He was slumped in the chair by the door, his eyes bloodshot, bruises underneath indicating he hadn't slept.

"Did you see it happen?" I demanded. "Because they could've said anything, couldn't they? Maybe you were in the room when they pulled her out of me, but you weren't there when they disposed of her, so you don't know anything more than what they told you. Haven't you ever been lied to?"

"Stop," he pleaded.

I heard my voice rising but couldn't control that any more than I could control the rage. "Stop wanting to know the truth about where my baby is? What a selfish bitch I am. You know what she is to them, don't you? Medical waste."

"For God's sake, stop."

"Twentieth-century laws were already claiming that anything cut out of you was the establishment's to do with as they wished. My rights, your rights, her rights are nonexistent. If they want to dissect her or use her DNA to grow tissues to sell for transplant, there's nothing we can do about it."

"Ty."

"These people don't recognize human rights. I never should've let you bring me here. At least out where we were, I would've miscarried and we would've kept her safe, buried her with proper death rites. I trusted you to

41

watch my back, to watch hers, too, and you let them take her."

"Stop it. You know I loved her—"

"Prove it. Prove you didn't take their word for what happened to her." Two med techs had responded to my shrill voice, and when I saw the syringe, I snarled, "Don't you dare. I'm not out of control, and I'm entitled to some righteous anger."

Cris stepped between them and me. "It's not necessary. Please. Let me talk to her."

"If we hear her voice raised one more time, she's getting the sedative. There are other patients here."

"Did you steal their babies for medical experimentation, too?" I asked.

Cris ushered them from the room and leaned against the door, facing me, grief tightening the lines of his face. His eyes were dry, but the darkness in them was unmistakable.

I waited.

"I was in the room with you," he said. "I was supposed to leave, but when I tried, the door was pushed open from the other side, and I was forced into the corner while people rushed in. You were screaming and fighting them, so they sedated you. She came out whole, but she was malformed. Don't ask me to describe how because I can't bring myself to think about it. They said women's bodies usually abort fetuses with her condition within a month or two."

"So you're blaming me," I snapped. "If I'd known I was pregnant sooner, we could've treated her. That she lasted so long tells me she wasn't as defective as they first said."

He gave me a helpless look. "Ty, no. I don't know how many times I have to say it. There's nothing they could've done. Nothing *you* could've done."

"I sincerely doubt that."

He let it go. "They cleaned her up, wrapped her in a little blanket so only her face showed, and they gave her to me to hold. She... Look, trust that I saw her being cremated."

"Without me."

He wouldn't look at me.

"You bastard."

His gaze shot to mine. "It wasn't the plan. They all spoke as if nothing more would happen until you woke up. They sent me to the chapel with her to wait for the padre. A man showed up. He wouldn't say who he was or who he worked for, but he told me that miscarried and aborted fetuses were usually examined for suitability for any organ donation. He said that's one of the options the padre would discuss with us. To get our consent. Although, according to him, they really don't need it. I didn't think they would've found anything of use, but I could've accepted a piece of her living on, helping someone else's baby live."

"A piece of her. A piece. Well, I wouldn't have let them guilt me into allowing them to hack up my baby."

"*Our* baby. She was *ours*, Ty. Look, the padre was taking a long time, and the man was tense about the delay. So was I. I thought they should've put her in a refrigerator to keep her parts viable for transplant, but they didn't. If the holdup was because she lasted so long when she shouldn't have, maybe they had sent for a university team to retrieve her. I couldn't handle that. Saving another baby was okay, but I didn't want her dissected."

His voice was raspy, getting worse with each word, and he took a drink of water from my glass.

"When I asked the man if there was anything we could do, he checked to see if you were awake yet, but you weren't. He snuck me down into the biological waste incinerator in the basement. He said the death rites, and I kissed her before he took her from me and fed her in. I've got no ashes. It wasn't a proper crematorium. It burned fast and hot, and she was so little that her ashes fell through the grate to mix with the others before I realized I wasn't going to be able to capture them. They caught us as we left the incinerator bay, and the man told me to return to you while he dealt with them, so I did. I can't prove any of this to you."

"What did the man look like?"

"That's all you have to say to me? Our child is dead. We've got no ashes to add to the Chavez crypt where she would've been watched over by my ancestors. And you want to know what the guy who burned her up looked like? Why? So you can make him feel like shit, too? I doubt I would recognize him if I saw him again. Believe it or not, I was paying far more attention to our daughter." He scrubbed his fingers through his hair. "Christ, this is a nightmare."

What did he know about nightmares?

"What did you name her?"

"What?"

"You let some strange man incinerate her without even naming her? What the hell did you call her during the death rites, Baby Girl Chavez?"

"Of course not. Amy. I called her Amy. I don't know why. It popped into my head."

"Short for Amelia, after Amelia Earhart," I decided. "She died before completing her intended path, too. She tried like hell to, though."

"Amelia," he said, breathing the word like it was the first respite he'd had in days.

"Amelia," I wailed, bursting into tears.

CHAPTER 7

BLACK AND WHITE

An hour later, when Cris left my hospital room to consult with the social worker in private, Domino stepped in and shut the door.

My heart gave a weak, panicked throb at the presence of the lab's chief of security. The urge to fight to get past him so I could flee was still there, but thanks to my hysterical sobbing, they'd been heavy-handed with the sedatives. Now there was a massive disconnect between what I wanted to do and what I was capable of executing. I couldn't even find the energy to cross the room and throw away the tiny bouquet of marigolds that had mysteriously appeared in my room, not even when I looked up their meaning in the Victorian world—grief, cruelty—and wondered whether that was an accusation or sympathy.

Domino wasn't giving me the space to escape anyway. Built big like Cris, the man blocked the only door out of the room. I was trapped. Random flutters of panic appeared in my belly only to get crushed underneath the heavy, fuzzy feeling of the drugs.

But they could've sent someone far worse than him. There had been a time when I might've called him a friend, but perhaps that was too nostalgic of a term. Perhaps he had been nothing more than the enemy of my enemy.

"How did you escape Mauss?" he asked without preamble.

I returned his regard wearily.

The mint in his mouth clicked against his teeth, warning of his impatience. "You used the same name you chose in the lab. As if that wasn't enough, they ran your DNA. What result could you possibly have expected other than this one?"

"Obviously, I wasn't thinking. I was trying to save someone's life."

"Lucas saw Mauss shoot you in the chest three times from about a meter away and drag your body away. We thought you were dead. But that was another one of Finley's illusions, wasn't it? How did you and Mauss communicate? Where is he?"

Sharp pains in my chest made me glance down, and with dull surprise, I saw a hospital gown instead of a jacket punctured with a trio of holes. I could still smell the gunpowder and blood, though. "He didn't know I had body armor."

"Where did you get it?" he demanded. "Were you in contact with Jason Chavez?"

"What? No, I got it at a thrift store. It was in a motorcycle jacket. They felt like the standard safety panels so no one recognized them for what they were."

"Where is Mauss?"

"Look, when I regained consciousness, I was alone in the incinerator room," I said tiredly. "I guess he thought I was dead and went back to kill Lucas. I don't know. The door was locked or blocked and my palmer was gone so I had to squeeze through the walls to try to get topside. I lost a lot of blood, and I passed out while I was still in the insulation. By the time I found my way out and got back to where I left my motorcycle, it was gone. Everyone was. I haven't seen sign of Mauss since."

At least I'd ended with a truthful statement. I'd meant to subdue my tormentor for Domino to interrogate, but I'd accidentally killed Mauss. His corpse had been turned to ash in the incinerator he had lit for mine.

"Are you here to take me back?" I asked dully.

I hadn't meant to ask that, hadn't meant to remind him that was an option.

"I came here to clean up a mess," he said bluntly. "Your unauthorized pregnancy, for one. Have you ever heard of a condom?"

My eyelids felt like stone, and with comments like that there was no incentive to keep my eyes open. "You can go now."

"Not yet." He handed me a new palmer. "My phone number is in there. You can use it for a recall for safety or medical reasons."

"I don't want your help."

"So don't use it. It wasn't my idea anyway. And speaking of ideas that aren't mine, you have to report to the security station two blocks from here within twenty-four hours of your release from the hospital for a PIT bracelet with a poison core."

Dread filled me. The lab wanted a personal information transmitter they could remove at a moment's notice so I could be taken anywhere and anytime. God forbid I should have a citizen's PIT embedded in my hip where it might lead someone to the lab's location before they could cut it out of me.

The Hernandez had implanted a poison core version in my hip, but it had been easy enough to excise. Guessing it was sensitive to both drops in body temperature and exposure to air, I had quickly carved out a large chunk of my ass so the transmitter was completely surrounded by warm flesh until it was free of my body. Granted, it had still deployed, but not fast enough to kill me.

Cutting the bracelet on this new one or picking the lock would no doubt trigger the release of the contents. But no matter how poisonous the bracelet, likely all I had to do was create a matching biomagnetic signature along the inside of the bracelet to prevent the secondary trigger from firing and then break the bones in my hand to make it fit through the bracelet's opening. Too easy.

But the idea of it, the idea of the lab reaching up from the bowels of the earth to reclaim me was impossible to dismiss as easily.

"It'll make me look like a felon," I said.

"It looks like jewelry. It's tough, too. The chances of it accidentally triggering are astronomical."

I snorted. "A lot of what's happened to me had astronomical odds. Why would they risk poisoning me?"

"Better dead than in custody of another clan."

I pushed the sweaty hair off my neck. "Domino, I don't bother anybody. I don't deserve this."

"The world isn't a fair place. But they've prepped some good offers for you."

"I'm not working for them. I don't want another of their free makeovers either."

"Not everyone is out to screw you over."

"No, I know who I can trust. Get out."

He narrowed his eyes at me. "It didn't take you long to forget who tried to help you."

"You're helping me into a poison core bracelet. Get out before I scream for Cris."

He shrugged that weird one-shouldered shrug of his. "Get the bracelet or don't. I don't care. You're a grown woman capable of making your own decisions and reaping the consequences of them. I didn't like having to drop everything to ferry messages to you, and it would suit me fine if you handled your own life so I could go back to handling mine."

"What am I supposed to tell Cris about having to report to a security station for that bracelet? Or where I got the money for a palmer?"

"Your lies aren't my problem."

"Why are you so pissed at me? First off, I already said no one was around when I came to. Was I supposed to turn myself in to the locals and ask for the secret government laboratory that owned me to be notified? Secondly, even if I hid until I could escape, would you have done any different? Knowing you'd otherwise spend the rest of your life locked up in that lab for no other reason than your biological uniqueness?"

"You have no idea how much you've complicated your position. How can anyone argue for your maturity, trustworthiness, or respect for local laws now?"

"Since when does any of that matter? I'm legally biotech property, aren't I? A rare laboratory monkey? Stripped of my rights and locked in a cage, I was never in a position to earn my freedom with good behavior. If they wanted to react to my rude behavior, there was only so much they could do without creating more work for themselves. I have no delusions it will be any different the next time I wake in that place."

"Do you ever stop thinking about yourself? Can you imagine what their reaction is going to be when I don't return with that fetus? How much I set back science and how many laws I broke to keep her from lab hands while you were incapacitated and unable to do your own fighting? After talking to you, can you imagine how much I regret taking that risk?"

Hot color flooded my cheeks. "I'm sorry. I don't have words to adequately express my appreciation for what you did for us."

"Save it. Consider that the last time I go to bat for you."

He turned to leave, and I said to his back, "Like it or not, the time is coming when you're going to have to pick a side. I mean, can you even see a set of twins without wondering if they're clones instead?"

He looked at me over his shoulder. "No, I can't."

"There are rumors in the outlands about cloned parts available on the black market."

His eyes closed for a moment, and his hand tightened on the doorknob.

"Is it true?" I asked.

He was silent for a long time before admitting, "I don't know. For what it's worth, I think it's highly unlikely that any cloned parts out there are yours."

"Oh? Because the major reason both Texas and the Hernandez went to so much effort to acquire me was my DNA strand is the only one known to respond favorably to the cloning process."

"It's suspected there are other cloning labs throughout the clans. There must be other genetically compatible material out there. Or maybe their techniques have a higher success rate with any available strand."

"Or perhaps my genetic code is being spread across the land one black market organ at a time."

"I don't believe that."

I smiled slightly. "You don't want to. One of me is already a giant pain in your ass."

He grunted. "Get some rest."

"The world isn't ready for this," I called after him.

"That's not going to stop it from happening anyway."

CHAPTER 8

ANGRY AT GOD

A week after my release from the hospital, I stood on the porch of our house with a blanket pulled tight around me. It was sunrise, but the clouds were oppressive, allowing the sky to brighten but never letting me see the fiery orb or feel its warmth.

The boards creaked as Cris stepped behind me. He wrapped his arms around me, ever careful not to touch my abdomen, but in avoiding it, he only drew attention to it.

"You're thinking about leaving, aren't you?" he murmured. "You don't have to. Not on my account. We could stay married, I mean."

"Why?"

"To avoid a massive fine and jail time when they find out we got married to get you medical care, for one," he teased, his beard like a soft brush against my cheek. He'd been too distracted to shave since the day we'd driven to Austin for the bioscan.

"You've got the family connections to get out of that."

"I'm worried about you. I wake up each morning wondering if you took off during the night, but you're always out here staring at the sun. You eat and sleep and work out, but I can tell you're going through the motions. You don't even read anymore."

"Cris—"

"You should be around people who care about you right now, so tell me you're not thinking about leaving."

I stepped out of his arms and faced him. "I can take care of myself."

"You could let me take care of you a little, too." He chewed on his hangnail. "I feel helpless."

"I take your shelter and your protection and the food you pay for."

"I want to give you more. Companionship. Comfort."

"Comfort?" I snapped. "Do you think there's anything you can do or say that will ease my pain?"

"I'm hurting, too," he said quietly. "She was ours, not yours alone. And the way you're acting, it's like I lost you, too, that day."

I shut my eyes against the look on his face.

"Please, don't leave," he said.

The boards creaked as he went back into the house.

I leaned against the pillar holding up the porch roof and flattened my hand over the belly where my child should've been growing.

I had been so certain absolution was possible. God had smiled on me, blessed me so beautifully.

I hated Him for teasing me with the hope for an ordinary life.

But maybe that had been the point. To illustrate the difference between the selfish desires of a quiet life raising a child with a man I adored versus looking beyond my inner circle to address the troubles within my community and my clan.

Why hadn't it been enough that I'd figured out who Finley truly was before he kidnapped and killed anyone else? Why hadn't it been enough that I took three bullets in the chest when I figured out where Mauss was hiding?

And why bring anyone else into it? Cris hadn't deserved to go through a miscarriage. My poor daughter didn't deserve what happened to her either. Perhaps she would've been a monster, but she was still a person and we had loved her.

What had God been thinking letting her die like that? I feared the possibility His plan was a little more complicated than simply preventing my half-clone child to be viable. Perhaps He saw me turn away from that news program covering bioengineering legislation like I didn't have firsthand knowledge how wrong it could go. When I tried to live a simple life isolated from the sophisticated issues of the rest of Texas, did He think I was wasting the gifts He'd given me?

God had definitely made it personal, made it visceral.

Made me bleed again.

Christ, I was so tired of the blood. That coppery smell, that distinctive consistency, that awful color. Blood from my womb, blood from my heart.

Needing the reassurance that my boundaries were intact, I looked at my wrist and saw the blue veins through my pale skin as they carried away the deoxygenated blood from my hand.

Her hand. The clone's hand. That poor girl. The baby had been hers as much as mine. Perhaps more.

Grief ripped through me at the loss of all that life, and I collapsed to my knees.

Cris's arms were hard and strong like an oak, but it was his living heat I clung to as I sobbed.

"I have to leave," I cried. "I wasn't meant for this life."

"Shh, of course you were," he murmured. "Life is what we make of it. That's the beauty of free will. If you want to stay here with me, you can."

"Free will applies to other people. Ordinary people. Some of us don't have a choice. We have everything stripped away over and over again so we understand where our path must lie."

He chuckled and held me tighter. "Free will is for everybody, angel. Take responsibility for your life and choose your own path."

CHAPTER 9

THE SKY AND THE EARTH

It wasn't more than a few weeks after the miscarriage that the doctor studied the bioscanner's results and lifted all restrictions on me, citing my remarkable recovery. Cris raised an eyebrow about that even though he had commented on it himself.

Granted, the lab had told me my genetic code contained an anomaly that seemed to be linked to rapid healing, but I preferred to believe most of the reason I was back on my feet so fast was that I did my homework. Meals were chosen so the key nutrients and building blocks were available for repairs, rehab exercises pertinent to the injury were performed, and naps were scheduled to provide adequate rest. I even visualized how my body was healing instead of dwelling on the pain. My body knew how to fix itself. I simply provided the conditions, materials, and mindset to encourage it.

We stepped outside the clinic, and Cris paused, tipping his face toward the sun with his eyes closed. He was clean-shaven so I could see the full outline of his mouth as he smiled.

God, he had a beautiful mouth. It was wide and had just the right amount of fullness. I couldn't look at it without wanting to kiss it.

"What do you want to do today?" he murmured.

"Pretty much everything."

Cris's smile started burning. I loved that smile, that show of irony, male heat, and humor. "Pilgrimage to the Harbinger-Ellis museum?"

"Perfect."

But when we got there, the white tile of the women's bathroom or the scent of the disinfectant or the hue of the lights overhead made me press back into the corner of the stall, trying to calm down.

It wasn't the lab. I wasn't in the lab. I knew that.

But it was here, around me, dragging me under again.

I would've screamed for Cris if I could've drawn breath.

I shut my eyes.

Center yourself. Can you smell that? There's some mold or mildew in here somewhere. There was never any of that in the lab. Can you hear that hum? You never heard that sound in the lab either. Calm down and think. Figure out where you're at, and you'll be fine.

I forced my hands to unclench and felt my wedding ring shift, catching on the knuckle. No groove on this one. It wasn't the one from Paul then, but Cris.

The moment I thought of him, I felt a burst of heat and heard echoes of laughter accompanied by the image of intelligent brown eyes.

Cris. Okay. That's right. I'm in a building in the H-E compound. Once I leave the bathroom, I will be surrounded by artifacts of the post-American history of aviation. I am free to come and go. I am safe. I am whole.

My hands pressed against my flat belly.

No, not whole.

Maybe that wasn't God's fault so much as the lab's.

That goddamned lab. They'd broken me somehow, broken my body with their ceaseless surgeries to see what could and couldn't be done. The merger of human and clone, the merger of machine and flesh, the combat of torn flesh and science stitching it back together again. They had done that to me, and more. No wonder I couldn't grow a child.

They had promised me everything when I woke in their care, but they had robbed me of everything instead: my name, my citizenship, my body, my privacy, my ability to carry a child, everything.

Worse yet, they'd gotten away with it. They hadn't started with me, and they weren't going to end with me. Somebody had to act. Someone had to expose them and stop it. The outlands were full of people the lab could steal and experiment on and break the babies of and—

The pounding on the door made my heart leap into my throat, and my legs almost buckled.

"Ty, are you okay in there?"

I swallowed the lump in my throat, trying to find my voice. "Yes," I croaked. "I'm coming."

As soon as I opened the door, Cris took my arm. "You're white as salt."

"I need to sit down for a minute."

At the nearest bench, he pulled me across his lap, and I rested my head on his shoulder.

He stroked my hair, murmuring, "We should go. This was too much, too soon."

"No, this is perfect," I said, eyes falling on the static display of an Axe. "I love these planes. Look at how beautiful they are."

"Are you sure?"

I nodded, feeling better. Deep breaths brought the distant scent of jet fuel to my nostrils, and my soul thrummed with pleasure. I'd handled an Axe like that one. I'd been awesome at it. I'd handled the Hernandez Ministry of Defense, too, made them acknowledge that I was so much more than the genetic profile they'd used to define me.

I looked over at Cris, and the similarity of his features to Jason's made me smile. Jason had known I was capable of anything. If anyone could handle the lab, it would be me.

Thinking of my gregarious husband's vast social network, I said, "Hey, do you happen to know any reporters? Not one in aviation?"

"Not with that caveat, no. Why?"

But who would believe me about the lab without proof? I wasn't proof. The clone used for my overhaul had the same DNA as mine. How would I prove what was cloned and what wasn't if there weren't markers of some kind, markers that would've defeated the lab's desperate need to mask the extent of the repairs done with illegal tissues?

I needed to find the lab. Let them try to explain that basement full of occupied cryogenics tubes and all that cloning equipment to a bunch of reporters and human rights activists. Let them explain the missing lab employees who made the mistake of asking questions or the ones Mauss had murdered.

As I thought about the possibilities of how the demise of the lab would play out, I couldn't help smiling. Would they drag Isidro out in handcuffs, his wiry hair in shambles and his lab coat smudged? Would Sam, my former counselor, cry as they led him to a squad car?

And as for me, I'd probably make it onto a talk show. I bit my lip at the thought of all that attention. But it was for the greater good, so I would do it. The world would thank me for exposing the atrocities that occurred down there. I would become a Rosa Parks or Susan B. Anthony, or some other woman who stood up against all odds and inspired the world to change.

The hue and cry after the lab's exposure would lead to new laws, tighter laws with massive penalties and a lot more oversight until no one in the clans could do human experimentation like that. They would say cloning was unethical, period. No matter what the situation, it was morally reprehensible to grow a human being to be used as parts for another. It was repugnant for corporations who owned the technology that fixed someone to have any say in what the person did if his repaired or replaced parts exceeded fifty percent.

But how does one go about finding a secret underground laboratory? I'd been unconscious each time I entered it and unconscious each time I was removed from it.

"What about a geologist?" I asked my husband. "Do you know any of those?"

"Oh, I remember it well," the old lady said, leaning forward and tapping her spoon on the scarred kitchen table for emphasis. Splatters of peppermint tea flew off the spoon and seeped into the table where the finish had worn away. "It was a small, secret government bunker with high-tech medical gear. Few patients. Ones crucial to the war effort."

I was leaning so far forward I felt the edge of the table dig into my belly. Collecting oral histories from the oldest people I could find was paying off with astonishing speed. "And you saw it yourself?"

"Just the once. I must've been seventeen or eighteen, and the guy I was dating was the son of some important general. When he got badly injured, he had me take him there."

"Do you know where it was? Like the precise location?"

"Well, it was only the one time, and it was underground, you know? I remember the general area, but I couldn't tell you where the entrance was exactly."

I slid a pack of wild-harvested marshmallow her way. "It'll soothe your throat."

Her cackle turned into a cough. "We're just talking, girl. I don't need bribes. But I'll take it," she said, scooping up the packet before I could retrieve it. "It's up in Oklahoma City."

Damn.

I sat back, trying to hide my dismay. I'd been to the lab she described. Lucas and I had found Mauss there, and I'd been shot. Domino must've found the lowermost level, too, along with the fifty corpses Finley and Mauss left behind. Given that one of those bodies belonged to the Assistant Defense Minister Harry Fischer, that hidden lab was a significant find, but it wasn't my home lab.

That was all right. One of these outlands old-timers would eventually reveal information I could use. Statistics promised me that.

CHAPTER 10

STIRRINGS

The following week, I heard the ragged growl of the Beast and ran outside to greet Cris. He'd been gone for three days on a contract job to install some solar panels.

"You're early," I said, throwing my arms around his neck. I'd just returned home myself, timing that had barely spared me from having to explain to him why one of my bags of groceries had contained an assault rifle.

Weeks ago, I'd been scouting one county over for herbs or other plants I could dry and use for trade, and I'd stumbled across the carnage of a turf or gang war. I'd taken the one weapon I was most likely able to find ammo for and left the rest. I'd been leery of bringing the gun all the way home until I had a good hiding place for it because if Cris saw it, he would've insisted I turn it in to the police like the law required. Instead, it was safely hidden behind a toe kick beneath one of the kitchen cabinets.

"I can't stand being away from you," he said, nibbling on my lower lip. "Take off your pants. Mine, too. I've got a present for you."

"Have you ever seen the start of a revolution?" I asked Cris around a mouthful of chili. I hadn't meant to ask the question, but the sex had been so awkward that we'd been eating dinner in a strained silence I couldn't stand.

"What do you mean?"

I squirmed under his regard and felt the ache between my legs. Why wasn't the sex getting any easier?

"I mean, have you ever witnessed a nearly tangible change of a society when people were done tolerating the injustices they had been living under?"

"No."

"Me neither. Why do you think that is? Why is complaining enough? Why is shouting and throwing bricks through windows enough? Why is venting with people of a similar mind people enough? When do people reach a point where they would die for what they believe in?"

"It's a turbulent world already. I can't imagine the chaos of an uprising."

"Can't you? It's your heritage, isn't it? Your ancestors can trace your fight for Texas all the way back to its independence from Mexico in 1836. Chavezes have been flying combat aircraft since World War II. When the wars moved stateside, your family continued to engage the enemy. You've got two active-duty siblings who safeguard the airspace overhead right now. Growing up with all those stories, you're telling me you still can't imagine flying over ground littered with broken bodies and torn flags?"

"What on earth have you been reading?"

"Robert Frost, actually."

He burst out laughing.

But later, as Cris sorted laundry, he asked, "Seriously, why is revolution on your mind? We agreed not to read anything incendiary for the rest of the month after we both got so butt hurt during the Nietzsche argument."

"I was trapped at the grocer's with some irate locals sparring with some protesters headed for that biotech firm."

"Which firm?"

"The one in Fort Worth that's under investigation for overcharging for organs grown on synthetic matrices."

"They're going all the way to Fort Worth? That's a lot of rage."

"They're right, though."

"Don't tell me you got sucked in by the propaganda."

The truth was it had taken a lot not to join up with them. From the front of the pack, I wanted to scream at the corporation to make those bioprinted replacement organs readily available. I wanted the recipients to own them free and clear, too, instead of incurring an annual bill or service fee or whatever they wanted to call it. If the person wasn't paid up when he died, the biotech firm could seize the remains and harvest what they wanted. I understood a company's need to recoup some of the money spent on research, but they'd made their money back on those bioprinters decades ago.

It was far too risky for me to get involved in that demonstration, though. Incarceration would've been miserable enough, but what if the cops processing me discovered I was legally listed as biotech property? What if instead of being a voice in the debate, I became the subject of it?

Cris paused with a pair of dirty jeans in his hand. "Ty, you can't believe everything you hear."

"Please don't forget to empty your pockets. I don't want another rusty nail incident."

He dutifully went through his pockets in front of me but pulled out nothing but lint.

Satisfied I wouldn't need a tetanus shot to do laundry, I said, "And you have to allow for the possibility there's a lot of truth in the points the protesters are bringing up."

He balled up his jeans and slung them into the basket of darks. "What if there is? I don't have the time or energy to fight every battle that needs fighting. I focus on the causes I have the education and experience to address. I'm sorry, but this isn't one of them."

"Don't be sorry," I said even though he'd just jumped off the pedestal I liked putting him on. "You're right. The wrong people involved could make the matter worse."

CHAPTER 11

ORION'S CHILD

Flat on my belly, I pulled myself through the dirt until I could peer over the crest. Excitement made my heart race. This was it. This was the place. I'd found the lab.

It had taken months of studying geology, geothermal power, tectonic plates, and old military bunker designs to isolate some areas where my lab could exist. That information combined with a choice interview led me straight to this unremarkable patch of land. In fact, it was that bland landscape that thrilled me the most because I considered it the hallmark of a remarkable secret being hidden beneath.

The old man I'd spoken to had been clear about the entrance location, and I found the area unobstructed. He'd been a worker there long ago, a domestic in a secret underground laboratory set up by the government to carry out illegal experiments in cloning tissues. They'd been attempting to repair genetic damage of key personnel caused by a particularly nasty chemical warfare agent during the Clan Wars. The domestic said they'd been unsuccessful, and he recalled the horrible sight of the patients when they first came in and the monstrous sight of the patients after the genetic repairs failed. I'd tried to guide the conversation to the structure of the place, but he'd been caught up in his memories of the people he'd known.

However, he'd confirmed the existence of a main room in the common area with corridors radiating like spokes. The main room had been called the atrium, and the lights in there were full spectrum to accommodate the pots of plants growing there. In my lab, the atrium had large tanks of animals as well as plants in beds, but I could see his atrium being the larval stage for mine.

Wait a minute. What the hell?

A ground hatch opened, and my gut sank when teen-agers spilled out. They laughed and shoved each other, some stumbling drunkenly, some strolling with their arms around the waists or shoulders of their significant others. They threw off camouflage tarps to reveal assorted off-road vehicles. A few grabbed brooms and returned to the hatch. After closing it, they brushed away their tracks while others tossed dirt over the path to further obscure it. When they left, they leap-frogged, some vehicles moving ahead while the youths masked their tracks, then getting into their trucks and pulling ahead while the next crew obscured theirs. Through binoculars, I watched them all the way to the paved road. They were good, too. I saw no trace they'd ever been there.

The hatch wasn't locked. For my recon trip, I hadn't planned to do anything more than watch for signs of life from a distance, so I had nothing more than Mauss's gun and my small, ever-present emergency kit. I opened the hatch, and my nostrils flared from the strange scents: a dusty smoke, the fresh green scent of plants, and an herbal scent I couldn't identify. No smell of death, though. I shone the flashlight down the hole and descended the short ladder to the ramp. Lights came on automatically, an indication the geothermal power system still operated. The corridor hadn't been swept or mopped in years. The peeling paint on the walls further told me this wasn't my lab.

The lights of the atrium were still on, and I saw a timer. I roamed around the small atrium, fingering some of the narrow, serrated leaves of the crowded plants. The burning herbal smell made sense. They had a nice little marijuana farm growing here.

Listlessly, I checked out the rest of the lab, but there wasn't much left to explore. Parts were caved in or doors rusted shut despite obvious efforts to pry them open. All the medical equipment had been removed long ago, the marks on the floor covered with decades of dirt. The kids had added some chairs and a lot of cushions, but it was surprisingly free of trash. The air recyclers were still working, but it was plain from the taste of the air that the filters hadn't been changed in decades.

Disappointment and frustration nearly bringing me to my knees, I felt an almost overwhelming impulse to trash the place and topple the kids' empire. If they'd been into computers, I would've done it, but I didn't have the heart to destroy the lush vegetation.

I didn't hide my tracks. I left the hatch wide open, leaving the farm to the whims of man and weather.

I pulled the hem of my shirt over the gun stuck in my waistband as I strode away.

Stop fussing. You ruled out a few more acres of Texas. That's more than you had yesterday.

Later than I expected, I slipped though the basement door of the learning center in the nearest town.

I shook Edgy awake. "Everything okay?"

Her gap-toothed smile made me grind my own per-fect teeth in annoyance.

"All good," she said, presenting her arm and pushing back her sleeve to reveal my PIT bracelet.

I examined it carefully, but the smart girl hadn't messed with it. With her large wrist and tiny hand, she definitely had the better end of the deal. I took several fast breaths and then jerked my thumb out of joint. I saw stars. Without hesitating, she grabbed my hand and jerked the PIT down over her hand, over mine, and up past my wrist.

Whimpering, tears streaming, I forced my thumb back into place and cradled my hand to my chest.

She pried it free and checked the bracelet. "Didn't break. You'd better get home before your husband finds out you've been messing around with someone else."

I pinned her with my gaze.

"Wedding ring," she explained, touching the groove where my ring usually sat.

With a shaking hand, I dug out a cash card and gave it to her. As an afterthought, I added a second one to encourage her to keep her mouth shut about my alleged affair.

"See a dentist."

She grinned at me, then whistled through the gap in her smile.

The constellation Orion reclined along the horizon as I trotted toward the house. I was exhausted and my thumb throbbed with every step, but compared to the vastness of the universe, my discomfort was trivial and thus easily borne.

However, I did swear as I approached the house and saw Cris's vehicle parked out back. I jumped when the motion sensor lights came on. Had he heard my dirt bike? Its hiding spot was a few kilometers away but sometimes sound carried funny.

Cris opened the door to greet me. "There you are."

"I thought you wouldn't be back from helping Jiminez until tomorrow afternoon," I said, discreetly checking my finger to make sure I'd remembered to put my ring back on. I hadn't wanted the sun to pick up on the shiny metal and give away my position.

"He and Mindas got into a fight so I told them I'd come back when they could settle their differences like adults. Where were you? And what's the matter with your hand?"

"I dislocated my thumb and couldn't get it back into place, so I hiked toward Doc's. Then I realized he'd charge me far more than the service was worth, so I went to the creek to soak my thumb to keep the swelling down so I could try to get it back into joint. Took me a while, but I got it," I said, showing him the inflamed joint.

He kissed it. "You should've called me. I could've handled Doc."

Unhappy, I followed him into the house. I hated lying to him.

Someday you'll understand, Cris. Hopefully you'll have loved me enough by then to be able to forgive me. Perhaps someday I'll be able to forgive myself, too.

CHAPTER 12

UNWANTED OPPORTUNITIES

Texas spread out in front of our homestead in a dusty disarray of concrete pads and distant mountain peaks. The sky was that bluebonnet blue I loved, but it wasn't as deep a blue as Domino's hair now that he was coloring it again. The hue brought out the blue flecks in his hazel eyes.

I stood on my front porch with my hands on my hips as he came to a stop in front of me. The quality of his charcoal pinstripe was slightly better than average but not by much. He didn't wear it with ease, though. I'd never seen him in clothes he looked comfortable in.

I certainly was wearing an item I wasn't comfortable with.

I thrust my hand in his face, making him see the poison core bracelet I wore thanks to his previous visit. It wasn't a sign of compliance so much as an accusation, and he knew it.

"Wasn't my deal," he said bluntly. "Let me in."

"Why is it you only show after my husband is gone? Are you afraid of him or simply avoiding having to explain who you are?"

"I'm giving you the opportunity to be questioned in private. I can drag you to the nearest security office in handcuffs if you want."

Questioned?

I went to the kitchen and poured myself a glass of water. I heard Domino enter the house and shut the door, locking it behind him. I didn't see it as intent to restrain or intimidate me as much as an automatic measure to protect a high-priority lab asset.

I rapidly thought through everything I'd done since the last time I'd seen him. How thorough was his surveillance? Would the oral histories be suspicious? I hadn't limited what the subject was, so I had catalogued a decent variety of discussions. Or had he seen me hiking around the outlands? Surely I had enough drying herbs around here to prove it was a legitimate enterprise.

He said, "I'm supposed to believe you don't know why I'm here?"

"Perhaps you should tell me," I said without heat, indicating he was welcome to sit at the kitchen table.

The chair scraped across the floor as he accepted. "There was a bombing last night."

"How deliciously vague."

He waited.

My eyes widened. "You think I'm a bomb maker?"

"You're saying you couldn't be?"

It was horrifying to realize that if I thought about it long enough I probably could figure out how to make one. "Would you believe I'm far more interested in keeping the raccoons out of my cold frame?"

"Your what?"

"Tiny unheated greenhouse where my salad greens are wintering. Cris built it for me."

I don't know why I added that last part. It sounded corny.

"Do you have an alibi for the time of the bombing or not?" Before I could ask, he said, "This past Tuesday, late morning."

"Sort of an odd time, isn't it?"

"They were in the middle of a VIP walkthrough. Do you have an alibi or not?"

"Would it matter? Bombs can be put on timers, can't they?" I asked. "Why are you asking me about this anyway? Now that you know I'm guilty of escaping the lab, am I going to be blamed for every crime that doesn't have an obvious perpetrator?"

"The target was Genseed's research labs."

"Genseed. Genesis seed. Genetic. It's a biotech firm? Genetic manipulation?"

He nodded.

I drained my glass of water to stop myself from asking anything more, but I couldn't prevent the flurry of connections being made between random data in my head.

"No comment?" he said.

"Well, whatever happens to that company doesn't directly affect me so I see no need to think about it. Choosing what to make for dinner has far more impact."

"Being a suspect doesn't affect you?"

I shook my head. "Faulty logic. The company didn't affect me enough for me to go to the trouble of bombing it in the first place. Who on earth said I should be a suspect?"

I didn't expect a reply, and I didn't get one.

His gaze strayed and landed on a trite novel. "Don't you get bored trying to be a housewife?"

"There are moments I am," I allowed.

"A lot of people died in that bombing. If your big brain slips and accidentally latches on a clue I need to know about—"

"I seriously doubt the lab wants me to get involved in anything as dangerous as trying to track down a bomber. Look what happened with Finley and Mauss. I almost got fragged, and more than once. That reminds me. Any sign of Mauss?"

I congratulated myself for remembering to ask about him like I didn't already know where he was.

Domino shook his head. "I was going to ask you that. Now that your name appeared in the provisional database, it will be easier for him to find you."

"Any chance I get a gun yet? Or is Lucas out there watching me? It feels like someone is."

"Call me if there's trouble."

For a moment, I considered amusing myself with the bombing data while I continued to refine the way I would tell my story as a lab victim to the reporters.

Through my shirt, I touched the scars to remind myself what happened the last time I followed a puzzle into a dark corner. Pressing harder, I felt my clone heart throb. It was no wonder I ended up on the list of suspects in that bombing. Despite being saved by it, I would never be a supporter of the genetic manipulation used to repair me.

Domino's eyes rested on my chest, although it was in no way a sexual overture. His cheek twitched as his candy migrated to that part of his mouth. I couldn't smell wintergreen without thinking of him.

"Does it still hurt?" he asked.

"No, it's nothing but scar tissue and healed bone."

He shook off whatever he'd been thinking, his gaze lifting to my eyes again.

"Domino, what am I supposed to do about this push to get medical checks on outlanders?"

"It doesn't affect you."

"Do the people running that program know that?"

He ignored that as if he'd already addressed the issue. "Are you ready to let me give you some options?"

"Yes," I said warily.

He set a sizable envelope on the table in front of me. "Do you still have the palmer I gave you? You've never turned it on, but you still have it, right?"

I nodded.

"Call me if you have questions," he said. "Don't call me if you have complaints because I didn't generate these offers. When you've made your decision, call me to pick up anything you don't use from that packet. If you mean to use all of it, I don't need to be notified. Just use it."

I nodded.

His nose wrinkled. "Okay, I tried not to say it because it's obvious, but I can't help it. Your husband doesn't—"

"I won't do anything in regards to those offers that strikes him as strange."

Satisfied, he left the table and headed for the door.

I trailed after him. "Domino? Is Lucas okay?"

He glanced over his shoulder at me, eyebrows lifted. "Either you're in or you're out."

"I'm out. I want him to be okay. That's all. I'm glad you are."

He gave me a long, strange look and left the house. That was my first warning I wasn't going to like what was in that envelope.

I broke the seal and dumped the contents on the kitchen table. Most of the paperwork was routine hardcopies with special imprints that authorized me to be within the border. They were not citizenship papers, I noticed with anger, but they did constitute official recognition and tolerance of my presence within Texas's borders. Was the receipt for an enormous bank deposit to an account in my name meant to soften that blow?

The instructions on the disc indicated it would build on the other paperwork and unlock files across the various Ministry databases as soon as I inserted it into my palmer. Within seconds, I would have a history that would stand up to anyone's scrutiny. Still not citizenship, but it created the profile of someone who had complied with Texan laws and expectations since the accepted date of my birth.

Bastards.

I'd been kidnapped in 2014 and had awakened into a world where the U.S. had fallen and the survivors of that war had created a confederation of seventeen clans, Texas being the biggest.

Citizenship was different under the new governments. If a person wasn't born to a citizen in good standing, his rights had to be earned. I'd been grandfathered in as a Texas citizen since the lab I was cryo preserved in was within the borders, but since almost all of the cryo victims died so soon after being hatched, the lab didn't rush to officially file any of that paperwork.

Actually, as far as I knew, they'd never filed it for any of us, and I doubted that the offer of official recognition of existence originated from them. Despite everything I'd done for the clan, that disc was probably the means to the most rights I would ever be offered.

Domino had been wise to leave before I saw this.

Figuring it couldn't get any worse, I didn't hesitate to open the first of two small boxes from the envelope. It contained a pair of brown contact lenses, a sure sign they meant for me to keep masking my distinctive gold irises. I'd escaped the lab wearing an issued set, so I was glad to have a fresh pair in the same color. They were top of the line and would no doubt fit perfectly. Those were definitely from the lab.

The source and purpose of the contents of the other box were far less apparent.

Seven bullets of varying calibers and composition were nestled in cutouts in the foam lining the bottom of the small wooden box. Their settings indicated I wasn't supposed to use the bullets. It was more like they were trophies or something. I didn't quite know what to make of it.

I was grinding corn into meal for tortillas when Cris came home.

"Are you early, or am I late?" I asked him after he kissed me hello.

"I can't finish the repair until they get the parts in. Let me get cleaned up, and I'll finish the corn so you can start on the filling. I'm starving."

It should've been pleasant working side by side as we prepared our dinner, but I could feel the heat of him and my body stirred in a confusion of alarm and lust.

"You know how the hospital sampled my DNA during the miscarriage?" I said blandly, stepping away to get the cutting board and setting it up at the opposite end of the kitchen. "Well, you know they test it for various key codings and— Well, I don't know if they test everybody's. Why would they?"

"It's not like you to babble."

"I received a notice they want me to go in for further testing. There's nothing wrong with me or anything. I mean for a career. Some of my genetic sequences lean toward something—"

"Something? It's not like you to be imprecise either. What's going on?"

I set down the knife and faced him. "I have the option of reporting to the testing office in Austin for my suitability to attend a military flight school."

His mouth flattened. "Angel, if they came all this way out here to deliver a summons, I feel comfortable saying it's not a request. There's no need to get upset, though. Unless they gave you a particular date, make the appointment as soon as possible and get it over with. Without any prep work, you'll fail and that will be the end of it."

"You sound upset."

"I thought I left that world behind, but now it's coming for my wife. They must be desperate."

I jerked at the insult.

"No," he said firmly. "Of course I think you're incredible, or I wouldn't be with you. I meant that they generally don't shop for flyer DNA in provisional outlanders. First, the health screenings of young registered outlanders and now this. Something's up."

CHAPTER 13

JASON

Cris and I had to go all the way to Austin for my evaluation, and he said less and less with each kilometer that brought us closer to the glimmering cityscape.

"You don't have to come with me," I reminded him as he pulled into a parking space in front of the testing office.

"I want to," he said flatly.

When Cris and I were shown the results of my written test a few hours later, it was obvious he wasn't the least bit pleased with me. Proud that I was intelligent but upset it was out there for everyone to see.

"Did you even try?" he asked me, and the test presenter looked at him like he was the biggest douche in the world for appearing to expect even more of me.

I pulled Cris aside. "I'm sorry. I'm an OCD test taker. If I see a correct answer, I have to mark it as such."

"Ty, I want you to do what you want to do, not what they want you to do. I've been there and done that."

"Nothing's set in stone yet. I can still bomb the following test."

"And probably will. The oral exam will have you stand there with no references or aids of any kind while you answer math and tech questions. The test ends when you make your third mistake. It won't last long and it'll sting your pride, but don't take it personally. Everyone sucks at it. I don't even know why they still do it unless they want to see how you handle pressure."

Cris was allowed to accompany me to the next testing brief, and his frown deepened when the list of interviewers for the oral exam was revealed.

Shifting his gaze to the presenter, he said, "I have to point out a conflict of interest here. This is my wife, and Jason Chavez is my brother. He can't be one of her interviewers."

"He's our best interviewer for this segment. He made a list of questions from his previous oral examinations. The MoD chose from that list. Someone else will be evaluating the solutions, but he asked to be there to provide any necessary clarification of the question or the answer. This was all approved by the MoD."

Cris's lips pressed tightly together, and he led me to the waiting area.

I asked, "Are you worried he'll be too easy on me or too demanding?"

"I expect him to do whatever the hell he wants without regard for how it affects other people. This may actually be a blessing, though. If he thinks we shouldn't have gotten married, he'll make you look stupid so I'll think twice about staying married to you." He flashed me an apologetic smile. "Sorry."

My name was called, and I stood.

He took my hand. "I'll going to go stretch my legs, so call me when you're done, okay?"

I nodded.

He hesitated. "Try not to cry in front of him. He'll laugh."

"Why would I cry?"

"Frustration, humiliation, fear of failure, whatever. It happens more than you'd think. Some people want those wings very badly and study for years to get into that room."

Shaking my head and smiling at the idea of letting the interviewers make me lose my cool, I turned away.

The room for the oral test was cramped with stacks of chairs. Jason pushed a table against the wall to create some space in front of the table of interviewers.

"Still stalking me, I see," he said, swiping his hands over his immaculate suit to make it hang correctly again. "Somehow I knew I would need a restraining order at some point."

"Only a man with your arrogance would think a woman eating a sandwich at a bistro across the street had plotted to watch you be worshipped by your tailor."

Which I had, actually. He'd disappeared after I'd been pronounced dead at Greyson, and I'd needed to see that my former partner and mentor was safe. However, when he'd failed to recognize me through the results of all the reconstructive surgeries, we'd parted ways spitting threats at each other like angry cats.

"You two have met?" one of the interviewers asked with far more drama than the situation called for. "I thought you said you hadn't met your brother's wife. We can't do this."

Jason said, "Relax. We spoke briefly once, but she failed to properly introduce herself so there was no way for me to recognize her name when the file for Cris's wife came across my desk. All the usual safeguards are already in effect. This changes nothing." He turned his gaze back to me, his fingers light on the back of a chair. "Will you be sitting or standing?"

"Standing, thank you."

"I will not be involved in the interviews unless they ask a question or you give an answer that requires a translator. I do not affect the outcome here."

"Sure you do. Just not as much as you'd like," I said, earning me a flashing grin.

"Whenever you're ready, Ms. Chavez," the woman at the center told me.

"Hit me."

Of course, it wasn't over as fast as Cris anticipated. Or hoped. These tests were the first real mental challenges I'd had since trying to figure out where Mauss had been hiding. I felt my whole being flex and sigh in gratitude like I'd been released from a cramped box. I could've gone on forever, especially after Jason got bored sitting on the sidelines and started throwing me tantalizing off-menu questions. The other interviewers sat back and watched as I solved problems by writing across the air and telling them my thought processes.

When Jason gave me a regretful look and the signal to wrap it up, I did feel that urge to cry. I didn't want to go back into my box.

"One more," I pleaded, thumbing the tear out of my eye.

He laughed. "No. The test is capped at four hours."

"Just to break for lunch, right? I can wait here until you guys get finished."

"The test is over," he said firmly.

"I don't want it to be over," I said. "The others can go, but you're fresh as a daisy. I'll give you ten minutes to use the bathroom, but then you come back here."

"No, but I do like how rabid you are. You should receive a generous offer from the flight academy."

I blinked.

"That was the goal here," he reminded me. "Don't you remember?"

Crap.

Nevertheless, delight coursed through me as the other interviewers congratulated me on their way out the door.

Jason remained. He handed me a bottle of water from his briefcase, saying, "Your throat must be dry. You seem unable to form words."

I broke the seal and took a long pull on the bottle.

"You seem to be waiting for me to comment on your performance," he said. "If you are pleased with what you did, that should be enough for you. Can't you see that?"

You try being devalued as a human being for five years and see how much clarity you have. It's not wrong to want others to tell me I am valued for traits beyond the genetic or physiological.

He was far too self-assured to comprehend, so I didn't bother saying it.

"I don't have to take the offer, do I?" I asked.

"You can remain brain-dead in the outlands if you prefer. Cris has stacks of books. For a while, that might be enough to take the edge off your obvious need to be challenged. But you have to ask yourself if it is truly worth it."

"You want me to go to flight school."

"Since I teach there, yes, I do. I love to see people working toward reaching their potential instead of squashing it because they are lazy, scared, or worried about following a path their husbands disapprove of."

"It's not like that."

82

"Of course it is," he said, taking the empty water bottle off me like he expected me to throw it at him instead of toss it in the recycler. "Tycho—"

"Ty."

"Don't interrupt me. When we met, I negated your argument that your genes proved you'd be an excellent pilot. However, your grasp of math, physics, and aerodynamics makes it obvious you do have the potential to be an amazing aviator. If you want to be. Make up your own mind about it, though."

"Cris isn't pushing his agenda on me."

"He uses his bitterness about MoD expectations to reject opportunities he would jump on if they came from another agency. If I never see your name on the roster at either of the flight academies, I would prefer to believe it is because it was what you chose, not what you let him decide for you."

Waiting on the sidewalk for a traffic light to change so I could cross the intersection, a glance at a storefront reminded me I had higher priorities than flight school. I could see my image in a pane of glass as well as a ghost image in the rear pane. Would the word *clone* ever stop flashing at the forefront of my mind when I saw multiple images of myself?

Who would try to stop cloning if not me? What I was doing hadn't been successful so far, though. Not that I was with Cris for his social network or vast knowledge, but I was disappointed about how little I'd been able to use his strengths to bring me closer to finding the lab.

Jason, on the other hand, might be far more useful. I thought I would be able to survive his astute analysis of my motives. If my genuine disinterest in furthering myself socially or financially showed, if my pleasure for planes but not glory showed, I might be able to get close enough to him to present an argument for why the lab needed to be found. After all, they'd made a synthetic copy of him to use for their own end. Hopefully, he wouldn't like that. It was possible he'd want some kind of revenge of his own.

Cris wasn't going to like us working together, though. The pulse of his cheek muscle whenever his brother's name was used in the same sentence as mine warned me how Cris would feel, even if Jason and I were teacher and student. I did want to keep Cris in my life. He made me remember the lab hadn't been able to rob me of the ability to have romantic love as well as a rich, fulfilling life of service to others.

No, this path was not going to be easy. Was it truly worth the risk of losing Cris, losing the part of me that felt alive when he was near? After all, Domino had told me my DNA was coveted because it had a rare ability not to succumb to the malfunctions that brought down all the other DNA strands they tried to create full clones with. After Mauss and Finley had rammed home how violently people could feel about the technology, perhaps the government finally understood that even cloning me alone created too many moral and ethical questions for modern society to contend with at the time. Maybe the cloning program had been dialed back, eliminated even.

Multiple reflections gazed back at me.

My palmer chimed with Cris's ring tone, and my heart clenched like it was seized in a fist.

"I'm across the street."

I turned, and he waved at me from outside a I. I hoped he'd already eaten because my stomach was roiling.

His smile faded as I came close enough for him to read my expression.

"You were in there a long time," he said. "I thought you might be hiding in the bathroom too embarrassed about your performance to face me. At one point, I even wished you were fighting with Jason over being married to me. But that wasn't it at all, was it?"

CHAPTER 14

BOUNDARIES

At the end of my first day at the military fight school in Austin, I took in the sight of their library. Natural light glinted off transparent sculptures representing flight that were hung from the arching ceiling. New, high-end computer equipment was nestled in each of the spotless study areas. At the far end, modern furniture placed in airy clusters accommodated group projects.

Jason appeared beside me. "It is beautiful, isn't it?"

With my school bag slung over my shoulder so I could brace my hands on my hips, I doubted my stance conveyed approval. "As a room, sure. As a library, it sucks. There's not a book in sight."

"The number and quality of books you can access in this room and only in this room make it a phenomenal library."

"No, it's a data access point," I said, turning away.

It was sunny and clear out, but I'd fallen for the traitorous view this morning and knew to button my coat all the way up before I stepped out into the January day. But knowing how frigid it was outside, I couldn't bring myself to leave the building.

Jason appeared at my side. "What did Cris say when you accepted the offer to attend?"

Cris had said I would do well. Really, what could he say? The decision had been made.

I asked, "Am I your brother's wife or am I your student? Because if I'm to be your student, I don't want to have conversations about Cris."

"You are both," he said, "and I will discuss whatever I want whenever it is relevant."

"His reaction to my decision is not at all relevant to you. Your curiosity is not my problem."

Christ, I didn't mean to say it like that even if it were true.

Jason's eyes were narrowed.

"How's your sex life?" I asked him.

His frown deepened. "Nonexistent, unless you include the eternal question whether to use my left hand or my right. Why?"

I fanned my hot cheeks with my hand. "I thought I was illustrating how inappropriate personal topics were, but I chose poorly. The two questions aren't comparable on a scale of intimacy. Thanks for the visual, by the way. I'm never going to be able to look at your hands again."

"What is a prude like you doing with a sexually adventurous man like him?"

"Missionary style, of course. Are we even yet?"

"No, not since I now have to go to the trouble of deleting this conversation from the security feed."

"All you had to do was stick to proper topics, and none of this would've happened."

86

Narrowed eyes again, damn it. I had started the year arguing with Cris in the morning and now Jason in the afternoon.

My agitation had to be a reaction to all the people. Austin's inhabitants surrounded me, bumping, crowding, and overwhelming me at every turn. I ached to flee back to the outlands where I could breathe.

"I will use my left hand tonight," Jason told me. "And I will be thinking of you when I do it."

This was not happening. He did not just say that to me.

"Wow," he commented, peering at me. "You really can turn a deeper shade of red."

"I hate you."

He burst out laughing.

I pushed through the door, and the glacial air pierced my lungs and drove all thoughts of him from my head.

Cris was waiting for me.

Jason appeared at my side. "Imagine that," he murmured. "Do you think he was looking through the window and watching us have the kind of discussion so personal that even a confident woman ends up blushing?"

Without waiting for my scathing reply, he descended the steps and shook his brother's hand in greeting. "I thought you were meeting with H-E Corporate today."

"I did," Cris said. "I figured my wife would visit the library as soon as she was free to."

Was there unnecessary emphasis on the word *wife*? I thought so.

His smile warmed considerably when he turned to me. "And how was it?"

"Disappointing."

He flicked a glance at his brother as if I'd disparaged him, too, and Cris's laughter split the air.

He took my hand and tugged me toward the parking lot.

"She is in uniform," Jason said sharply.

"She's my wife," Cris threw back.

Not caring for the way either man was acting, I took my hand back. "I actually am in uniform, and I do mean to adhere to local rules of etiquette."

Jason shot Cris a triumphant look.

"I am not your toy," I snarled at Jason. "I'm not here because of you or for you. I'm here to do a job."

"Then I suggest you stop standing there with your breasts jutting out as if your aim is to incite us into fighting over you," he said and sauntered away.

"I have perfect posture," I yelled after him. "Nothing sticks out that shouldn't."

He turned to raise an eyebrow at me. "True, you do have wonderful posture, but your manners need work. Shrieking after your instructors is not acceptable."

"You can't win," Cris told me, steering me in the opposite direction. "Just try not to react to whatever he says."

My noisy exhale condensed into a white cloud, and I batted it away. "I hate being cold."

"Is he really your instructor? I knew he taught basic theory, but he's not the only one."

"I'm in his class. They sorted us alphabetically, which I don't like. I'm seated beside another female Chavez. When the instructor calls for Ms. Chavez, I don't know who they are referring to."

"For what it's worth, he's a good instructor as long as you don't piss him off."

"That particular ship has sailed, so now what?"

He glanced at me in surprise. "That was nothing. When he's angry, I promise you'll know it."

I chose the wording of my next sentences carefully. "I appreciate you showing up here, but I can handle any conflicts that come along. There was no need to reschedule your H-E meeting. It must've caused no small problem."

He looked like he was about to protest, but then he shrugged. "I don't trust him."

"Well, Cris, there's nothing you can do about him, is there? He's obviously not cowed by the reminder that you're in my corner. In fact, your presence probably brought out worse behavior in him."

He glowered at me.

"You can't smack me," I said primly. "I'm in uniform."

His smile was reluctant. "I forgot to tell you how lovely you look."

"You were mad I was in uniform at all. I get it. But my breasts aren't sticking out too far, are they? He's got me worried now. Do I need to slouch? I don't think I can slouch."

"Perfect posture and perfect breasts," he assured me. "Don't let him get to you."

"Funny. That's what I was about to tell you."

"It'll work out. He'll get bored with you if you act professionally."

Somehow I doubted that.

"It would help if you didn't show up here like this," I remarked.

Yet even as I said it somehow I doubted that would stop either.

I sighed and batted away at the white plume my breath made while Cris chuckled.

CHAPTER 15

NOT MY MONKEY

March tenth, Cris ran laps beside me, not bothering with his usual scowl at the academy boys whose gaze usually lingered on me too long. It wouldn't have mattered if he noticed them; his big build, outlaw's stubble, and tight mouth were intimidating enough.

Jason fell into step on Cris's other side. "Well, this is ominous."

"Nothing concrete," Cris said. "Just a few rumblings of an ugly cargo."

"Emmy Driscoll was just appointed to lead the committee," Jason said.

Cris swore and picked up the pace. I didn't. I'd strained my knee the week before and wasn't willing to overdo it.

I told Jason, "You know that bitterness about familial obligation to the MoD you spoke of? Constantly reminding him of the Ministry by discussing it like it's a rogue family member you have to keep tabs on doesn't help that bitterness fade. He doesn't work for them anymore. Change the subject."

Jason ignored that and sprinted to catch up with Cris.

I finished my laps and retired to the sidelines to stretch and watch the brothers run while they compared notes about what was going on in the Ministry of Defense. Jason's stride was cleaner, but Cris's definitely showed power. Still, Jason could outrun his brother. A health and fitness freak, Jason could race past everyone here.

His stride made me uneasy, though. Mine was precise like that, too, thanks to the muscle memory exercises in the lab. In fact, my life within the structure of flight school brought out many unsettling reminders of having been in the lab. Without thinking, I ate what my overbearing surgeon had made me eat in the lab, no more and no less, right down to the days of the week certain foods had been dispensed.

Even in the areas of my life where I had no schedule, I waited to be told where to go and what to do like I was still in the lab. I used personal products that had the same smell—or lack of—as those the lab forced me to use to control which chemicals passed through my skin. Off-duty, my clothes were light and flowing as if I still had fresh incisions that would be irritated by anything tighter. In our sparsely furnished apartment, the bedroom wall screen showed a forest glade animation populated by fairies, like I'd had in the lab, and our ceiling held the familiar starry sky animation.

As soon as I recognized what I'd done, I would liberate myself, but it was usually within days that I was back to living in the way the brutal lab had enforced. If Cris happened to be gone while I was home, it took mere hours before I was reliving my lab life.

As if remembering what happened after I'd called the surgeon a foul name for subjecting me to an indignity, my left eye twitched. Isidro had smiled so strangely then, his eyes burning so brightly as he told his techs to cut out one of mine. Christ, I didn't even want to contemplate what he would do to me if he thought I was challenging his right to practice his mad science.

Thoughts of him scattered when Cris came to a stop in front of me, gulping down air. Jason continued his laps.

"What do you think about that plane crash?" Cris asked me, swiping his forearm across his brow.

"I don't."

He wrinkled his nose. "There's no room for superstition."

"It's not that. So what if one of the Clan Wilson's planes crashed on the Texas side of the border? Accidents happen. It's not like the clan boundaries are painted on the ground, and it's not like you have a lot of options when your plane is crashing."

"This from you? You had all kinds of conspiracy theories when we lived out west."

"Conspiracy hypotheses," I corrected. "Theories are hypotheses that have been tried experimentally and proven to be sound. Mine were never proven in any way."

"Look, whether this crash was an accident or not doesn't matter as much as whether it was perceived to be an accident. That plane had hazardous chemicals on board, and they're making the argument that the spilling of those chemicals on Texas land wasn't an accident at all."

"Why would anyone believe they deliberately crashed their plane in Texas to spill a few chemicals?"

"It's a significant watershed."

When I saw Cris's gaze flick toward a classmate with breasts so large even a sports bra couldn't hide her endowments, I looped my arms around his neck and pulled him down for a kiss.

"Don't let Jason rile you with MoD rumors. That plane crash is nothing," I said. "Look, I'm sorry we live in Austin where the MoD is constantly in your face. I can try again to switch over to the Galveston academy if you want."

"No, it's plain they want you here."

But it wasn't the academy he looked at when he said that; it was Jason.

"Why did you stop flying?" I asked. "I'm going to be very disappointed if you say it has anything to do with him."

"I was bored with living up to expectations. When Jason came on active duty all fired up to conquer the universe, I finally had the chance to bow out and chase other—"

"Skirts?" I offered, giving one of my instructors a cool glance that she totally missed because she was surveying Cris like he was a particularly big mountain she wanted to climb.

"Is that Donna Kintos? Wow. I went through flight school with her," he said, bemused.

"Did you have sex with her?"

"I don't remember," he said diplomatically, giving her a cordial smile before turning his full attention back to me.

"You did, didn't you? Was it in the shed beneath the bleachers?"

It must've been a direct hit because horrified laughter escaped him. "Wow, look at those snowflakes. Looks like the forecasters were mistaken again."

I snorted and let the matter drop. I turned to say something and saw Jason surveying the scene, frowning as he looked between Ms. Kintos and us. I felt a trickle of dread. Cris saw my face and whirled around.

Jason wasted no time joining us.

"Did she make you uncomfortable?" he asked me.

"What are you talking about?" Cris demanded.

Jason's gaze didn't waver. "Did it make you uncomfortable to have your instructor blatantly drooling over your husband?"

"It's nothing," I said.

"Jason, don't," Cris said. "I was with her a long time ago. She was probably startled to see me here. For Christ's sake, she just looked at me."

Jason left without a word.

It wasn't two days later that a bewildered Ms. Kintos was arrested in the middle of class for allegedly embezzling nearly a million dollars from the academy's coffers.

When I left the classroom, I saw Jason standing there. Our eyes met for a moment, and then he sauntered away.

After Cris heard what had happened, his hands shook as he ran them through his hair.

"You don't honestly think Jason arranged that, do you?"

Cris pretended he didn't hear me.

"Well, do you?"

"He's got the ability and the petty temperament to do it, but I doubt there will ever be any proof he was involved."

"Why would he do this? Because she was unprofessional while in uniform? Seriously? I mean, this wasn't just because I didn't care for the way she looked at you, right? Because that's insane."

His gaze shot to mine.

I tipped my head at him, studying him. "Wait a minute, this was directed at you, too, wasn't it? It was a hint of what he'll do to you if you act in a way that jeopardizes my slot in flight school. Did you flex that big social network of yours to see if I could be removed from this program without penalty?"

"This plane crash is a big deal," he told me, his tone frantic. "I'm trying to remove you from the game board while the MoD decides which way to play it."

"It's my decision to make," I snapped. "When I want your help, I will ask for it. Agreed? And I need you to agree because it's right, not because you're afraid of what Jason will do if he catches you interfering again."

"Ty."

"No, don't use puppy dog eyes on me. You treated me like a child incapable of making a competent decision. The whole time in the outlands you praised my intellect, but now it's obvious you think I have none."

"That's not true."

"So what's true? That I'm a pretty trinket who can't possibly stand up to hard use? That I'm book smart so I can't possibly be street smart? That loving me means robbing me of my rights so I'm safe from possible harm? What on earth makes you think I'll tolerate that? It's my life and I will make my own decisions how to use it. If you can't handle that, you need to leave and find some fool who'll be flattered by your desire to wrap her in cotton and put her high on a shelf."

"I'm sorry if what I did gave you that impression. I respect your strength—"

"Even as you wish I didn't have it," I snapped.

"Okay, if you want an apology, you've got to be willing to hear me out."

"Honestly, I'm afraid of what you'll say next. I need to calm down. I'm going for a run."

"Do you want me to come with you?"

I shot him a frigid look. "So you can save me by block-ing off half the traffic in Austin so I can't be hit by a car? No, thank you. I have my palmer, and I'm only going to the fountain and back. I'll be back within the hour."

"Fine, but you have to realize that this plane crash does concern you. Think about that on your run."

CHAPTER 16

VERITAS

By the end of the month, my relationship with Cris had recovered from his abuse of power, although he continued to assert that I didn't appreciate MoD machinations the way he did. He stopped showing up at the academy, though. Jason had retreated as well, perhaps feeling he had made his point.

Or perhaps Jason was simply preparing for the next round.

The steely-eyed gazes of the security team followed me as I paid the taxi and approached the entrance to the gated community.

I gave my name and showed my identification, and they escorted me to the golf cart that would deliver me to my destination. The houses revealed the wealth of the owners, but the subtle elegance of the neighborhood suited Jason perfectly.

He stood in the open doorway to his home, a neutral smile pasted on his lips.

"This is very untoward," I told him as I followed him through the sleekly furnished house.

"No one forced you to come," Jason said, motioning me toward a seat on the couch in his study.

I tore my gaze from his well-stocked bookshelves and sat. "Turn down a summons from a man who's as notorious for being as powerful as he is petty?"

He didn't grace me with even a fraction of a smile, so I stopped the foreplay.

"What's going on?" I asked, leaning forward, elbows on my knees.

"What program are you choosing next week?"

"Axe pilot program."

"Good," he said. "I would've vetoed anything else."

My lips pressed together at his highhandedness. "You wasted my time bringing me here to ask me something we could've discussed on campus?"

"There's no discussion."

His jaw was set, not that I needed any confirmation he felt even more strongly about which plane and position I ended up in than I did.

"I still don't see why this couldn't have been said on campus."

"If you fought me, I was going to have to point out that your DNA matches that of a certain dead Hernandez visa holder. I doubt you want to risk anyone overhearing that."

I froze.

Before I could ask, he explained, "I took your water bottle after the oral test so I could perform a DNA analysis on your saliva and sweat."

It took me a moment to find my voice. "And what is your conclusion?"

"What is your explanation?"

"Perhaps you could start by telling me why this is coming up at this moment."

Jason's patience wore thin. Loosening his tie impatiently, he said, "Today, Texas ended trade with the Clan Wilson despite our Confed treaty."

I regarded him blankly.

With acute condescension, he said, "Remember the plane Wilson said was sabotaged to go down on Texan lands? The one Texas said Wilson sent down on our lands on purpose to poison our watershed? ADM Harry Fischer, hands down our best negotiator in the past two decades, had the ill grace to have a heart attack and die in his bed less than two years ago..."

Harry Fischer? His idea of a negotiation was to steal me from the medical lab and serve me on a platter to the Hernandez. The man who had kidnapped me from my original life took offense to the theft and killed the ADM along with everyone else involved. I'd seen his corpse myself.

"Pay attention to me," Jason snarled. "The new ADM is only making matters worse. Confederation negotiations completely failed. We are on the precipice of a war. You need to fly a Battle Axe."

"Calm down. I already said that is what I mean to choose."

"I will not tolerate anything else. I will block every other option if I have to."

"Understood," I said, standing up.

"We need to address the matter of your DNA."

After a moment's thought, I shook my head. "I don't intend to."

"Unacceptable."

"You've got a reputation as a hacker, so I've got no doubt you can come up with more answers than I'm able to give you."

"You knew at the tailor's. You knew it then."

One of the lights on my palmer flashed, and I glanced over the new message. "My husband is wondering why I'm late getting home."

"My Miranda Donovan has precedence over his Tycho Walker Chavez."

I rubbed my temple, already feeling a tension headache coming on. I hadn't slept well the night before, awakened by dreams of abandoning my child to Isidro's cruel smile and the whims of the lab. "Jason, there are only four possible explanations for your findings indicating I have Miranda Donovan's DNA: I am her, I'm her identical twin, I'm her clone, or someone switched samples. I don't care which scenario you choose."

"I will expose you."

My hand stilled. He couldn't be serious. He had to know I no longer claimed to be Miranda Donovan in any way.

Christ, if he exposed the duplicity of my DNA, I was in real trouble. Once the Hernandez found out, I would get sued for breach of contract, and I could very well find myself back on their lands at the hands of a furious Defense Minister, a man I all but told to bugger off when he finally offered me citizenship.

"So be it," I said.

"I will do it."

"Oh, I totally believe you have the ability and willingness to do that, but, Christ, you must've figured out by now I'm no stranger to taking a hit."

He continued to glare at me. I hadn't given him any explanations, justifications, lies, or pleas. No matter how much he thought he knew, I still had more to hide.

I said, "Is there anything else? No? I'll be on my way then."

When I walked into our apartment, Cris was standing at the window staring moodily at the traffic below. Hardened by work and and darkened by so much sun exposure, he looked out of place in the pale rental. Needing the feeling of space more than ever, I'd pleaded to have only essential furnishings, nothing remotely dark or heavy, and he'd humored me.

Without preamble, he said, "Does the MoD have any reason to single you out for military service?"

"Obviously, since the academy bypassed the waiting list so I could start this term."

He flashed me a sharp look. "Something other than your testing."

"Why don't you tell me what you suspect instead of waltzing around it?"

"I'm afraid they deliberately hunted you down in the outlands because they knew you had a special skill set even before they tested you. You've proven yourself before. For the Hernandez."

"How so?"

"You're Miranda Donovan," he said, the words coming at me hard and fast like punches. "And they're going to do anything to get you into an Axe cockpit."

His voice broke on the last word.

"Cris."

"Don't deny it. I read Jason's file on you. I know who you are. I don't quite understand how it's possible you're her, but you are. It's supposed to be your choice what you want to fly, but they're not going to give you any say about it at all."

"Are you that worried about Texas breaking the trade treaty with Wilson?"

"Don't change the subject."

"I'm not. Jason just got finished using that reason to justify grilling me about what I would decide. Cris, don't worry about me being in an Axe. It's as natural to me as breathing."

He whirled and pinned me with his gaze. "That's supposed to reassure me? They're sending my wife to a combat zone, but she's so talented there will never be a freak fault or lucky shot that downs her?"

I hugged him. It was like embracing a mountain. "You know it's not your fault, right? We tried to prevent pregnancy, but it happened anyway so I ended up in the system. If it weren't that, something else eventually would've happened to tell them exactly where I was. It's going to be all right. I'm young and healthy."

He pushed me back so he could make me see his seriousness. "You better have one hell of a memory because I wouldn't be surprised if they pull you out of school early. You already know how to fly. But don't tell Jason who you are."

"He found out my DNA matches his samples for hers. That's why I was late getting home. He had to be sure I was still parking my ass in an Axe for king and country."

"Choose another plane," he said, desperation driving his voice to a higher octave. "A cargo."

I smiled at the idea. "They're never going to let that happen. You know that. Even if the MoD allowed it, Jason wouldn't."

He spat his brother's name.

"Cris, it's nothing I can't handle."

"Don't underestimate him."

"I meant flying the Axe in a war. No one can handle Jason," I said with a ghost of a smile. "He's threatened to leak the comparison of the two DNA samples."

He nearly vibrated with pent-up frustration and fear.

"Cris—"

"Stop saying my name so much. It is that difficult to tell us apart?"

"I like saying your name," I said with a shrug.

He whirled and grabbed me forcefully. My heart had leaped into my throat before I realized he wasn't attacking me but yanking me into his embrace.

I uncurled my fists and put my arms around him. "You're so warm," I said, burrowing in closer.

"And you're a cool shadow on a hot summer day."

His heart beat strongly, drowning out the sound of mine. I opened my mouth to tell him ADM Fischer was killed because of me so I pretty much started a war, but his tongue slipped between my lips. I groaned and deepened the kiss.

"Slow down," he murmured, bending down to nibble down my neck. "I want to kiss you everywhere. I want you so melting and aching ready for me that you can't stand that I'm not inside you."

Maybe this time. Maybe I would unfurl like a flower blossom to the touch of the sun when the touch became intimate. Maybe this time Cris's passion wouldn't overwhelm me. Maybe, just maybe, I could forget the past and would be wet enough this time, relaxed enough. Maybe this time I loved him enough that my body would finally welcome him.

Or not, I thought as the first flash of pain made my fingernails flex into his shoulders.

Cris withdrew slowly, not from reluctance so much as an effort not to hurt me worse.

I let out a shaky breath. "I'm okay. Let me shift, and we'll try it again."

How many times had I said that before?

He rolled onto his back.

"Hey, where are you going?" I protested, already feeling like I'd been dumped in icy water.

"I love that you keep trying, but we both know this isn't working. You need to see a therapist."

I yanked the sheet up to cover myself, crying, "Stop saying that. I don't need a therapist or gynecologist or any other specialist you've shoved at me."

He stared at the uneven texture on the bedroom ceiling. Cautiously, he said, "I've been with a lot of women, and I've worked to be good at pleasing them."

"I'm aware of your reputation," I said nastily. "As soon as we moved to Austin the women threw a parade."

His mouth twitched. "I'm sorry."

"That you're God's gift to women? Why on earth would you apologize?"

"No, that we returned to a place where I dated a lot. Angel, I'm sorry for needing to say this, but I'm experienced enough to know what's wrong between us is not going away without someone's help. I don't know if you're scared I'm going to get you pregnant again or if you've got some kind of nerve malfunction that makes penetration hurt. I'm not blaming you. Not even a little bit. I just want to fix this."

"I'm perfectly functional," I gritted out. "There is nothing stopping us from having sex."

"Nothing but the suspicion I'm hurting you a lot more than you want me to believe when I'm inside you? Oh, and the suspicion that you fake an orgasm when I put my mouth on you instead?"

The color drained from my cheeks and then returned full force.

"It doesn't have to be like this," he told me as he got out of bed. I knew he was going to sleep on the couch again. "I want you to be able to enjoy it. Can't you see that?"

104

"Maybe I'm too freaked out today between Jason's threats and your saying I'm Miranda Donovan to want sex, that's all."

"Are you denying that you're her?"

Suddenly, I wanted to tell him everything. Well, not everything, of course, but the highlights.

Without letting myself overanalyze it, I blurted it out. "I'm her. I was kidnapped and put into stasis for more than a hundred years. I woke on Hernandez lands and was hidden by one of the emergency personnel until it was too late for their DM to hide me in his illegal cloning research lab as planned. He wanted me as a source of quality, unregistered DNA."

"Ty—"

"Then they let me enter flight school, assuming I would fail because I was so damaged from the cryo. I proved my worth to them at Greyson and they offered citizenship, but I'd already found out what they originally meant to use me for so I was pissed enough to decline. I was already dying from the stasis project, but what killed me was the retrieval attempt by the Texas lab that hatched me from the damned experiment in the first place."

"Ty—"

"They rebuilt me, but they didn't let me go. They never meant to let me go. I eventually escaped. I wanted to be happy for a change so I looked for you, figuring I'd ride it out until you were tired of me."

"You expect me to believe that?"

"If I wanted you to believe me, I would've told you a lie," I snarled. "Sometimes you find yourself in strange circumstances. You have to give me that much. You have to admit that no matter how remote it is, there is still a possibility that everything I said is true."

He considered it, then shook his head. "No, I really don't."

"I can go into detail."

"I'm sure you can. I'll go so far as to say that it sounds like you think what you said is true. But I don't. What I believe is that you, Miranda, were a wreck by the time they pronounced you dead at Greyson, and that because of the level of your flying and Jason's interest in you that my clan spent a fortune to rebuild you. You tried to lie low in the outlands, but you and I clicked, which led to your pregnancy, which led to the clan remembering that you were an untapped asset and forcing you into flight school."

"I can understand why you think that, but will you at least hear me out? I really need to tell you all this now that you know who I am."

He kissed my forehead. "When are you going to learn that you don't need to lie to be with me? Who you are needs no embellishing in or out of bed."

"The science is there," I yelled at his back. "You know it is."

"Goodnight, Ty," he said before shutting the bedroom door between us.

With a sinking feeling, I realized that when even the people who loved me wouldn't listen, the chances of a stranger accepting the story without proof and publishing it for all to see were roughly zero.

Maybe even less.

CHAPTER 17

RISK OF EXPOSURE

The last day of March in 2128, the Republic of Texas declared war against the Clan Wilson, and our military personnel established six firebases along the northern border. The MoD even drew people and planes from the pair of Texas aircraft carriers in the Gulf of Mexico.

For several tense days, Cris and I waited to find out if I would be activated early. I felt my anxiety grow until I couldn't help but fall back into all the behavior patterns groomed in the lab because they were familiar.

Seething at my weakness, I did the most prohibited activity I could think of on the third day of waiting.

"What are you doing?" Cris snapped, his frustration showing in his scattered reference materials and finger-twisted hair. "Please, it's clean enough."

"I wasn't allowed to clean. I wasn't allowed to do laundry. I wasn't allowed to—"

"Just because your parents were control freaks, it doesn't mean you have to take a toothbrush to the tile to prove you're capable of getting the floor clean. Do some schoolwork."

"I finished my homework. It was too easy. It's always too easy."

He confiscated my toothbrush and snatched a book from the stack. "Read that."

"I can't sit still. Let me clean. I'll just dust something. Well, everything."

Ten minutes later, I found the first pest repellent device. At least that's what I thought the tiny button of hardware pressed under the kitchen cabinet was for. I'd cleaned the apartment when we'd first moved in, and thanks to my paranoia, I'd been thorough in hunting for crevices where a past tenant could've left behind drugs or other contraband that could've been used to incriminate me.

I was about to show the device to Cris when I thought better of it. Under the guise of cleaning, I located ones in the living room, the dining room, our bedroom, and even our bathroom.

I spied the small can of ant spray Cris had in the back of the bathroom cabinet. "Do we have a pest issue here on the third floor? Why didn't you call the super?"

"No need. There were a few ants by the window," he called out. "I took care of it."

"You sprayed? That's a little inhumane for you. I expected you to us those sonic or pheromone repellent devices instead."

"I would if they worked."

So much for that theory.

I sat back on my heels. "Have you let anyone in the apartment lately?"

"A few days ago, yeah. The guy needed to check for water leaks."

108

"Did you leave him alone?"

He peered around the corner at me. "I had to. The call from the MoD was too sensitive for him to overhear. What's missing?"

"What did he look like?"

"I don't know. A normal guy with a flu mask on. Should I call security?"

I reached under the sink, pushing items aside. "No, never mind. Here it is," I said, holding up the container holding my menstrual cup. "I couldn't figure out why some maintenance man would need this."

Cris chuckled and returned to the living room.

So those buttons weren't for insect control. Deep down, I'd known that from the moment I found the first one.

I was under surveillance.

The following day, we got confirmation that the MoD was leaving me in school, much to Cris's wary relief.

As I desired and everyone expected, I signed up for the Battle Axe pilot program and started with a new crew of instructors. Perhaps I should've been thankful to be out from under Jason's piercing gaze—he taught only basic flight theory and then the Axe gunner end—but letting him out of my sight left me jumpy and unsettled.

I tried several more times to share my past with Cris, coming at it from different angles so at least some of my story would make it through his smiling, patient refusal. Finally, he told me the war had exponentially increased his workload at H-E as the MoD tried to force war plane upgrades from the planning phase to the production phase. In other words, he barely had time to scarf down his meals, let alone listen to some storytelling.

I saw his point, but hell, why would I keep insisting he needed to know about my past if I didn't think it was important for understanding me? He was the one who'd wanted to stay married to me.

Well, okay, I wanted to stay married to him, too. The sex still sucked, but I knew it would get better. He was skilled and patient, and each time I was with him, I had to be developing more trust in him.

Good Lord, will you stop thinking about your husband for ten seconds and get some work done?

Rubbing my arms, I glanced around the academy library. One of my larger classmates was nearby, and I was tempted to sit beside him, but I would've needed to be awkwardly close in order to feel his heat. I found a seat by the window and moved until sunlight streamed over me again. I closed my eyes and let the warmth penetrate me. Better.

I made a high, startled sound as a book hit the table in front of me. Jason spun it around so the title was facing me.

"I need you to concern yourself with the marked passages," he told me.

"Shouldn't this be passed to my instructors to disseminate over the whole pilot class?"

"It's advanced theory. They aren't ready for it. The students aren't either."

I strangled a laugh.

Obviously not caring who might be watching us fraternize, he sat opposite me. "What are your concerns?"

"As far as?"

"Are you acting this stupid to piss me off? I'm referring to you being an Axe pilot."

I bit back a scathing remark and considered the question seriously. "Weakness in the training and outdated mods to the Axes. Texas hasn't done well at the Comp since your win and definitely wasn't doing well at the Comp before it. I appreciate the limitations of that

110

competition, but there's a reason people use it to gauge clan strengths and weaknesses. Are our sheer numbers supposed to balance Texas's weaknesses?"

"They won't hurt."

I tapped my stylus restlessly on the table. "They won't mean anything if the Clan Hernandez gets involved."

"I am aware of that."

See, now that would've been the perfect time for him to tell me he didn't expect it to come to that. The Clan Wilson was not an especially large clan, nor was it known for its military strength. Cris and Jason seemed to be the only ones who didn't expect the war to be over as quickly as it had started.

Given his reaction, I had to ask, "I'm being fast-tracked, aren't I?"

"Not if I can help it. I want confirmation of your strengths each step of the way. But considering the worst case scenario is always necessary."

"Agreed." I added his book to my bag. "Thanks."

His shrewd gaze rested on my eyes. "Just say it."

"Hmm?"

"You seem to be biting your tongue."

"Okay, fine. Why are you bugging my apartment?"

His gaze sharpened on mine. "You would not have found them if they were mine."

Damn. It would've been so much easier if it had been him.

"Did you save one?" he asked.

"Why would I keep spyware?"

"So I could trace it back to a user. Come to my office after school today, and I'll tell you other places to look for them."

After a moment, I said, "I don't want to get caught looking through Cris's possessions."

"But you've done it all the same, haven't you?"

I didn't reply. At one time my morality had been firm, but circumstances had eroded it a fair bit. Most survivors probably felt the same way.

But I didn't have to embrace my dark side the way Jason did.

"Invite me over to dinner tonight," he told me.

I shook my head. "Cris has a meeting."

"All the more reason to have me over. I'll be there at seven."

Hands twisted together, I sat on the bed that evening while Jason went through Cris's belongings. It bothered me a lot more than when he went through mine. I had no attachment to anything Cris labeled as mine. Having to start over from nothing over and over again left me with a certain perspective as far as ownership was concerned. But Cris cared about what he owned, and I didn't enjoy betraying his trust that I would respect his privacy and ensure that our house guests did as well.

"No sex toys? I need to see everything."

"I don't like to be crowded, so Cris keeps most of his stuff at his old condo across town."

"That failed to answer my question."

"I don't use sex toys, and I don't permit them to be used on me. They aren't necessary for having a satisfying carnal relationship."

"Carnal," he repeated like he was tasting the word. "I like that. Must be the purring sound in the middle. The end of the word *sex* is a nasty hiss. And I know your sex life is not satisfying, so there is no need to lie."

"It is."

"Possibly for you, but he's quivering with built-up sexual tension like he hasn't been sated in some time."

At my expression, he reminded me, "He's my brother. It's easy for me to read him. Is it the size of his dick?"

I felt the blush heat my cheeks. "If Cris wanted you to know about our sex life, I'm confident he would tell you himself. Not that it's any of your business."

He straightened up. "I've finished. You're clean."

"Thank you," I gritted out.

He stood in front of me, studying me. "I've never had a woman in my bedroom. Intellectually, I know it's a room with furniture like any other room in my house, but it's also where I sleep. I'm exposed. Unguarded. Vulnerable. I cannot let anyone in there."

I raised an eyebrow at that. Did he forget I'd been in his bed when we'd been at Greyson?

"Don't be ashamed of the limitations you require to feel safe," he said, giving my hot cheeks a fleeting caress.

"Why does it matter to you what I feel?" I whispered.

He smiled. "I need you to be focused on flying, not your miserable sex life."

"That'll be easier now that you're not my instructor anymore. You have a beautiful mouth. If I kissed you now, what would you taste like?"

His smiled faded. "Don't bait me."

"Shall I be like a sister to you? You have a sister my age, don't you?"

He recoiled in horrified disgust, no doubt feeling his erection shrivel up and die.

"Don't want to be my big brother? Then keep the conversations about flying," I suggested. "Let me escort you out."

"Don't come near me."

"Don't make excuses to touch me in my bedroom while my husband is gone."

"Don't encourage me to."

113

I followed him through the apartment, grinning. Maybe another woman who wanted his attention would've resorted to sex or stroking his pride, but Jason knew all the tricks. It was better if I remained spontaneous and artless until I was sure he was on my side.

"Big brother, will you read that book to me while I sit on your lap?"

"You do not want to start this with me, Tycho. You really don't."

"Tycho? Don't you know? I'm your precious Miranda, and I've got the DNA to prove it."

He spun and got in my face, eyes dark with fury. His hot breath hit me in waves.

Cris chose that moment to arrive.

"What did you just say to me?" Jason demanded of me.

Without backing away, I told him, "I said I learned where the line is. I won't cross it again."

The terrible energy drained from him. "I indulged you tonight, but I won't again."

"You know what, Jason? I indulged you, too," I snarled.

He smiled. "I know."

Cris's voice was sharp when he said his brother's name.

The air crackled with tension, but I chose to believe it was because of the thunderstorm's electrical disturbance because ten thousand volts of current would've been easier to deal with compared to the animosity and jealousy growing between the two Chavez brothers. In a perfect world, it would've been easy. I adored Cris and could easily shut Jason down.

But Cris wasn't the one who was going to get me to my goal.

114

Love and duty. What a tired conflict. But this wasn't a game, and I had no intention of giving up my advantage with either man if I didn't have to. Cris was a morally upright person with a vast social network, yet Jason had not only technological skill but also the immorality that allowed him to use it in ways Cris never would've.

I already knew I wasn't going to like myself by the time the lab issue was concluded, but that wasn't the point. Ending the lab was.

So the air crackled and the men fumed, and I did nothing to defuse it. Neither man seemed to be in a mood to surrender his claim on me for the sake of familial love, either.

Eventually, I got bored. "Can I get anyone anything to drink?"

Cris's smile flexed in a way that never reached his eyes. "Hemlock, Jason?"

Jason didn't rise to the bait. He didn't have to. I suspected Cris was already threatened by his suspicion that Jason and I had been lovers.

But I thought Jason felt threatened—as little as he ever was—by Cris's prowess with women. And frankly, Cris was the one I had married.

Married. Christ; I was still married. How different this marriage was from my last. I had no business being here with either man, not really. No business being in school, promising I would fight in their battles when I was only there laying the groundwork with Jason to fight my own battle.

No, I didn't like myself.

But I wasn't going to stop, either.

Jason ignored me and nodded at his brother on the way out.

Cris raised an eyebrow at me.

"As an instructor, he's amazing," I muttered. "As a mentor, he's brutal but worth it. As anything else, he's a capricious god with too much power and too much knowledge. Don't mention Miranda Donovan to him, by the way. It's a trigger."

He set his bag on the coffee table, his usual workspace. "Why was he here?"

I held up the book Jason had given me. "He gave me homework."

He flipped to the marked pages and frowned. "This is way too advanced for you. I'll speak to him."

"Good luck with that. While he was being born, he probably told your mom and the doctor how he could've been delivered better."

Chuckling, he tossed the book into his bag and pulled me into his arms. "Forget about his stupid homework. He can't make you do anything."

The following morning, Jason approached me on my study break. Maybe it should've been awkward, but he acted like it had never happened. I certainly wasn't going to bring it up.

He held out the book to me again.

"Thank you," I said, relieved. Cris had fallen asleep on the couch, stirring each time I'd tried to get close enough to snag it from his bag.

"Why did you fail to tell him you could handle the material?"

"He wouldn't have believed me."

He gave me a strange look. "Even knowing who you are? Why are you with a man who thinks you are capable of so little?"

"Just to piss you off."

He snorted. "Consider your mission successful. My turn. You will be divorced by this time next year."

"When you talk like that, it makes me stubborn about proving you wrong."

"Fine. You will still be together by this time next year."

I ground my teeth. "Just bring me more books, please."

"I've got the first ten books ready. I'll evaluate you after you've gone through those, so by late next week."

My heart leapt. That was a lot of work. Dormant parts of my brain came awake with a burst of gratification at the prospect of being put to use again.

He grinned at my response. "Do not hesitate to ask me questions."

I nodded and said honestly, "I look forward to your insight."

CHAPTER 18

A WARM WINTER

It was less than two weeks into the Axe pilot program that I noticed one of my classmates was watching me like I watched him.

I liked the way Winter McIntyre moved. It was as if he had no fear, but he wasn't stomping around like he was trying to impress anyone. He was as young as the rest of my classmates, who fell between seventeen and twenty, but the look in his gray eyes suggested he'd been on his own for a long time. Self-reliant, uncompromising, and even a bit hard, the young man couldn't have blended in with the crowd if he wanted to. Fortunately, he had no interest in that.

Unfortunately, he was training to be another Axe pilot instead of an Axe gunner. I would've liked him to be my flight partner.

"I want you to go out with me," he told me outside the cafeteria.

I held up my left hand, making a show of my wedding band.

He said, "Are you going to answer me or not?"

"My marriage signifies a decision to remain with one man."

"I know what a wedding ring is," he said, pushing his hand through his chestnut hair. The longer top layers had red highlights from sun exposure. Despite always smelling like sunscreen, his fair skin had a light tan. "I also know it has little to do with a woman's answer."

"It has everything to do with this woman's answer."

"When a woman doesn't say she's in love with her husband, it makes me think she got married for another reason."

I stiffened.

"Look," he said. "I'm from the outlands. I understand doing what it takes to survive. I'm saying you don't have to pretend with me."

"I'm trying to make it work with him," I gritted out.

He nodded and pushed away from the wall. "I can respect that. You let me know if you change your mind."

"I don't bounce around from man to man," I snarled after him.

"Nothing about you made me think you did," he said, turning with his arms out wide.

Brow furrowed, I bit my lip. He was leaving, and I didn't want him to. "Your call sign doesn't suit you."

He turned back, puzzled.

"You're not a Winter."

"I didn't remember my real first name, and the orphanage people had to call me something. I didn't like it there, so I only went back to it when it was too cold to camp out. You know. In winter."

119

I watched him stride away again. I should've felt some pity or something, but instead I buzzed with pleasure at his strength.

My palmer signaled an incoming call, and I opened the connection.

"That didn't work? Seriously?" Winter said. "It's true and everything, but I generally don't whip it out like that unless I'm desperate enough to try for a pity date."

"Watch yourself, boy-o. This is becoming harassment. How did you even get this number?"

"We exchanged them last week when we were paired up for that project. Don't be pissed. I like what I see in you, and I had to try. I'll see you in study hall."

Oddly enough, the exchange made me smile. He was direct, honest, and unswayed by the drama of our classmates, and I ended up genuinely enjoying him as a partner for our class project.

After enduring the frivolous conversation at the next table in study hall one day months later, Winter said, "The culling tests weren't brutal enough. There are way too many babies that we're told to trust with our defense."

"You're what, eighteen? Nineteen?"

"It's not the years, but the experience. I'm like a thousand times older than them."

"Their reflexes are phenomenal."

"Their hormones are phenomenal," he said in disgust. "It's all about drinking and groping with those babies."

Amused at his response, I tapped his screen. "Let's get back to work."

He continued to frown at the giggling youths. "We deserve better than to be stuck with them in the air."

"Just because they've lasted this long doesn't mean they'll make it to the end."

He brightened at that and returned to the project at hand.

His words still hung heavily in the air. Sending children to war didn't sit well with me. Granted, almost all of them already had their two- or four-year college degrees, but that made them educated, not mature. Some of the youngest ones were from prominent MoD families. If my child had lived, the combination of Chavez genes with mine would've guaranteed pressure to prep her for early admission to flight school.

My hand was on my abdomen, searching, forever searching for that missing piece of me.

I haven't forgotten you, little love, and your daddy and I would've hidden you instead of handing you over to the MoD meat grinder.

I also haven't forgotten my promise that I'd make the lab pay for whatever it is they did that made me unable to properly nurture you within me. Your death is their fault. I'm still trying to find them, I swear to God. I go cross-eyed from poring over maps and legends of lost underground war bunkers. Someday I will prove the lab exists, and they will be forced to close down. No one else will be subjected to the cutting and sewing and breaking and rebuilding just to see if it could be done. No other poor girls will be—

"Ty?"

I blinked, and the youthful I fell back into place. I smiled brightly at Winter out of habit, but it was a wasted effort. He seemed to be able to see through some of my lies to the scar tissue underneath.

He motioned at my cheek his with his stylus and said in a matter-of-fact voice, "I want to kiss your freckles."

I let him see my annoyance. "Back to work."

When I got home with a bag full of take-out, Cris was sitting on the couch reading his screen with a smile on his lips that wouldn't go away.

I came to him from behind, kissing the top of his head.

He tipped the screen my way to show the image of Miranda Donovan curled up in a chair in the sun in her Hernandez cadet uniform. It looked like the library at the academy there.

I'd been awfully skinny then but no longer skeletal, and the smooth line of my nose indicated the photo had been taken before Kairo Ashton punched me in the face and broke my nose. Late summer 2120 perhaps.

"That feels like a thousand years ago," I murmured. "I don't remember anyone ever taking a picture of me. Where did you get it?"

"Jason's file," he said, leaving the couch, nose twitching at the tantalizing scent of Chinese food.

I scrolled through the archive, shocked at the number of photos Jason had taken, but it was nothing compared to the sheer number of text files he had on me. It had been no secret he'd saved and analyzed my academic work, but nearly half the portfolio was about me personally. The narrative was surprisingly insightful given how little I'd told him, but it was biased and indulgent, too, as it described my nearly two-year fight to gain acceptance from the notoriously demanding clan.

I should've guessed Jason had created a dossier about me to show his Defense Minister when he said he wanted me to think about returning to Texas with him, but this went far beyond a simple dossier. It was like reading a novel someone had written about my life.

An idealized one.

A fantasy that my husband seemed to favor over reality. In some ways, he was more immature than Winter was despite the difference in their ages.

"I've changed a lot since then," I had to point out. I heard the strain in my voice. "Even if I wanted to go back to being like the woman in that file, I couldn't. You know that, don't you? He left out the incidents that made me look like a stubborn child and behavior that made me look paranoid and crazy and weak. You're seeing an advertisement for a pilot Jason wanted to use to buy back the DM's love."

He laughed and collected the screen from me like he expected me to delete that file. To delete her.

Smart man.

CHAPTER 19

A Blow to Mecca

Early in September, I woke to the sound of Cris moving around the bedroom with purpose. It was almost two o'clock in the morning. While Cris usually worked well into the night, especially if the engineering muse or MoD demands dictated, this time I felt his urgency.

"You okay?" I murmured.

"Harbinger-Ellis's western compound has been bombed. I need to fly out."

I pushed to a sitting position and turned on the light to look at him. He wore nothing but his jeans, and his hair was all tousled like he'd been scrubbing his hands through it. God did like throwing me reminders of how sexy my husband could be without trying, that was for sure.

I said, "Like the MoD tasked you with going or like—"

"Like I've worked with the H-E people for years, they're my friends and colleagues, and I have both the ability and desire to help them," he said, moving his duffle to the bed now that he could see. His duffle was already so full of computers and parts that it was difficult for him to wedge in a change of clothes.

I rolled out of bed and dug through my backpack. I handed him a pack of moist cleaning towels, guessing that being bombed meant there probably was limited water. As an afterthought, I added my first aid kit.

"Thanks," he said, pressing a kiss to my lips that made the usual flicker of dread appear before logic dictated he was unlikely to want sex at the moment. "And thanks for understanding why I have to go. I don't know when I'll be back."

"Do what you need to do, but be careful, okay?"

I don't know why I added that last part. Cris was more than competent to handle himself. It was one of the characteristics I loved about him.

"I will," he said dutifully.

His palmer vibrated, and his eyes went to its face. "My ride's downstairs. I'll call you when I can."

"I would appreciate that. Hey, take this," I said, forcing him to take my barest emergency pack. "One day of water and a week's worth of water purification tablets. Each of those food pills is 400 calories. There's a little electrolyte powder in there, too."

He stuffed the supplies in the cargo pockets of his pants. "Thanks. Love you."

And then he was gone.

I felt bereft, unsettled.

Cursing, I dug the emergency products overflow box out from under the bed and hurriedly prepared another water and calorie pack to replace the one I had given him. Only when that was done did I feel the harsh talons of panic release me. After I built another first aid and sanitation pack and put them in their assigned places in my backpack, my breathing and heart rate slowed to normal rhythms.

Almost.

I dug out Mauss's pistol—was I ever going to think of it as mine?—and checked the clip. Nine rounds in their immaculate cocoon.

Satisfied that I was statistically favored to survive what might come, I crawled back into bed.

In the morning on the crowded train, I had to reevaluate my chances as the man sitting beside me drew a knife on the man opposite. It was like I was some kind of magnet for crap like this.

The woman on the other side of me screamed in my ear and grabbed me like I was a shield, which just made the escalating situation more irritating. Yelling at her to let me go, I shoved back against her in an attempt to get out of range of the blade.

The train's marshal was trying to get to us, but a few helpful people were intent on disarming the knife-wielding man in the meantime.

Predictably, I got nicked, a shallow slice across my forearm that splattered red on my white uniform before the knife was knocked from his hand and landed on my lap. And really, there's nothing like several good Samaritans grabbing at your crotch for a weapon while a train car lurches to your stop.

"You're late," Winter said without looking up as I tossed my bag on the table beside him.

"You know, I really can't decide if I have bad luck or good. Plainly terrible because of the situations I find myself in, but it must be good because I always survive them."

His eyebrow rose when he saw the stains on my uniform and the matching mark on my arm.

"You okay?

"Knife-wielding nut on the train this morning."

"Ah. Must be Wednesday," he said, making me laugh. For some reason, it was funnier coming from him than if someone else had said it.

"Did you handle it?" he asked.

"The marshal was there."

He snorted, his eyes going to the cut on my arm. "Takes less time to get stabbed than it does for the law to show up to prevent it. Seriously, why didn't you do anything? If you were that close to the action, you could've handled it before anyone got hurt."

"Partially because some lady was clutching my dominant arm to make sure that if anybody got stabbed it wasn't going to be her," I said, annoyed by the question because it sort of felt like I was being accused of being a coward. "The rest of it was that if I interfered and ended up killing that guy or some innocent bystander, there would be repercussions. It was better to try to get out of range instead of jumping on that dog pile."

He shook his head at my reasoning but let it go.

I didn't even finish unpacking my study materials before I packed them up again. "I can't handle seeing my own blood like this."

"It's a few drops."

"But they're my drops. I'm changing clothes."

"You can't see them through the table."

"Doesn't matter. I know they're there."

He shot me an exasperated look and waved me away.

After I had changed into an academy logo T-shirt and sweatpants, I stopped by Jason's office to pick up another book, but his door was locked tight. The message on his door said he was going to be out for the rest of the week and referred his students to another instructor.

127

Uneasy, I thought of the implications. Jason didn't deviate from a schedule on a whim. In fact, the atomic clock could be set by his classes. He wouldn't have surrendered his syllabus to another instructor even for a few days during peacetime, let alone while Texas was on a war footing. It had to be the H-E bombing, although I couldn't imagine him climbing over rubble to salvage the computers and get them back in the network. Was he over at the MoD?

Damn, I wished I'd heeded their warning that I pay more attention to what was going on in the Ministry of Defense. Between researching respected journalists with open minds who might believe me without proof and trying to find the lab itself, I had barely touched the sticky web of Ministry dealings.

No, the Chavez family had their feelers attuned to that place. I was the only one who was trying to expose the lab. I couldn't get distracted.

Down in the quad, students swirled around me with self-important masks for expressions. How little they truly knew.

As I watched, two youths started shoving each other while the object of their affection smirked from the sidelines.

Was humanity already lost? Was there any real possibility of saving humanity from its own mistakes?

Or was I arrogant for thinking I had the power to make a difference? Was it even possible for one person to take on a task this big? I was one person. One gun.

Was that part of it? That I needed to believe I was put on earth for a reason? That the misery and torture and time displacement had all been part of a grander design to bring me to the very point I was at, on the very edge of the action I contemplated? Everywhere I looked, I saw connections where no one else seemed to. Was it a curse or a gift? Or once given the gift, had God created

128

the situation to make certain my gift was not wasted on reading mystery novels and winning trivia games?

I thought of the deaths I had caused, the deaths I had witnessed, the deaths that had happened on my behalf. Were those losses meant to drive me to the point where I would prevent far more? It made a cruel sort of sense.

One of the instructors arrived and the fight broke up, but the kids seemed to know he was feckless because they started up again almost immediately. Hell, the man seemed to know how little he was respected, too. He ignored their taunts and trudged away as soon as the security personnel were close.

Did I envy the drones dragging themselves through ordinary lives toward unremarkable deaths? Perhaps.

However, another part of me burned with pleasure at the challenge of incapacitating the lab. Too bad Finley had chosen to take a bullet when he realized he was caught. I would've liked to pit myself against him again.

When I entered my apartment building, the concierge flagged me down.

"These came for you this morning," Kiki said, opening a white box to reveal a slim bouquet of blue-violet flowers. "Is it your anniversary?"

"Good evening, Ms. Kiki," I said, softening the evasion with a smile as I closed the lid.

Up in my apartment, I emptied the box onto the kitchen counter, using a pair of chopsticks to poke the stems apart and look for surveillance, a note, or anything to explain their presence in my life. If Jason had been of a mind to send flowers, they would've been exquisite, the money spent on them obvious. Cris felt guilty about the mutilation of plants for their pretty parts and would've taken me to a botanical garden instead.

I didn't recognize the flowers. Each stem had several downward-facing florets, gorgeous for their indigo coloration but not particularly handsome in form.

An online search indicated it was aconite. Also known as monkshood for the shape of the flowers or wolf's bane because they were poisonous. Damned poisonous. Deadly. In the Victorian language of flowers, they represented distrust or contempt of mankind.

What the hell what that supposed to mean?

I checked the box but found nothing more than the generic font of the label that listed my name and when the flowers were to be delivered.

I returned to the desk and asked Kiki about it under the pretense of wanting to get a tip to the delivery guy. She showed me the footage of the messenger, and I bit back a gasp as I recognized him.

I made it back to my apartment on wooden legs.

It couldn't be him. It wasn't him. It had to be a mask. Of course it was a mask. The physique of the delivery man was athletic and slim, not the soft build of an administrator.

Harry Fischer, the dead ADM, had not delivered flowers for me.

But who had?

Chapter 20

Dodging a Bullet

That Saturday evening, the feeling on the flight academy campus became slower, more low-key. We worked thirteen days on and one off, but it was a true day off for most of us—no homework and no projects to prep for. With tomorrow being the fourteenth day of the cycle, everyone could finally sleep in.

Students and instructors trickled down the main staircase in the library building, their conversations covering both the war and the baseball game. From my seat in one of the study pits, I could look through the window and see the exodus continue toward the train station. I wondered if I should be among them.

Winter caught me surreptitiously rubbing my temple.

"Still have a headache? Go home," he suggested. "Should be nice and quiet with your husband gone."

I shifted my tired, bloodshot eyes to his. "Enough about my headache. I just want to finish prepping next week's work before I leave."

"Then why are you reviewing the optional exercises from last month?" he said, leaning over the coffee table to read my work upside down. "The ones you said were useless?"

I swore.

"Go home," he repeated.

I bared my teeth at him, but at least now I could abandon the pretense and use both hands to press circles into my temples. "Stupid eye strain."

"Take some pain meds and get some sleep."

"I know what to do," I snarled.

He smiled at me. "See you on Monday."

"Don't be nice when I'm nasty. It confuses me."

By the time I got home, it felt like fat, knobby roots were trying to grow in the crevices of my gray matter. I took the maximum dose of nonprescription painkillers and went to bed with a wet cloth over my eyes.

It was dark when I woke, and it took me far longer than it should've to remember who and where I was. The pain in my skull was becoming debilitating, and I grabbed for my hidden palmer, needing two hands to hold it.

Domino answered on the second ring.

"I need a doctor," I managed to say. "There's a glitch in my head. The pain is..."

I couldn't think of a way to describe it.

"I'm so hot," I moaned. "My head..."

"I'm on my way," he promised, his voice rushed.

Bits and flashes of the night made it through the agony in my head. Domino's concerned hazel eyes and dark blue hair. The sweep of the bioscanner. The sting of needles. The mention of transport back to the lab so they could operate immediately. My fear becoming lost in the maelstrom of skull-fracturing pain.

When I woke, my vision was filled with Domino's face. His mouth was tight, his eyes like flint. The oxygen feed to my nostrils didn't block the scent of antiseptic.

My eyelids felt like stone, but I was determined to keep them raised. "No need to give me the stink eye. I didn't throw a cog on purpose."

"You have bacterial meningitis," he told me.

I tried to think around the pain in my head. It was nowhere near as crippling as it had been, but it was still twisting in there, making it a struggle to hang on to a thought. "So why did I need surgery? Didn't someone say I was having surgery?"

"You don't need it. The lab misdiagnosed it to get you underground again. They've been saying for some time that you're too valuable to risk losing in a war."

I tried to puzzle it out, but seeing my difficulty, he filled in the gaps.

"I think they arranged to get that bacteria into you in the hopes it would manifest to the point where you had to call us. They've probably tried a few times since you started flight school, but this time they got it to stick," he said, gesturing at the cut on my arm.

"Definitely. I wasn't sure I was going to make it through the night."

"When they gave me the code to take off your transmitter bracelet so I could bring you to them, I figured I could get you to my doctor for a second opinion before they realized what was going on. There's no doubt it's bacterial meningitis."

"Well, good."

"Not really. It's still a lot more dangerous than the usual viral kind. People do die from it."

I closed my eyes, smiling slightly. "Those bastards. First the shooting at Greyson and now this. I suffer a lot from their attempts to save me from a life topside. Thanks, Domino."

"I'm surprised you called me."

"Isn't that what I'm meant to do?"

"Yeah, but I never thought you'd risk it."

"Domino," I sighed, "you witnessed the only change in my condition that would've made me that desperate. Once my brain malfunctions to the point where I can't think, it's worth anything to save. It's my only original body part left, after all. So what did your doctor say when he saw me under the microscope? Does what I am show?"

"He's independent of the lab, and I trust him."

I digested his emphasis on the word *trust*. "So the cloning shows?"

"I don't know. Maybe it only shows at the chromosomal level."

"When Mauss targeted Lucas for a forced blood donation, the medical center said I was blacklisted."

He nodded. "You're exempt from all tissue harvesting. Prohibited from donating, too."

"Because I'm tainted."

"Because you're classified as being too valuable to risk having parts of you removed."

"But not so valuable they won't risk poison-core bracelets and a vicious brain-destroying bacteria," I said with a grim smile.

"I'm not putting the bracelet back on you."

My gaze was steady on his. "Whose decision is that? Because as much as I hate it, it does prevent them from snatching me off the street when they get tired of trying to entice me into calling them."

"The laws have changed slightly since yours went on. I was able to prove that it is now illegal. If the lab didn't tell me to take it off, there was nothing I could do, but since they told me to take it off, the law prevents me from putting it back on." He hesitated. "I don't know how long that'll last. The lawyers are fighting it out. I didn't know you wanted it."

"I don't. I want them to leave me alone."

"Until your head hurts?"

"I didn't call them. I called you," I said pointedly.

"I work for them."

"You're still sticking with that story? How can the lab not be suspicious yet?"

His eyes narrowed. "They knew when they hired me I stick to the law."

"No matter how unethical it is," I snarled. "What happened to me—"

"I do the best I can to protect you," he said tiredly. "But it will be within the law."

He opened the door and motioned people into my room. After he introduced me to the doctor and two nurses to personally vouch for them, he checked that the security measures were in place and then left.

When I let myself into the apartment Monday afternoon, Cris rushed me, his hair wild.

"Where have you been? Why didn't you have your phone?"

"I forgot my phone when I went to the medical center. I have meningitis."

"What? Why didn't they notify me? I'm listed as your next of kin. Which center did you go to? I called all of them."

I pointed to the counter where my wallet and phone were. "My head was all jacked up. Maybe I gave them the wrong name or no name or whatever. Look, I'm sorry. Will you let me in so I can get off my feet? I feel like crap."

He backpedaled, taking the bag of antibiotics off me to free my hands. "Go get settled in bed. I'll bring you some tea."

"I would like that."

"I'll ensure the academy isn't listing you as a no-show, too."

"Thanks."

Along with my Earl Grey, he brought me cookies, and I munched on one.

"I'm really sorry I wasn't home," he told me. "Did you call Jason?"

"Jason's been out all week. Probably due to H-E. I don't know that I would've called him anyway. It was just a matter of going to the doctor."

"Well, I want to introduce you to my brother Shaun. If you can't get a hold of Jason or me, he'll be happy to help. You're one of us."

"I like the way you said that like you're some brain-washed cult."

He grinned at me. "You said it, not me." He brushed the crumbs off the blanket. "You should nap."

"I'd rather hear how your trip to H-E went. Mind if I close my eyes while you talk, though?"

He took my hand, stroking it lightly, twisting the ring on my finger. "I did some checking. Discreetly, of course. About what you told me."

I opened my eyes.

"Do you want to discuss this later?" he asked.

"No, now."

"Well, it's sometimes easy to forget how advanced the ancient Romans were because of how backward the Dark Ages were after Rome fell. I made that same mistake with the Clan Wars. I don't think you know how much information was lost when the American digital world fell. Add a worldwide recession after that, and well, let's say I'm sorry for making some assumptions about the technology available in the beginning of the twenty-first century."

I froze, suspended between hope and disbelief.

He smiled. "I believe it's possible you were put in some kind of underground cryo preservation and forgotten about while the Clan Wars were happening above you."

I closed my hand around his and squeezed. Of anyone, he was the one I needed to believe me, and we were all but there.

"I have some questions," he said.

"Thank you," I whispered, tears stinging my eyes.

It still took a lot for him to suspend disbelief, so I didn't mention Finley or Mauss. I stuck to what I knew about my Hernandez era, and that meshed with what Jason wrote about me, so for now, it was enough. I glossed over my time in the lab after that, simply saying it took a long time for them to stabilize and rebuild me given how ill I was before I died.

"I want to find the lab," I told him. "This meningitis business makes it obvious if I do have some major malfunction, I've got no way to get a hold of them for help. I have to trust they will show up on their own. Will you help me figure out where they are?"

He shook his head. "I don't want you to look for them. A place built on secrets is far more likely to see your attempts to find them as a way to bring unwanted attention to them deliberately or accidentally. I mean, Jason was completely shocked when you resurfaced, which means that despite all his tricks he couldn't find any sign of you. That tells me these are some very careful people. Try to find them, and they might just grab you to protect their secrecy instead. I'd never see you again."

Damn.

"Are you mad?" he asked.

"I don't know," I said irritably. "You might be right."

"Where's your bracelet?" he asked, lacing his fingers with mine.

"It broke."

"Where is it? I'll take a look," he said, plainly looking for a peace offering.

"No, I got rid of it. I decided I like my wrist bare after all."

Wow. How much of our marriage was built on the lies we told each other and the lies we told ourselves?

Around midnight, my stomach was growling with painful need, and I left the bedroom as quietly as I could, figuring Cris was catching up on some much-needed sleep.

He stirred on the couch, shifting his phone to the other ear. "No, I told you I can't tonight," he murmured. "My wife is sick." He bit back a groan and adjusted his growing arousal. "You're such a tease. Look, I'll call you when she goes back to school."

My belly now felt hollow, and my hands curled into fists. I slipped back into the bedroom and got into bed.

So what if it sounded like he was getting sex on the side? Wasn't I grateful he wasn't bothering me for it? Wasn't I thrilled he'd stopped pestering me about getting counseling? Didn't he still go out of his way to bring me books and do other sweet things? And hell, wasn't he even starting to believe the crazier parts of my past?

And didn't this problem have a ridiculously easy fix? All I had to do was take the bullet and come on to him and moan like a whore when he was inside me. And it was just when he was inside me that really bothered me. I loved making out with him. I loved feeling the muscles in his arms flex when he embraced me. I loved the feel of his hair between my fingers and the rumble in his chest when he laughed. I even loved the magic of his dick going from limp flesh to hot steel.

But I never got used to him penetrating me, nor did I look forward to the next attempt.

Was it a feeling of vulnerability like Jason had that prevented him from letting a woman in his bedroom? I didn't know. It had been there before the miscarriage, I knew that.

I rolled onto my side, staring at the shaft of moonlight falling on his work boots. They were sturdy and scuffed from hard, honest work. People didn't always agree with Cris, but even his enemies had to admit he gave it his all at his contracted jobs and charity work both. He was a good man. He deserved good sex. Hell, yes, I felt betrayed, but if I weren't willing to even try any of the solutions he offered to fix me, could I really begrudge my husband some extracurricular attention?

Yes. I could.

I smothered my sigh in my pillow.

CHAPTER 21

VIGILANTE

I didn't get much studying done in the main hall the day I got back to school. I knew Cris was meeting with Jason upstairs, so my eyes kept returning to the staircase to look for him. Eventually, I saw his dark hair, and I waved like mad to get his attention.

"Come sit," I said, trying to avoid the kiss he aimed at my cheek. Why did he keep trying to kiss me in uniform? "You remember Winter, right?"

"Sure."

"Winter's got some fascinating ideas about self-governance in the outlands."

Cris's handshake froze, and his manner cooled considerably. Nevertheless, he sat down with us. "I heard them all when we lived out there. Small communities self-policing in the absence of appointed or elected officials is nothing but vigilantism. What happened to a fair trial?"

I snorted. "That works fine when the world isn't split into metropolis areas and wastelands. Texas is a big place, and they aren't treating the outlying areas equally. Should they wait until the big cities get around to processing their information and setting up a trial? Do you know how long that takes?"

"The computers don't differentiate between a crime committed in one district and the next. Murder is murder, and once a suspect is arrested, a public defender is assigned if they can't afford it. Locals who decide to ignore the process because they consider it too inconvenient are committing a crime, too. How would you like it if you were accused, convicted, and punished without having the fair trial the Texas constitution promised you?"

"But if you know someone did something—"

"Know? Really? Because the evidence you're looking at was obtained in a legal way and you've obtained the qualifications to perform an official analysis of it?" he said, frowning at me. "Things aren't necessarily what they seem."

"Sometimes they are exactly what they seem."

"Which is why we have a Ministry of Justice, jails, and a thriving lawyer population. Sometimes people get away with crimes. Sometimes innocent people get convicted. No system is perfect. But there's no excuse for vigilantism. None."

"Sometimes it's the only way to—"

"To rob people of their inalienable right to a fair trial?" he asked me. "What if, for instance, you come across the victim of a stabbing? It's someone you know, someone you don't really like, but hell, they're in trouble so you rush in to help him. The next person to show up finds you with a dead body and blood on your hands. What they are likely to see is that you had another fight and in a heat of anger, it became physical and you killed him."

I smiled. "You underestimate people's intelligence."

"I'm confident if you look in the histories, you'll find a similar case that resulted in the death penalty. So the locals can say the precedent is set and they shoot you in the head. After all, they have the right to self-police because there's a backlog, no one in town has the fuel or time to drive you to a proper judicial center for processing in a larger city, and everyone knows exactly what happened, don't they?"

"Sometimes—"

"Sometimes people commit atrocities in the sincere effort to protect their community. Well-intentioned murder is still murder."

"Capital punishment."

"I was waiting for you to bring that up. The decision of the proper authorities to terminate the life of a prisoner convicted in a proper trial is still a long, thoughtful process. It's not done as a convenience or a tool to get reelected."

He pinned me with his gaze.

"There's no excuse for vigilantism. It's easy, but it's not right."

I sat back, a smile teasing my lips. Cris was fabulous. He really was. Sometimes I wound him up just to hear what he had to say.

"I've seen self-policing get out of control," Winter said, his voice quieter but no less certain than Cris's. "But I've also seen what happens to a community when the gangs or cartels moved in and the townspeople followed the laws. They reported what they saw to the proper agency and had their houses burned down and their families murdered for their trouble. The lawmen were bought off or killed off until someone bought off wore the badge. Trial dates were set, but by that point most people were too terrified to testify. The rest mysteriously vanished before they could give testimony. Those are the areas in Texas people know not to go to."

Cris acknowledged that with a nod.

Winter said, "People have a responsibility to make up for the shortfalls in their community. You must think so with all the charity work you do. The government programs are in place, but they are underfunded and understaffed, so people like you pick up the slack. Why? Because if you didn't, your communities would rot, right?"

"Charity is done within the law's boundaries. Self-policing is illegal. How can there be true justice when those people lack the authority to act?"

"Cris, have you seen the ratio of lawmen to inhabitants in the outlands communities? How is one person meant to serve and protect all those people even if he has the best technology? From what I've seen, self-policing is the only reason some of those places can be traveled through without the protection of an army. When the clan expands and updates the police force so it can actually live up to its mandate, I'll be the first person to step aside. But until then, people like me will step in to pick up the slack like they do when someone is hungry or needs a place to live."

I had no doubt each man had repeatedly acted according to his beliefs, and it made me proud of both of them.

"Are you headed home?" I asked Cris when he stood. When he nodded, I returned my books to my bag so I could join him. As we left the building, I said, "He's interesting, isn't he? To be so fully formed at such a young age?"

"I don't think he got to be a kid for very long," Cris said, pity in his voice. "But if one of these pups has to be flying on your wing, I definitely want it to be him."

"He does have an air of competence, doesn't he?"

"Definitely."

Thinking of the meeting with Jason, I said, "Is the H-E situation handled or are you leaving again now that you and Jason have compared notes?"

"That depends on you."

"I feel fine. The doctor said there's no permanent damage."

"I meant about how you feel about us, but we'll discuss that at home, okay?"

So I stewed about it on the ride home, unable to think past Cris's conversation with his lover.

At the apartment, he started making sandwiches, slapping them together without thought as if he needed to occupy his hands while he decided how to approach it.

Eventually, he ran out of bread.

"For a while now, I've felt like there's a distance growing between us," he told me, hands braced on the counter.

Silent, I slowly sank into my chair, listening with knotted hands.

"I'm not leaving you," he assured me. "Until the clan gives you more protections under the law, I'm uncomfortable bailing on you."

Wow, that so wasn't the reason I hoped he would use to stay.

"Cris."

"Please let me finish," he said. "I've been thinking about what you told me about your past for days now, trying to pick it apart or sort through the timeline or weigh the possible repercussions if this or that got out. But then it hit me like a lightning bolt that you trusted me with all this. You opened yourself and told me what you haven't told anyone else. It made me see that you're still invested in us."

"Don't you want me to be?"

He nodded.

Why didn't I feel better?

CHAPTER 22

BUR

In December, I felt Jason's eyes on me more often than not during the Resist, Escape, and Evade section of my academy training. Learning how to handle myself on enemy lands after being shot down was a requirement, and it was the very point where I fell apart in my Hernandez training. Thanks to some astute questioning by Jason while I was so torn up I couldn't remember who or where I was, he'd been able to unlock a bank of memories about my first husband's death.

However, a lot had happened since I had squeaked by my Hernandez REE training. This time the pistols, knives, and hand-to-hand felt far more comfortable. I was plainly no expert, but I didn't hesitate to go for the throat either. Winter was pleased and helped me clean up my technique.

Jason, however, looked unsettled as he watched me in action. Did I look bloodthirsty to him?

"The evaluator said those strikes were confident and accurate," I told Jason after the second week of REE. "I thought that would make you happy."

"You know me. I like my violence to be as a last resort."

"Is that why you're such a strong runner?"

His gaze sharpened at being called a coward, but his lips twisted in humor. Only for a moment, though. "Do you still think about Paul?"

I was surprised Jason remembered his name. "No, actually, I don't. I was afraid I was holding him here, and there were elements of my life I didn't want him to see."

"He would not expect you to be celibate for the rest of your life."

"No, I was trying to spare him the knowledge of what was being done to me, because he couldn't have stopped it. I don't expect you to understand."

"Then you underestimate me," he said. "You are still too right-hand dominant, by the way. What if your right hand is incapacitated?"

I paused. He made a good point. During my rebuild, I'd had a lot of issues with the nerves in my left arm and hand, so whatever gains I'd made to improve my weaker side had been lost.

He motioned for me to join him as he stepped away from the tidy piles of dummy knives. "I want to speak to you about the graduation offers they are prepping for you."

"Offers? I thought this was straightforward. If I meet the graduation requirements, I get my diploma and my partner, and once we finish the simulations, I get my wings and my flight assignment."

"That's the route for citizens."

My teeth gnashed. "I can't tell you how tired I am of having to prove my worth."

"I'm not thrilled about it either, Tycho."

I jerked at my name falling from his lips. I didn't know why I expected him to still call me Miranda. He knew the risk, which was why his promise to expose me at the time of his choosing was such a potent threat.

I asked, "You've seen the offers? Are you involved in shaping them?"

He shook his head. "And that is another aspect that is pissing me off. One of them is complete, though, and that is the one I want to discuss."

I sat in front of his desk while he closed the door to his office.

After he had checked his surveillance blockers, he said, "You can talk freely in here, but not very loud. They are going to offer you guaranteed entrance to advanced aviation or aviation engineering degree programs. They will fund it entirely. If you want to do both tracks, they will pay for both all the way through the doctorate level. The only stipulation is that you never get in a plane. Simulators are allowed, but absolutely no aerial work."

"I can't control getting drafted."

"You are not a citizen, so you cannot be drafted under Texas law."

"So it's my choice," I said, savoring the idea. "And there's no way that offer was created by the MoD."

"Are you interested?"

I made a noncommittal noise. "Am I to assume that the MoD's offer will be like the Hernandez work visa, essentially hiring me as a mercenary to fight in their war?"

"Probably."

"Complete with the tease that if I do well enough, I will be offered citizenship?"

"That is the part that is still being crafted."

"Why are they hesitating?"

"I have the impression the MoD wants you sworn in as a citizen as soon as possible so your involvement in the war is guaranteed."

It was the lab, I realized. Because almost every part of me had originated as cloned tissue, they had legal standing to classify me as their biotech property and retain all rights to how I would be used. That the cloning itself had been illegal in the first place had no bearing on the situation.

I suspected that whoever Domino actually worked for—the Ministry of Justice?—offered that scholarly option to bridge the gap between treating me as a person like I deserved and placating the lab's need to keep me out of the war.

And honestly, I was ravenous for all that schooling. The days at Greyson when I split my time between the library and the simulator to pursue my own agenda had been the most satisfying of my life.

But.

Man, oh, man, did I relish the idea of denying the lab what it wanted. The satisfaction of serving the country, living with a purpose beyond that of a lab rat, and screwing the lab at the same time?

"Which way are you leaning?" Jason asked. "Talk me through it."

I shook my head. "There are factors that aren't public knowledge. I'm confident I can reach a decision without assistance."

"Your choice does affect me," he said, the corners of his lips turned down. "I would like to be your instructor again, and the earlier I know your plans, the better I can position myself."

"Mentor," I corrected. "Your role as a mentor is expansive compared to that of an instructor. And I'm flattered you want to continue building on our professional relationship, but there are still two weeks before I'll get to see those offers. They may change considerably in tone and intent before then, so I'd be a fool to set my heart on one or the other."

"I hate the way you sit there with that smug little smile knowing damned well you have made your decision and won't deign to tell me because you like having the upper hand."

"When have I ever had the better position?" I teased. "You already know where you want me and how to make sure I get there, so why play at asking me? Skip to the notification, will you? I'm hungry."

He didn't smile back.

I sat back in my chair, regarding him. In a more serious tone, I said, "It's a difficult call. There are massive advantages and disadvantages to both."

"Do you have any loyalty to Texas?"

"Not enough for it to affect my decision."

"I want to protect my clan."

"You're debating whether or not you're getting back in the cockpit, aren't you? If I go on active duty, you want to be my gunner again, and if I stay a student, you want to be my mentor."

He nodded.

"I'm willing to listen to your arguments either way," I said.

"No, I need you to make this decision on your own. Like you said, there are pertinent elements to this that are unknown to me."

"That hasn't stopped you before."

He sucked in his breath.

"Or would you like to pretend that your ignorant mishandling of my life didn't have anything to do with the catastrophic events at Greyson?"

"I cannot be held responsible for—"

"You got me killed," I snapped. "You falsified those lab results to favor me, but those doctors weren't the only ones you fooled. I thought my kidneys were better. The Hernandez MoD gave me the option of testing for citizenship the day of Marco's funeral, but because of that stupid flight physical I thought I was strong enough to take the Greyson trip and get more experience before I did a simulation for them. How do you think I felt when I found out I was dying, Jason? How do you think I felt when I learned what you did to me?"

The color drained from his cheeks.

I blew out a sharp breath. "I'm sorry. I thought I forgave you for that a long time ago. I know we both did what we thought was best given the information we had. Let's leave it at that."

"Ask me where I went after Greyson."

"Jason, I'm not doing this. I need to focus on what's directly in front of me. Thank you for the heads up about my offers, but now I need to take off and start thinking it through."

I stopped with my hand on the door handle, thinking of that falsified flight physical lab work. "For what it's worth, I would trust you in my cockpit again. Perhaps you should ask yourself if you can trust me. I wasn't the least bit upfront about my illness with you. I meant to tell you after I had citizenship, but until then, I couldn't risk you abandoning me."

"I trust you," he said, his voice husky with emotion. "You only did that one flight, the one before you found out you couldn't honestly pass a physical. I know you wouldn't have risked my life."

I still couldn't bring myself to leave.

When he stood beside me, he was so close I could feel his heat.

"Miranda," he said, his voice like black silk. "I will follow you. But the moment the situation starts getting out of control again, I will act whether I have all the information or not. While you have so graciously forgiven me for trying to cover your ass when I knew you failed an essential flight physical, I have not forgotten or forgiven you for bringing down Greyson, the only multi-clan aviation school in North America."

I spluttered, "You can't forgive me? For what? I died."

"It was not the dying as much as the murder. You knew someone dangerous had tracked you across clan borders, but you neglected to warn Pooka so he could increase his security. You refused to notify me either, and you know I can make changes happen when others cannot. No, you carried a loaded pistol in defiance of Greyson's rules, and you—a Hernandez visa holder—murdered two Texan citizens on Pooka's campus."

"It was self-defense."

"It was clear their sole intent was to kidnap you. Those were not disabling shots you fired but intentional kills."

"I warned them those tranqs were lethal in my condition. They fired first."

"Well, you showed them, now, didn't you?"

My stare was as impassive as his.

The truth was we needed each other. He needed me as his pilot to keep his ass alive in a war, and I needed him to help me find the lab since Cris wouldn't.

But needing someone and trusting them were two completely different facets to a relationship.

"Can you even pass a flight physical?" I asked tightly. He was thirty-seven now. He seemed as fit and strong as when I first met him, but looks might not mean much.

"Yes. I am not in the top percentile anymore, but I am better than anyone else you're going to find. What about you?"

I searched his face. No gray at his temples, no lines around his eyes, no sign he had aged at all.

"I don't like the idea of you aging," I said.

"Sugar, I'm not fond of it either. You should give me the name of your doctor," he teased. "Then I can turn back the clock until I'm twenty-one, too."

Ice flooded my veins at the idea of Isidro working on Jason.

Jason's smile faded.

"I'll take your needs into consideration," I told him, my voice sounding flat and strange. "After I read the offers, you'll be the first to know what I decide."

CHAPTER 23

TOE TO TOE

Because it was right after Christmas, my graduation party at the Chavez house was probably going to be the last time the family was going to be together for a while. Risa, the youngest child and the only girl, was my apparent age. She was a cheerful but mediocre Axe pilot stationed at Forward Operating Base Six over by Albuquerque. Also home on leave was the next youngest, Trey, an Axe pilot stationed halfway across the northern border at FOB Three. He had the reputation of being stable and competent, although he credited his calm personal life to his penchant for dating imbeciles.

Jason, the third son, was my partner, and he'd pulled strings to ensure we'd be stationed at FOB Six, too, so he could try to keep Risa from getting herself killed.

The second son, Cris—

Christ, he'd been livid when he found out Jason and I were flying together again. Jason had reportedly said he had no intention of getting back in the cockpit, and for some reason Cris had believed his brother.

Cris was going to be working near us at H-E's battered western plant, retrofitting Axes and designing patchwork modifications to link incompatible systems.

The oldest sibling, Shaun, was a shrewd tactician but wouldn't be flying in the war either. Due to his asthma, he'd never been in the cockpit but fulfilled the usual expectations as a Chavez by working for the MoD like his parents.

I'd liked the hard-working, humble patriarch, Alex, from the moment I'd shaken his hand, but the Chavez matriarch had hated me on sight. Jason told me in private Renee had had her wings repeatedly pulled over the MoD insistence that she get pregnant with the next generation of flyers instead of selfishly trying to advance her own career.

When people found out I'd married into the family, they inundated me with stories and malicious gossip about the Chavezes, but the most persistent rumor was about the fabled bastard. Renee had been so very resentful about the MoD choosing a husband for her, after all. When I regarded the five siblings, not one of them looked so different their paternity was in obvious doubt, but the gossipers were quick to point out that Alex had brothers and cousins who looked similar. Each child was markedly different from the other Chavezes in my eyes, so I could argue that any one of them was the bastard if I'd been so inclined. Only a DNA test would clear it up, and the Chavez children's test results had all been sealed by the order of the Defense Minister. I'd asked Cris about that last part, and he'd confirmed it along with his fears that he was the bastard.

I lingered on the stoop of the Chavez house with my snack of almonds and raisins, mentally bracing myself before rejoining the turbulent family. At the sound of Cris's raised voice, I scrambled to my feet and pushed through the front door.

"You promised me," Cris yelled, striding across the dining room to get in Jason's face.

"Things changed," Jason said. "Why are you so angry with me? Not only did I arrange to get assigned to Risa's firebase, but flying with me increases Tycho's chances of survival exponentially. And speaking of her, does she know you volunteered to haul your wrinkled old ass back into an Axe?"

I pushed past Risa to stare at Cris.

"You are so jealous you called in every favor you could to get assigned to our firebase so you could keep an eye on us," Jason threw at his brother. "You are thirty-nine years old, Cris. What were you thinking?"

"Cris," I said in a cutting voice. "Is that true?"

"You both can blow it out your ass," he said, dividing his stony gaze between us. "I've logged more simulator time and actual airtime in an Axe at H-E than the two of you combined."

Jason raised an eyebrow. "All that experience, yet you had no intention of getting in the cockpit until you found out we were partners. What are you trying to prove?"

I asked Cris, "This is a done deal? You've passed your combat flight physical and everything?"

He gave me a look that could've frozen Hell. "I had no issues passing the physical."

"I was ascertaining your present stage in the process, not your ability to make it through the process."

"My orders are cut. I will be stationed at the same firebase you are." He glanced past me to Jason. "So I can protect my wife in the air."

"You are jealous," Jason taunted. "You are risking your life in an effort to prevent us from picking up where we left off."

156

"Prevent what?" I said, wide-eyed. "You were my mentor and sometimes my friend. I expect you to stay in those roles."

Both men looked at me like I had insulted their intelligence.

"Ty," Alex murmured from the doorway. "Come have a drink with me, and let the boys hash this out on their own."

Alex's study was an eerie reflection of Jason's with overstuffed bookshelves and sophisticated computers.

He poured a whiskey and held it out to me.

"No, thank you," I said. "I don't drink."

"Married into this family, you should start," he said, pushing the glass into my hand.

When the liquor flowed over my tongue, thoughts flew out of my head.

"This is good," I said in surprise.

"It's MacArrans," he told me.

I pushed my glass at him for a refill, and he chuckled.

The sound of raised voices made his smile fade. "So you're the legendary Miranda Donovan. After Jason dropped everything to follow you to Greyson, we thought it would be a matter of weeks before we met you. I was sorry to hear about your death."

"Me, too. It definitely complicated matters. But what they're fighting about isn't an issue. Jason and I weren't a couple then, and we won't be now."

If anything, that made him look uneasy. "I wondered. Jason's innocent when it comes to love."

I choked on my drink. "I don't think anyone's ever called him that before."

"Instinctively, he's always known how to guard himself against the people trying to use him for his money,

157

his talent, and our name. The only love he knows is ours. Familial, I mean. If you'd been a man, he would've considered you a brother. He's never been affected by women before, but since his dick seems to have taken a liking to you, what lies between you must be romantic. There's innocence to his logic."

"Can't you speak to him?"

He laughed as if I'd asked him to fly by flapping his arms. "Can't you?"

I frowned as the heated argument in the dining room turned into torrents of rude language. Cris was swearing in Spanish, but Jason was disparaging his brother in—

"Is that Italian?" I asked Alex.

Alex and I jumped as Cris burst into the room.

"We're leaving," he told me.

I eyed him coolly.

"Don't start with me," he warned. "I can handle being in the air."

"I don't doubt that. It's what going to happen when we're all on the ground I'm worried about."

CHAPTER 24

A TIME TO KILL

Our firebase was nothing more than a thick band of security wire surrounding runways next to a few hastily constructed structures at the northwest end of Texas. There was a lot of complaining about the spartan outpost, but not from me. My cot was comfortable, the food was hearty, and Jason had obtained a great plane for us, so really, what was there to bitch about?

Most of my time was spent in my hangar or the chow hall. I was safe from both Jason and Cris's relentless claims for my attention in the women's barracks, but I found it worrisome to be apart from them, mostly because I didn't trust them to behave.

Being the focus of Jason's gaze felt like a spotlight shining on me. I could feel the heat and intensity of it while I listened to our crew chief update me on the status of *Good Night*, our Battle Axe.

There was no need to remind Jason that he should be listening, too. I had no doubt he could've briefed me about the condition of our plane even more thoroughly.

His professional thoroughness was one of his few admirable traits.

When finished, Michael nodded at us and replaced his baseball cap over his ginger hair as he turned his attention to other tasks. I glanced at Jason, expecting him to lecture the man about proper attire. Instead, he tipped his head to the side, and when I looked where he indicated, I saw Cris there, tight-featured and frowning. I hadn't felt him there like I usually did. Was Jason's presence so strong then? Did it matter? If push came to shove, I would side with the man who benefited me more. I had tried to live a traditional life with Cris, one of love, babies, and normal ambitions, but it was plain that was not the path I was intended to follow.

So be it.

But please, oh, please, Cris, don't push it.

Regardless of the rules about displays of affection in uniform, I approached him and lifted up on my toes to kiss him. It was like kissing a sun-warmed hunk of granite. "Have dinner with me tonight?"

"I'll be in the air," he said flatly.

"I'll wait."

He finally broke eye contact with Jason and smiled down at me. It wasn't much of a smile, but the shadows in his eyes eased somewhat. "No, don't. We could have breakfast together, though."

"I would love that."

Two hours after my first sortie, Jason took me outside the hangar, away from the noise.

"Do you need to discuss the flight?" he asked, zipping his jacket and turning his back to the wind.

Teeth chattering, I tucked my hands deep into my pockets. "We have to do this out here? It's freezing."

"Humor me."

"Were there better decisions I could've made during that mission? Yes. I could say that about any flight."

"I'm referring to the knowledge that you are directly responsible for taking two lives."

"It was self-defense."

"We went up there looking for a fight."

Ah, yes. There was that.

"You are level-headed, but you are still influenced by your surroundings," he told me. "In the few days since we arrived, I've noticed a culture of pride in the kills that honestly sickens me. I'm not saying you should go for a wounding shot if it jeopardizes our safety, but I want you to keep in mind that—"

"That what, Jason? Our enemies are people, too? People who love and have families? Why would reminding me of that make me a better wartime pilot? I mean, are you trying to persuade me into becoming a conscientious objector in the middle of a dogfight?"

"Don't be ridiculous. But I do not want you to get off on the kills."

"So, do it right, but don't be satisfied by that. Got it."

Frustration twisted his features. "Don't do that."

"What are you doing in the cockpit?" I asked, losing my patience. "Of all the flyers I've known, you're the best at what you do but the least happy with the job you took on. Those planes behind you? They were created to eliminate threats. Sounds pretty when you say it that way, doesn't it? The plain truth is that we load them with several ways to kill people, and we take them up into the air and we kill people. There is no glossing over that. It sounds like you're the one who needs the counselor, not me."

"I'm not the one who pulled the trigger in that dogfight."

"Oh, so they aren't your kills, right? What a convenient interpretation of the situation. You create the firing solutions for the big heavies, long-range targets, and secondary targets when we're outnumbered. Let me guess. Those are my kills, too, not yours. So be it. But you have to accept responsibility for me being in the cockpit at all. You got me into the Hernandez flight school, and you got me into the Texas one as well. You. You trained me to be a killer—"

"I trained you to be a pilot," he cried.

"Of a warplane," I snapped. "During a time when rising tensions and dwindling resources made war all but certain. You just didn't know who it was going to be with. You saw talent in me, and you used it for your own glory and now for the protection of your clan. I fly a Battle Axe, and I kill people, Jason. Honestly, I'm encouraged to because it means they can't come back to fight another day. So what I do is because of you. Don't you dare get squeamish on me now."

"Duty—"

"Distance," I corrected. "It's not like I looked that aircrew in the eye when I made the decision to switch from guns to missiles. By the time their plane detonated, you and I were headed in a different direction to evade another threat. In that respect, it was no different than any of the simulations I've done."

I wanted to smack that horrified, helpless look off his face.

"And get it together, will you? I interrupted you twice if not more, and you didn't yell at me the way you always have."

Cris strode around the corner where he must've been eavesdropping, took one glance at his brother's tortured face, and yanked him into a hug that forced the breath out of him.

Jason clung to his brother.

162

"Keep the faith, Jayce," Cris murmured, sending me a scathing look. "We're going to be all right. Beat up and scarred, no doubt, but we'll make it through."

Okay, so that made me feel like a bitch. I hated feeling that way, too, because I'd been right to say what I did.

Cris offered stupid, meaningless platitudes, but still, Jason seemed to be calming down. I recognized from Cris's expression that he expected me to reengage.

"Don't fret, Jason," I said, bouncing on the balls of my feet to try to stay warm. "If you are unable to perform your tasks because of your connection to the killing, I can switch to the emergency gunnery protocol and the computer can handle your end."

I was rewarded with twin looks of disbelief, fury, and affront. I almost laughed. The Chavez siblings looked a lot alike, but they had such different personalities that it was rare they wore the same expression.

"Umm... Keep the faith," I offered, smiling brightly.

"Go away," Cris suggested, looking embarrassed.

I slunk away.

"What was that all about?" Winter asked, falling into step beside me.

"I don't know. Some mental malfunction about the killing, I guess."

"Was it his first kill?"

I blinked in surprise. "I assumed not, but now I'm not so sure."

Winter glanced back at them with sympathy.

"Not you, too," I said.

"I don't have trouble pulling the trigger, but I'm not letting them stamp *Spider Monkey*'s fuselage with an airplane silhouette for each downed jet, either. I know a lot of these townies never saw a dead body, let alone caused one before they got here."

"Everyone's going to unnecessary extremes on the subject."

"Life and death are two extremes."

"No, those two conditions are infinitely variable," I said. "And that's half the problem."

CHAPTER 25

LOSING GROUND

Even in the noise of the hangar, the staccato beat of Tomai's little boots carried through the air like a rapid pulse in my head. The boss strode by without seeing me, her mouth pinched.

"She's probably caught up with Winter's situation," Risa explained without looking up from polishing her nails. The bubblegum pink looked horrible with her olive drab but matched the bra and panty set I'd seen her don in the morning. If she spent as much time on her flying as prepping for her social life, she wouldn't scare her brothers so much. "He had an in-flight emergency."

My heart skipped a beat, and I tried to reign in my response until it fell somewhere between Risa's casual acceptance and Tomai's worry. "How do you always know what's happened before anyone else?"

"I happened to be in the ready room when he called in. He was diverted to Firebase One."

"That's all the way over in old Oklahoma, isn't it? How was that the nearest place to land?"

"He was coming from Dallas, and there's a high wind storm system rolling across FOBs Two and Three," she said. She blew on her nails. It looked like she had bubblegum stuck on her fingertips.

"Winter and Fritz will appreciate your concern," I said dryly.

"What? The pattern was empty, and he had control. Besides, Winter doesn't want my concern. He wants yours. He knows you're married. He should leave you alone."

"He is," I said, frowning at her. "I made it plain to him I'm hot and heavy with Cris."

"Are you? I don't think Cris feels the heat."

"I'm not making out with him when we're both in uniform."

"When no one's looking, you'd better be or you'll find yourself without a husband."

I gave her a sharp look, and she shrugged.

"He's a man with needs. I'm sure he would prefer you being the one who fulfills them, but it's unfair to make him wait until you two can take leave. You're both pilots. Chances are they won't be able to release both of you at once."

"Risa."

"There are other women who can easily find fifteen minutes to trap him in a dark corner. That's all I'm saying."

"She's correct," Jason said. "You're losing him."

He didn't sound upset about that at all. In fact, he looked self-assured as usual. What tenderness he had felt had been masked since our fight after the first sortie, but I could still feel his eyes on me more often than not.

He grimaced at the sight of Risa's nails. "That color is unacceptable. Take it off."

"Ran out of polish remover," she said sweetly.

He pulled a small bottle from his chest pocket. "Nice try."

"I'm not changing it," she said, but then she ran away like a child.

He shook his head at her.

"Why give her crap about that?" I asked him. "It's a trivial bit of nonsense that makes her happy."

"She does nothing to address her cuticles or hang-nails. I gave her the tools to give herself a decent mani-cure in the field, but she slaps on the paint like a little girl. Let me see yours."

I pulled my hand away when he reached for it. "They're clean, bare, and neatly trimmed."

He snatched my hand and squeezed my fingernail against the finger for a moment. Gauging the speed of the blood fill to my nail bed, he said, "You are dehydrated. I expect that to be addressed before our next flight. Or is having sludgy fluid volume supposed to be a trivial bit of nonsense that makes you happy?"

I yanked free of him.

He glared at me. "Why is it a constant battle every time I give you the tools or observations with an end of optimizing your physical condition? If I showed signs of dehydration that provoked you to comment that I needed to get at least a liter of water into me by the next flight, I would thank you. Actually, no, I wouldn't, because it would never come to that. I carefully monitor my food and water intake along with the rest of my health to ensure I am fit to fly. It is not unreasonable to retain the right to comment when my life depends on your health."

"That doesn't give you the right to control every facet of my life. Or any of them, for that matter. And you agreeing with Risa about what I should do to keep Cris? How would you know? Seriously. The only time you had anything like a relationship was when Profit played the whore in the hopes you'd fly with her."

His startled look gave way to a pained one that made me blush.

"One of my Hernandez roommates was her crew chief. I knew where you spent your nights." Thinking about what Alex had said, I added, "I'm sorry, Jason, but I thought you knew what her game was."

"I did. I know Cris's intentions, too, and I've got a good read on the blonde who's desperate to ride his giant—"

"You're disgusting."

He gave me an odd smile. "How did you even get him to marry you? You're sexually repressed, and he could write the book on screwing."

"There's more to a relationship than sex."

"Oh, I know, but a romantic relationship does need some form of it."

"We have sex," I snapped.

He laughed. "No one in this hangar believes that."

"Just because we don't announce it when we have it, that doesn't mean we aren't intimate."

"No one," he repeated, smiling. "As soon as he finds a lover he wants for more than a few encounters, you'll find yourself being served with divorce papers."

He looked like he expected some kind of reaction, but I had nothing to say. The painful constriction of my heart warned me Jason had only pointed out what I was too proud and too angry to admit.

His haughtiness gave way to sympathy as he glanced over my body. "Nerve damage?"

I ran my hand through my hair. Some days I did want to confide in him, but these were things I should probably be discussing with Cris, not Jason.

"We need to get ready for our next flight," I said instead.

CHAPTER 26

ADRIFT

A week later, I saw Jason scanning the faces at the mess hall, and I almost smiled at the people whose hopeful expressions suggested they hoped he was looking to single them out. His Comp win was a long time ago, but no one doubted he could take someone to the top if he wanted to.

I lifted my arm to let him know where I was at. He approached me without anything resembling a smile.

"We need to talk," he told me. "When you are finished here, meet me in the observation lounge."

I pushed away from the table.

"I said when you are finished," he snarled, glancing at my half-eaten pasta.

I ignored that and left the building.

"Why do you have to be so stubborn?" he asked as he followed me out. "If I handed you an orange and said it was good for you, you would trade it in for an apple."

"Just tell me what the issue is. Not about my meal," I corrected.

"I will not do this in public."

His ass barely hit the stained weave of the chair in the observation lounge above our hangar before he asked, "Are you comfortable flying? Is the Axe responding predictably to you?"

"I'm not sure how to answer that. *Good Night* has some odd glitches at times, but I feel safe in the air with her, if that's what you mean. Did Michael find something?"

"What kind of glitches?"

"Uneven power distribution. Sometimes she's got less than I expect her to give, and sometimes she's got more. I researched her mods, but I've yet to find a possible explanation for the anomalies. I was going to speak to Cris about it when he had a minute."

"There is nothing wrong with *Good Night*, her series, or her mods. The problem is that you have been outflying your gunner."

I grinned. "Did you just refer to yourself in the third person?"

"I've got an above-average g-force tolerance, but you still take me past my limits."

I shook my head. "I keep a close eye on your medicals."

"When necessary, I bled power so you were incapable of driving the jet beyond what I could take."

The color drained from my cheeks at the seriousness of what he'd confessed. "You've been sabotaging my jet?"

"I did it so I could stay in your cockpit and give you the support you need."

I was so appalled I couldn't form words.

171

He explained, "It was only meant to be a temporary solution, and I only used it when I absolutely had to. It has created some inconsistencies in your flying, though, so the risk is now too great to continue doing it."

"Good," I snapped. "You should've told me."

His brows knit. "Why? There are probably a thousand adjustments I've made in that cockpit that you could argue you should have known about. You were in no more danger than I was, and you would have been far worse off with someone else in your gunnery."

"Why do I keep on believing that you're ever going to treat me right? You constantly pull crap like this behind my back, always telling me it's for my own good despite the evidence to the contrary. Have you ever been completely honest with me?"

"You, of all people, know how much honesty is overrated," he said dismissively. "Why are you taking this personally? No one is spared my machinations because I have a fondness for them. If anything, the affection drives me to get more involved in their lives."

"My life," I snapped. "My jet and my life. What on earth were you thinking, Jason?"

"I've already explained myself. I'm not going through it again because you failed to listen."

"I'm not flying with you anymore."

"You are not," he agreed. "I've turned in my wings."

Shock gave way to fear like I'd just lost my gun.

He let his mask drop a little, and I saw his pain there. Softly, he said, "This was a difficult decision to make. When it comes to keeping you alive, is it more important to have the best gunner or complete faith in how your plane is going to respond to your touch?"

I could only stare at him. This couldn't be happening.

172

He said, "I've been working with the MoD to find another gunner for you, but they have yet to find one with a higher G tolerance than I have. They do not expect to."

"Another gunner?" I repeated hoarsely.

"It's useless to worry the next one will bleed power without your knowledge. *Good Night* will respond true. No one else has the skill and finesse I do."

"Which is exactly why I need you back there. I can't believe you would risk my life with an inferior gunner."

Meeting my gaze squarely, he said, "I decided an inferior gunner is less a threat to your continued existence than a lack of understanding about your plane. Once you get used to flying without my interference, I expect you to come to the same conclusion."

"And if the decision you made about my life without even talking to me about it ends up getting me killed? Again?"

He smiled slightly. "Miranda, you must know by now I have no trouble falling asleep at night no matter what I do or who suffers from it. And if you are dead, you will be beyond caring. Or are you planning another miraculous resurrection?"

"I didn't plan the previous one," I snapped.

"Oh, and I am certain they felt your wrath about that," he teased.

"What would you know about it? You disappeared after Greyson. You put your family through hell because you couldn't be bothered to tell them you were sulking on Italy's sunny beaches after I ruined your plan to use me to get back in the MoD's good graces."

"That was not my intention."

"Of course it was. You won the Comp, but you did it in a way that guaranteed your partner wouldn't fly with you again. You can't tell me the MoD wasn't pissed."

Something flickered in his eyes, but before I could identify it, it disappeared behind a sardonic expression. "That is yet another reason why you should not assume my feelings for you guarantee a massive overhaul of my personality. You should ask yourself why you expect people to change to be with you instead of why you don't learn to accept people for who they are."

"Don't change the subject."

"Seriously, what did I do? Try to stay your gunner? Leave when I thought I was compromising your chances too much? What a self-serving bastard I am. Do you want me to selfishly continue to try to find you a gunner who can hang on? And once I find him or her, do you want me to selfishly tutor your new team member until I'm satisfied the replacement is competent?"

"Yes," I gritted out. "Please."

He grinned at me. "And here we are full circle, a-hugging and a-kissing again."

"Please don't be so cavalier about this."

His smile faded.

"What are you going to do now?" I asked him. "Oust Johnny? Or is being the XO not high enough on the food chain? Are you going after Tomai's position?"

He shook his head. "I have no interest in joining that tedious hierarchy. I will divide my time teaching at the flight academy and trying to persuade the MoD to ease down. This war never should have happened, and it needs to end as soon as possible. Someone there will respond to reason."

"It's difficult to hate you sometimes." I sighed.

"But you will keep trying, I'm sure," he said. "Miranda, I am not abandoning you. Do you understand that? You can call me whenever you want. I hope you will. Now if you'll excuse me, I have plenty to do before I leave on the shuttle."

174

Alone in the observation lounge, I curled my arms around my knees and tried to think past the strange sense of grief.

Suddenly, I needed Cris, needed him badly. I descended the stairs by twos to check the roster to see where he might be and saw that Jason's name had already been removed from the board. Feeling like the floor was dropping out from beneath my feet, I searched for Cris's name. He was off the roster for twenty-four hours.

I stuck my head in Tomai's office. "Is Cris sick? I don't see him on the schedule."

She frowned at the interruption. "Firebase One needed an engineer. He'll return tomorrow."

I should've known that. I was his wife, but there was so much distance between us that I hadn't even known he'd been called away.

It was the final straw. I was going to counseling so I could work toward a healthier sex life with him. The rest of the affection would return with that intimacy.

As I left the hangar, I stumbled and caught the door-frame to right myself until my wobbly legs could hold me again.

Jason was leaving. Everything I'd invested in him had been wasted. How would I find the lab now?

CHAPTER 27

STRIKING DISTANCE

Late the following day, I saw Cris striding toward my jet bay. Tomai must've told him I'd repeatedly pestered her about when he would get back from Firebase One.

Smiling, I hurried toward my husband, arms out.

His expression was shuttered, and his hug wasn't much of one, but I supposed I'd earned that for every moment I'd chosen to spend with Jason instead of my husband outside the cockpit.

"Cris," I murmured for the pleasure of saying his name. "I missed you."

"Did you?" he asked flatly.

"Yes, I really did. Look, I love you. I want to be your wife."

"We're already married," he said bluntly, frowning as he searched my face.

"I mean acting like one no matter who is watching."

"Acting? Well, you are a hell of an actor," he said.

"Don't be like that. I know I've struggled with my issues, but I want to go to therapy and—"

He knocked my hands aside when I reached for him again, his face showing his fury.

"What's going on?" I said, stunned.

He tried to leave, but I snatched his hand to get him to stop and speak to me. When my hand wrapped around his, he whirled and slapped me with such force I saw stars.

"You stay away from me, you evil fucking *bitch*."

"Cris," I said sharply as he strode away. "*Cris*." Winter had reached me, but I pushed him aside so my husband was still in my sightline. "*CRIS*."

"What the hell did you say to him?" Winter demanded.

"Nothing," I said, still stunned. "He went psycho on me."

"Do you want me to go talk to him?"

"I'll do it."

Slap.

Slap.

Slap after *slap* after *slap*.

Every time I approached Cris, his mood turned psychotically foul. He wouldn't listen to me, always demanding I stay away from him. He wouldn't discuss the matter with his friends, his boss, his siblings, or anyone else.

I didn't file charges against him. Officially, I explained away the damage by saying I'd tripped, even if there had been witnesses. When confronted, Cris refused to say anything.

Tomai approached me while I was watching the sunset less than a week later. It wasn't a particularly beautiful example of a sunset, but I never took it for granted I'd live to see the next one.

"Unacceptable."

"Ma'am, if he would sit down and tell me what was wrong, we could work it out."

"I told you to stay away from him."

"That's not going to happen. I need to find out what's going on. It must be some kind of misunderstanding."

"I can't have him hitting you."

I looked her straight in the eye. "He doesn't hit me."

She scowled but didn't contradict me. This time.

After she released me, I sighed and meandered through the hangar. At the farthest corner, *Spider Monkey* crouched in her bay. Despite the fuss they'd made over Winter at the academy, here he was given a dark, cramped bay to go along with his third-rate jet and fourth-rate mechanic. I suspected they thought his being from the outlands meant he was used to inferior goods and so the least likely to complain. It didn't bother Winter. He told me if nothing else, his bay was a good place to take a nap.

I crawled up on the wing to where he was stretched out.

He gave me a sleepy smile and reached out to push aside the hair that fell on my face, but I flinched before I could stop myself.

He sat up, snapping, "I'm not the one who hits you."

"You surprised me, that's all."

"How much longer are you going to let him do that to you?"

"Look, no one knows what he's pissed about, and the only way I'm going to learn what it is and figure out how to fix it is if I can get him to talk to me. He won't stay this mad forever. Have you heard anything?"

"The best guess I've heard is post-traumatic stress."

"But why target me?"

"No idea."

From there I searched out Ranger. He was a crash specialist from Harbinger-Ellis, but the bombing of the compound had resulted in the scattering of H-E personnel across half of Texas as they squatted in any hangar, barn, or large outbuilding they could find. Ranger had arrived with the remains of a downed Wilson jet, and Tomai had put them both in the last bay at the other end, assuring us there would be a jail sentence for anyone who crossed the line into his territory. I'd taken one look at the mess and told Ranger the plane had originated on Hernandez lands no matter what the flag on the fuselage indicated, but I couldn't have said how I knew.

At his jet, I called up to him, and he reluctantly peered over the fuselage at me.

"What's that look for?" I asked.

"What do you want?"

"Can we have a conversation about the possibilities of installing a governor on a Battle Axe?"

"Oh," he said, brightening. "Sure."

"What did you think I wanted to talk to you about?"

"Anything personal?" he said flippantly as he descended.

I told him what Jason had done to my plane, and what I was willing to do to get him back.

Ranger said, "A governor, huh? Makes sense. But we should include Cris in this conversation. That's more his end of engineering than mine."

"The thought did occur to me, but you'll understand the difficulties with that."

He shook that off. "This is business. He'll listen."

Fifteen minutes later, I was coming to, the sight of the hangar's struts overhead and the feel of concrete under the lump on the back of my head. That was nothing compared to the pain still shooting through my nose.

"Ty," Ranger said, his voice high and frantic, "are you okay?"

Feeling like I was drowning, I sat up too quickly and saw bright lights flashing on the backs of my eyelids. I swallowed and swallowed, but the coppery taste of blood was still strong.

"That *bastard*," I said. "Did he punch me in the face?"

"Yeah," Ranger said venomously. "Sorry. My mistake was in thinking he would act like an adult. C'mon, I'll get you to the medic. Not that you'll consent," he sighed.

"Yes, I want to see a medic. He might've broken my nose."

"Are you finally going to press charges?"

"And short the bay another pilot? Not a chance. But I'm not going out of my way to be in his path anymore. To hell with him."

By the time I was done with the medic and yet another meeting with Tomai and Johnny over Cris's behavior, Winter was back from his mission, fed, and stretched out on the far wing of his plane.

"Winter?" I whispered, not wanting to wake him if he was asleep, but not wanting to wait to speak to him if he wasn't quite asleep.

His mouth twitched toward an involuntary smile, but he wouldn't open his eyes.

"All right, I'll leave you be. I just wanted to tell you that you were right and I was mistaken anyway."

"About what?" he asked playfully as he rolled over, but at the sight of my black eyes, he started swearing.

"It's fine," I told him honestly. "I'm done."

He ruthlessly searched my face. "You're divorcing him?"

180

"Never will, if I can help it." He growled and jerked away from me, and I clambered across the wing. "It's not like that. I'm not a citizen, so being married to one gives me some medical and legal rights."

"Marry someone else. Marry Ranger. I hear he comes from a good family."

"I already spoke to him. He's not willing to risk his security clearance on me. When I tried to reason with him, he turned me down in five languages."

"What about Jason?" Even before I could reply to that, he sighed. "Never mind. He's worse than Cris. At least Cris can take his eyes off you from time to time." Then he looked at me with a different kind of intensity. "So there's nothing standing in the way of us getting together, is there?"

"There's nothing standing in the way of me thinking about it," I corrected. "But if you want to get laid and don't give a damn whether I'm enjoying myself or not, we can screw now and get it over with."

"Are you finished?"

"I don't know. Are you?"

"Am I supposed to waltz around the subject? For some people, sex feels good and they don't have to complicate it. We're friends, we want each other, and you know I'm not going to hurt you or announce our business to everyone, so I don't see what the problem is."

"The problem is I have just reached the point where it's even a possibility to me. That means I haven't let myself think about being with you, and I would like the chance to fantasize about what you taste like and what you'd feel like before I find out for real."

"I've already been waiting a while, Ty."

"Knowing I was married," I threw back. "Nothing's stopped you from having sex with someone else."

"Look, you can't blame me for—"

"Jumping on the widow two hours after the guy died?"

"I was being polite," he said outrageously. "For all I knew, you wanted to punish him by screwing someone else. Damned if that someone else would be anyone else."

"Can we just start with me fantasizing about you, Mr. McIntyre, sir?"

"I would like that," he said honestly.

I blushed hotly, and he laughed and sent me away so he could get some sleep.

I'd reached the door when my name was called out.

I shot Johnny an exasperated look. "No more."

He ignored that. "*Good Night*'s medical feeds show your new gunner passed out in your cockpit."

With reluctance, I took my hand off the doorknob. "He wasn't completely unconscious. I slowed as soon as I realized he was fading."

"Yeah, that shows, too, but it's clear this issue isn't going away. The Harbinger-Ellis people need to consult with you."

It didn't bode well that Johnny was the one telling me that. As second in command, the XO usually got stuck with the ugly tasks Tomai couldn't be bothered with. Were they going to pull my wings and offer me a desk job? Christ, I hoped not.

CHAPTER 28

GOVERNOR'S BALL

"H-E wants to discuss the governor," Johnny told me, checking his palmer as if to confirm that was the right term for it.

"I don't know what I can contribute to the conversation at H-E. I know what a governor does, but my conversation with Ranger proved that was the extent of my knowledge."

"They might want to do some tests to see how much they need to leash an Axe for you."

"Shouldn't they be testing my next gunner? It's his inability to stay conscious through powerful acceleration that's the problem, not me."

"Like they don't already know what the average tolerance is for an aviator? C'mon, they're offering you a reason to leave the firebase for a few days. Why not take it? You've got nothing better to do, do you?"

"Other than fight a war?" I said, frowning. "What's going on?"

He shrugged and sat down on the nearest bench. "We want to separate you from Cris while we figure out who to ship."

"My orders here were cut first. Plus Cris easily fits in anywhere. Everyone loves him."

"Go hang out with the H-E people for a couple of days. I've already scrubbed you from today's flights so you can leave on the supply truck."

I glanced at the clock, frowning. "Didn't it already leave?"

"It's waiting for you, so hurry up and pack."

"Thanks for nothing."

"Huh. I hear they have real books. I'll be lucky if I get you back."

The H-E compound looked like they'd just begun to clean it up from the bombing last year. As I followed the arrows pointing to the building I was to report to, I saw the museum Cris and I had visited the previous year had been leveled. Bulldozers pushed rubble to one side where long stakes in the ground warned not to make the piles any taller since the freshly patched runway was so close. I wondered which of the ruined buildings had been Ranger's and why he had been ostracized to a bay in our hangar instead of claiming space in the structures that remained.

After the interviews and tests, I was escorted to another building to wait. The room I was sitting in was about the size of a hangar, and half the missing roof had been replaced with a combination of tarps and plywood. Rubble and twisted metal had been shoved into one corner, including the ominous remains of at least three Battle Axes. The room seemed to be serving as a combination of a waiting room, some administrative offices, snack bar, and junk yard.

"Well, I've got good news and bad news," the H-E tech said to me two hours later as he sat, the metal buttons on his back pockets making a scraping sound against the orange plastic.

"I'm afraid to ask," I said, having thought over the possibilities and not liking what I'd come up with.

"We're vehemently opposed to installing a governor on an Axe for you or anybody else," he told me. "We've already said as much to the MoD."

I felt my shoulders sag. "So that's it then," I said flatly. "I'm done flying."

"Is that what they told you?" he asked, eyeing me curiously. "Because that's not how H-E is interpreting events."

"I'm sorry, I'm not following you. There's another way to bleed power? Did you speak to Jason Chavez then?"

"We're not advocating any limitations on the jet. You're up to the task at hand, and we build Axes that are just as capable. Since neither you nor the plane is the trouble, we're recommending you fly without a gunner."

"Easier said than done," I said. "Not to put too fine a point on it, but I fly combat and take damage. I'm uneasy having a computer program apply its one-size-fits-all solution to my problems."

"It's been argued that gunners fall back on patterns more than computers do."

"You need to be careful who you say that around."

"Jason Chavez is a notable exception," he admitted, flashing me a smile. "Will you humor us and try it out in the simulator for a few days?"

"That decision has to be made by my unit, not me. What's in it for you?"

"Not having to install a governor," he said, shooting me another grin. "It goes against everything we stand for to cripple a jet."

CHAPTER 29

RENDEZVOUS

Sensing movement, I glanced up, smiled at Winter, and went back to my book. Then I stopped and looked up, puzzled. "What're you doing at H-E?"

He sat heavily beside me, dumping his flight gear on the floor. "Your husband is getting an award."

"So?"

"So, they're making this big deal about him, calling him a saint, a hero, and demi-god."

"Nice exaggeration."

"It's not too far off the mark. I reminded them he punched you, and everyone looked at me like I had horns growing out of my head."

"Again, so? He spends more time in the air than anyone else, and he gets results. He also finds time to do a bunch of charity work and—"

"Teaches orphans to read and saves whales, yeah, yeah. Whatever. If it weren't for you, I wouldn't have a problem with him other than he seems to need people to tell him how amazing he is. But there was no call for him to pop you like that, and nothing they say is going to change my mind on that. If he didn't want to talk to you, all he had to do was get a restraining order."

"That still doesn't explain why you're here."

"Ranger said there was some recall *Monkey* should've been included in but wasn't. He doesn't have the tools for it, so since all jets are up and you're the only pilot out, he convinced Johnny to let me ferry *Monkey* here to have H-E fix it. They might've been afraid I was going to start something. I don't know why. Ranger's pissed at Cris, too, and has been a lot more vocal about it. My scumbag partner had no intention of coming to this crappy, bombed-out part of Texas, so I'm here alone. I'm telling you, Ty, this crap is getting old."

"That was quite a rant."

"You knew, didn't you? That they think so highly of Cris that even if you'd tried to press charges nothing ever would've happened?"

"Suspected, sure. Especially with Jason gone."

"Did you tell him what happened?"

"No. I doubted he would've believed it. I have it under control anyway."

His look suggested he didn't agree.

I asked, "How long are you here?"

"Day or two, I guess. You?"

"Maybe two days. They sent me back just long enough to pick up *Good Night* so they can run stress tests on her."

"Anything to do around here while we wait?"

"For me, sure. For you, not so much. Unless you're a lot more into old H-E books and historical relics than I'm giving you credit for."

He wrinkled his nose.

"There's a bar in town with live music tonight," the man behind the nearest desk said without looking up from his screen. "A few buildings down from a hotel, too. Since y'all aren't getting out of here in the next twenty-four, I figure you can get drunk and sleep it off before coming back here."

"We're not authorized to leave the grounds."

The guy shot me an amused look. "Who's going to report you? We're out in the sticks."

I looked over at Winter. "I'm game if you are."

"Oh, hell, yeah."

We changed into civilian clothes and hitched a ride off the H-E compound.

As soon as we got through the bar's door and he saw the line dancing, Winter told me, "We're doing that."

Startled laughter escaped me. "You mean you, yourself, and you, right? I've never done anything like that."

"Me neither, but it can't be that complicated."

"What about getting some beers?"

"It can wait," he said, grabbing my hand and dragging me toward the dance floor.

A few hours later, he finally let me snag a table and order a whiskey shot.

"Hey, look at those two go," he said, pointing out a particularly skilled pair of dancers. "They must do nothing else but practice that stuff."

Against my protestation, Winter picked up the tab for my drink. I realized the mistake in my order when I tasted it.

"Should've known better," I said when he saw my scrunched up expression. "I don't like whiskey; I like MacArrans whiskey."

"I'll check."

I pulled him back down to his seat. "I just want a water."

He gave me his. "Do you realize we are on our own until tomorrow morning? There are so many options. Can't draw too much attention to ourselves, of course, and I'm so wound up about the very idea of being away from that life for a few hours that I'll never be able to choose, but hell, at least we've got the chance, right?"

I laughed. "Finding military life a little constraining? And you've been at the firebase how long?"

"It's so... I don't know. I don't mind rules. They're there to protect me from stupid people mostly. It's just..." He shrugged.

"It's concrete and jet fuel fumes and steel and technology," I said with a grim smile, letting my gaze drift to the ceiling full of struts and speakers and lights and other club equipment when I would've preferred a sky full of stars. "That's what gets to me. It's too much human determination to master the universe and not enough organic spontaneity. I would've been okay if I'd never lived in the outlands and known what's possible."

"Do you want to leave?"

I wished he weren't so young. What I wanted from him wasn't right.

"Sorry. Didn't mean to ramble on like that. I'm tired," I said listlessly. "I'm going back to H-E to get some sleep. Have a beer on me, and I'll see you in the morning."

"I'll go with you."

"No worries. Thanks for offering, though."

"I'd feel better if I knew you made it back in one piece."

As soon as we stepped out of the bar, I inhaled deeply, catching the scent of the outlands amongst all the town smells. Polaris and the moon shined down from the sky, and I felt an ancient, primal heartstring being plucked inside me.

"I'm not going back," I said absently, scenting the air again. "Not going back into concrete and steel until morning."

"I'm going with you."

"You're not invited."

"I can either go with you or I can follow you. Your choice."

"I don't need your protection."

"Doesn't matter."

I shifted my gaze from the moon to his face. "You're too young for me, and you're not a big enough bastard to make me feel like I wouldn't be taking advantage of you. I mean, you've met both Jason and Cris. Did either strike you as particularly happy about having been with me? Be smart enough to learn from their mistakes."

"Be smart enough to learn from your own mistakes, and start hanging out with people who are more like you."

"I thought I was, especially with Cris."

He smiled his disbelief. "Prince Cris, Legendary Knight of the Realm? He can't see a crying little girl without fixing her toy or a limping dog without rushing him to the vet."

"I'm a good person, too."

"You two are completely different kinds of people. If you came across a woman who'd been raped and she pointed out the guy who did it, you would go after him. When he didn't give up when you confronted him, you would beat the crap out of him. Faced with the same situation, Cris would call the police, carry the victim to the hospital, and get her a good counselor. Hell, he'd remodel her house with the latest security stuff so she felt safe again. Punching you was probably the evilest he's ever been."

190

"I'm not evil," I snapped.

"I'm referring to people who've been in nasty situations and have found themselves acting in ways other people can't even bring themselves to consider. And you need to let go of my age. As far as experience is concerned, your boy Cris is the infant, not me. He's had the luxury of always being able to take the virtuous, moral path to be good. And I *am* following you. Get over it already."

"You're following me?" I said archly. "Well, now. Let's see if you can."

And with that, I took off running at full speed, heat rippling through my veins at the possibility of using everything I had and still being caught by him.

"God, I needed that," Winter groaned shortly afterwards, throwing an arm over his eyes to block out the bright moon. "Had no idea how much."

Plucking bits of dried vegetation from my hair, I said, "Thanks for not making me have to let you win."

He burst out laughing.

"So now what?" I asked awkwardly.

He sat up and burrowed his face into my hair until he could kiss my neck. "What do you mean?"

"I don't know what you expect of me."

"I expect you to stop worrying about what's expected of you and start doing what feels natural to you."

"Oh."

"You seriously don't have a clue, do you?"

"Nope," I sighed. "I did tell you I suck at sex."

"So stop calling it sex. We're friends, aren't we?"

"I'd like to think so."

"So as my friend, what do you want to do now?"

"Lick you someplace naughty," I said promptly, and he burst out laughing again. "Too soon?" I asked.

"Never," he promised me. Then, seriously, he said, "Anything you want. You know that, right?"

"Do you think we're going to be able to have nights like this at the firebase?"

"No, I don't."

"So this is probably the only night we're ever going to have?"

"I don't know about that. I hope not."

"But it could be."

"Sure, if one of us augers in."

"Then I want everything you've got," I said in a tiny voice. "I want to be sore for days. I want to feel so used up and worn out that I can't possibly believe I had more to give or that there was more to take."

He was silent for a long time after, long enough for the chill of the night to start seeping into my flesh. "Dangerous words," he said finally. "You sure you want to go there?"

"I'm not taking it back, Winter."

"I don't want you to," he said, reaching for me with raw, primal intensity.

As dawn approached, Winter and I strolled hand in hand toward the hotel, both of us moving with the surety that comes from years of hiking over uneven ground. I was beyond sore but still hungry for him. It was such a novel sensation that I was more thrilled by it than irritated.

Feeling my smile, he glanced over at me. "What?"

"I still want you."

"Glad the novelty hasn't worn off after a single night," he said dryly, "but I'd rather hear you admit that we're good together no matter what your logical arguments are."

192

I spun around and walked backward in front of him so I could face him. My hands on his hips, I started dancing, singing one of the songs we'd heard at the bar. Unable to resist, he danced with me, the lines of his face easing. He spun me and dipped me, kissing me on the way up.

"Say it."

"It," I said innocently.

"Say we're done with pretending—while we're alone anyway—and that you're going to stop letting them tell you how to fly. Take the lead. It's past time."

Startled, I stumbled. He hauled me to my feet, interlaced his fingers with mine, and continued walking back toward the war we'd left behind for a night.

CHAPTER 30

W + T

A month later, I felt all sorts of emotions I suspected were signs of happiness. I loved being in the air, loved flying without restrictions, and loved having a plane that took everything I had to give.

Hell, I loved having a lover who filled me so perfectly, too. I couldn't get enough of Winter. Cris took a lot of jobs at other firebases, so I barely even saw so much as his shadow during that time. When we did have to deal with each other, it was mercifully brief and professional.

Life was good.

One day, I'd had a great flight, and as I passed Winter on his way to *Spider Monkey* for his own upcoming sortie, he smiled at me. Without thought, I took his hand and pulled him into an open-mouthed kiss that he returned automatically, his free hand on my ass.

"Mmm, sweet," he commented appreciatively. "Oh, and Johnny's looking for you."

"Okay, thanks. Good hunting."

And as we started to go our separate ways, I froze, belatedly realizing we were in a bay full of people who were now staring at us. Winter turned to me, his raised eyebrow over his level gaze asking me how I wanted to play it. As the married officer, I had more to lose professionally if caught having an affair.

"Did you just French my wife?" The dark, ominous question hung in the air like a cloud of smoke.

I couldn't form words. There was no lying about this. Worse yet, I found I didn't want to.

Seeing my decision in my expression, Winter stepped up and faced Cris. "Your wife? She's a lot more my girlfriend than your wife."

Cris's eyebrows shot into his hairline. "What did you say?"

Winter didn't back down a bit. His eyes as cold and flinty as his name, he said, "Simple fact, man. And let me tell you, it isn't obligation that makes her take her pants off for me."

Cris's smile was one of amused tolerance. "If she actually had sex with you, it had nothing to do with lust."

"Believe what you want," Winter said, shrugging as if it didn't matter what Cris thought.

"You will stay away from her," Cris said, and the look on his face gave me the first prickle of fear.

"When she's done with me. Not until then."

"*What?*"

Recognizing Cris's temper had hit its flashpoint, I lunged between them, but Winter had anticipated that and swung me around, shoving me into the crowd. Cris's partner, Brody, caught me and for some unfathomable reason held me so tightly his grip sent pain shooting through my upper arms.

Cris's gaze locked onto mine, and he approached me as I tried to tear away from Brody.

"You've been fucking him all this time? You've been letting him inside you for no other reason than you wanted it? For how long? How long has my pretty, young wife been a whore?"

"For God's sake, Brody, let her go," Risa screamed, and Brody did, seeming surprised he was holding onto me.

"Oh, shut up, Ree," Cris snapped. Looking back at me, he said, "You will answer me. Have you been having an affair with this child—this hard-working, honest *kid*—for only a few hours? Or has it been a few days? Weeks? *Months*?"

I flinched. Winter had been on my mind from the start. Of course he had. Cris brought me closer to who I wanted to be, but with Winter, I could be who I truly was. He didn't flinch from a horrible truth, and he understood making ugly decisions to survive a terrible situation. Winter and I had secrets from each other but few lies.

Cris's eyes narrowed. He spoke in a low voice, but it carried in the awkward silence around us.

"That long, huh? What's the deal, wife? Because you made it plain to me long ago that you didn't want sex. I made it clear that you were still my first choice, yet you weren't adult enough to tell me you met someone and wanted a divorce."

Cris's smile was glacial.

"Haven't got him ready to put a gold ring on your finger yet? Maybe his citizenship isn't as sound as mine is, maybe his family isn't as connected, and maybe you can't use the surname McIntyre as much as you could Chavez."

"It's not like that."

"Of course it is. You use people. I knew you were using Jason and me, using us hard, but I believed you had the civility not to trash the lives of additional people when you already had us right where you wanted us."

"Cris, it's not like that."

"If you say that to me one more time, then so help me God, I will show you a new level of despair. I can prove how it's *just* like that. You have lied to me about very critical issues."

My ears pricked. Which lies had he discovered the truth of? Was he finally at a point where he would believe the whole story and help me?

"You have broken my trust over and over again," he told me. "You have wrung me out, but I stayed with you because I believed that once I scraped away all the lies I would find a woman who had been put through the wringer. I wanted to care for you, love you, and protect you. You know I did. I wanted to be everything a husband should be to his wife. But the deceptions and justifications kept pouring in. You never did understand that I would've loved you for the truth."

"I would like to discuss this with you in private—"

"I bet you would."

"—so you can explain to me exactly what I'm being accused of."

"So you can conveniently explain it all away like you always do? No, I'm not going through that again. I never have to go through that again. I'm filing. Jason's going to hear about all this—your lover and my overdue withdrawal from our marriage—by the end of the day, but it won't be from me."

His amused smile was nothing compared to the diamond glint of his stare.

"Your lover there is going to feel Jason's displeasure in force, and that will be your fault. But you already factored that in your equation when you spread your legs for him, didn't you?"

I felt like the bottom had dropped out, indicating how much I'd been relying on him. "Cris, please, can we go somewhere private. Nothing but honesty. Full disclosure about whatever it is you think I'm deceiving you about, I promise."

"Your promises are worthless," he said. I saw puzzling glimpses of sympathy within his righteous fury. "And you have bypassed many opportunities to be forthcoming with whatever it is you're suddenly dying to tell me now. And if your eagerness is solely derived from your fear that I will expose you, I'll let you know I have no interest in that. All I've wanted for months is to be free of you. Your troubles are your own. Hell, I'll be too grateful for having my own problems decrease to make trouble for you."

"What problems?"

"You can't be serious. It's been a constant battle with Jason from the day he found out I was married to you. Most recently I've had a retirement account wiped out and had a water pipe in my condo break that conveniently only ruined a favorite set of sketches a friend did for me. Oh, and I've been formally accused of burying evidence that the Delio modification was crap even when I supposedly knew air crews were going to die if it was put into production. Before the end of the week, I was expecting another rape accusation. They come every three months or so."

I wobbled and then sat down hard on the concrete. I hadn't known any of that. I knew Jason was a mean, petty bastard when he felt crossed, but he'd never punished me despite the occasional threats, so I thought Cris had been spared, too.

Cris crouched in front of me. "Why the feigned surprise? You've known all along that Jason does very little of his fighting face to face. But all my ills will magically be corrected the moment he hears I divorced you. Except for the sketches, of course. But we both know he'll buy me better ones. So you've got nothing to worry about from me, especially if you stay away from me. Are we clear on that?"

"Yes," I said hoarsely, "but you have to understand I can't totally avoid you. We work in the same place."

"I'm going to do whatever it takes to be reassigned. Until then, I'm taking some leave. I'm tempted to stick around and watch you reap what you've sown, but in the end, I'd rather have my life back."

Risa grabbed his arm when he tried leaving. Her voice was so quiet I barely heard it. "Don't be like Mom. You can fix this."

"I tried. Ask her."

"This is your wife, not your girlfriend. That means something."

"It's nothing more than a legal term at this point." Cris's anger faded into pity as he shifted his gaze to Winter. "You really think it'll be different with you, don't you? Bail while you still can, Winter."

"I don't need your advice, just your signature on that divorce paperwork."

"You have it," Cris promised.

I felt a searing pain in my heart each time it beat. Cris loved me. He wouldn't do this to me. Our relationship had issues, but he was the reason I had been able to drag myself back into humanity after the callousness and brutality of the lab. It would've been so easy to turn into a bitter, stony, dark being that gave in to anger and hatred, but because of him, I felt faith and hope about Texas's future despite all her broken parts. It was because of him and our child that I needed to end the lab's power.

Being with him had saved my soul. He couldn't be leaving me like this.

But he did.

Jason called me that night. His voice was stark, raw. "Is it true?"

My heart hammered in my chest in response to his emotion. "You wanted Cris to leave me."

"I wanted you both to come to the realization you weren't right for each other. I did not want you to start an affair with one of my former students. He is a child. What were you thinking, Miranda?"

"He's good for me," I snarled.

"How? Because you get to play at being a mommy?"

The color drained from my cheeks. It took several swallows before I found my voice. "Stay away from him."

"What is the worst I could do to him? Take his candy away?" he said, tension making his voice high and tight. "I cannot stand talking to you any longer. You are on your own."

"Jason, wait—"

He'd already terminated the call.

CHAPTER 31

SCAR TISSUE

"He's back."

I looked up from my text on the history of aerial combat. The arrival of only one person could make Winter's eyes scan the hangar with his hand jammed in his pockets to hide his fists.

"And he's looking for you," Winter added.

That made me set aside my book.

As I slid off *Spider Monkey*'s wing, he said, "You can't be serious."

"Whatever all this is about, I can hear it from him or I can sort through the rumors," I said. "Don't worry. The divorce is final, and I hear he's already got a girlfriend, so it's not like he wants to get back together with me."

Winter showed me his unhappiness, and I wondered if mine was well-masked. I wanted Cris to be happy, but the speed and ease with which he'd replaced me hurt me so much that some days I truly hated him.

"It'll be okay," I told myself as much as I told Winter.

I found Cris squatting by *Good Night*, his civilian clothes looking out of place in the hangar. He straightened when he saw me. Strange, intense emotion burned in his eyes, but only for a moment. Disappointment and anger quickly followed, only to be replaced with an unexpected flash of grief.

His blank mask finally dropped firmly into place.

At one time I would've thought that was interesting and actually would've been curious about all that emotion he was struggling with, but that was then. The part of my heart that was his was scarred over now, a hard shell protecting my wounds as they healed. If they healed.

"What's going on?" I asked him, hands on hips.

"I needed to speak to you in private," he said, tapping his ear to indicate it wasn't the kind of conversation anyone should overhear.

We moved outside, striding almost all the way to the perimeter fence before he spoke.

"When I asked you the other day whether or not you had told Winter anything, whether or not you were going to, you said no. You meant to go through life without telling another living soul about it."

"Things seem to have leveled out. No need for me to get blabby."

"I don't believe any of this is done for good. When trouble happens, you need someone who understands to help you out. Are you anticipating plenty of time during an emergency to explain it all over again to Winter or anyone else? That leaves me. Make no mistake, I have no intention of being a presence in your life. I don't want to be your husband, your lover, or your boon companion. I'm not even particularly interested in being your friend, although I'd prefer civility."

"You don't want to help me, don't want anything to do with me, but you're going to be my knight in shining armor anyway," I summed up. "Look, whatever you do is your decision. Yours. I didn't ask for you to spend the rest of your life riding shotgun against a threat that's likely nonexistent."

"You don't want me in that capacity?"

My mouth flattened. The truth was, I had wondered if everything was so quiet on the lab front because firebase security prevented them from using their surveillance and their petty tricks. Once the war was over, then what?

And frankly, I was already uneasy with two people knowing bits of my story. I didn't want to compound that by telling Winter anything, especially when I didn't know how long our relationship was going to last. My ability to trust had been severely stunted with Cris's desertion.

"I heard you have a new girlfriend," I said. "But I know you don't stay around either. If you're using me to avoid dealing with her or whatever, I'll have no part in it. I won't be a shoulder to cry on for you. Civility is fine, but I'm not interested in being your friend either."

"You know what? You can blow it out your ass," he snapped. "I broke up with her this morning because I can't reconcile the life I had with her and my unwanted obligation to you. Why do you think I hoped you'd passed this burden onto someone else?"

He was serious, I realized. He still felt some obligation to me when all I expected of him was to keep his mouth shut.

"Or has the situation changed?" he asked eagerly. "Would you be no worse off if we completely severed ties?"

"No," I said stonily, hating that I had to admit it. "If I ended up in a tight situation, I would not be better off without you."

"Well. There you go," he said flatly. "But I'll tell you flat out that I'm not taking any crap from Winter. If my presence in your life becomes necessary, you make it plain to him that my word is law after yours. And I expect you to notify me immediately if you change your mind and brief someone else."

"Because you want to get back to your girlfriend."

I hadn't meant for so much mockery to enter my voice, but I couldn't take it back.

"That's the truth," he said huskily. "She's a warm, passionate, fascinating, emotional, resilient woman full of humor and curiosity. She's full of life, not death. She's who I thought—"

He bit that off, but I knew what he meant. She was who he thought I was.

"She's a good woman," he said with forced calm. "If the situation were different, I would've liked for you to meet her."

"Why?" I blurted, disgusted at his sexual appetites.

"Because she would've been a good friend to you," he said tiredly. "I said what I needed to, so we're done here."

"Is she active duty? Are you now stationed with her?"

"I've gone off active duty," he said tightly.

"So you'll be at the H-E compound?"

"No, Austin."

"Why?"

"None of your business. Call me if you need me, but only if you truly need me. I'll always pick up."

I ached as I watched him leave. How could it have come to this? What lie had I used that when revealed could've provoked such a bitter response? In my memory, I felt his big hand wrap around mine in the outlands, cold but strong as he said the vows that bound us. I felt his hand on my belly and saw the smile on his face as he assured me he was happy about my pregnancy. I felt him inside me, too, doing everything he could to ease his passage so he wouldn't hurt me.

And by God, he had hurt me with that description of his girlfriend because he made it clear I was emotionless and unyielding, his personification of death.

But wasn't that what I wanted? Hadn't I deliberately chosen duty over love for the greater good? It's not like I thought I could return to his side like nothing had happened after I dealt with the lab.

With slow, heavy footsteps, I left the barracks and climbed the old, diseased oak behind the barracks. Hidden in the foliage, I tried to feel the earth move by placing my hands on the main trunk, but there was nothing but the roughness of the vertical grooves.

Cris. My husband.

The soundless plea made tears sting my eyes.

I was sacrificing everything, and for what?

Not for what. For whom. With sudden calm, I felt the rough bark digging into my clone hand, felt my clone heart beat for me as it had for her.

Thumbing away the tears, I knew what I had to do next, and it had nothing to do with my husband or my lover.

CHAPTER 32

DRY RUN

Five days later, my thigh muscles strained and my ass cramped from maintaining my position on the narrow ledge, but there was nowhere else I could perch that gave me the necessary view of the building opposite. I did a slow, shuffling turn to return the grip on the old doorframe to my left hand. It made my stance more of a challenge to maintain, but I couldn't let my dominant hand get fatigued.

As time stretched, I considered the possibility I was mistaken. After all, Lucas and I hadn't been through here in two years. Hell, it was possible the gossip he'd heard was about the local version of the boogeyman instead of being based on a real villain. And honestly, even the boogeyman didn't come out to play every single night.

It wasn't like I was a seasoned detective with a feel for people. I was nothing more than a woman with a mind where random facts stuck like splinters that shifted painfully one moment and disappeared when I tried to find them. They worried in deep, spearing and snagging other random bits of information until I woke up with a certainty that hadn't been there the night before.

I watched a man saunter by in his church clothes: a pale shirt and tie and dark pants. He was in his early twenties and a bit of a dandy given the way he kept checking his reflection in the windows and running his fingers through his hair. When he leaned against the building across the street and glanced around, it took everything I had not to press deeper into the shadows where the footing was a lot worse. I had scouted the site carefully and had to trust I was obscured by the shadows.

A little girl darted around the corner, making him jump, and he smiled broadly at her. If she spoke, her voice was too low to hear.

He pulled his hand from his pocket and showed her a bit of bright cellophane. When she reached for it, he held it high, laughing when she jumped for it. He didn't tease her long, and soon she was eagerly untwisting the candy wrapper. Hands back in his pockets, he grinned as she chomped on the treat, her expression rapturous.

My stomach threatened to flip over, and I exhaled slowly, deeply, trying to settle it.

The bright green wrapper fell to the ground as she approached him again. The sun glinted off the red wrapped candy in his hand, and when she lunged for it, he laughed and ran through the door into the abandoned building.

"Don't," I murmured.

The little girl chased after him.

Through the broken windows, I could see him again hold the sweet out of her reach, and I could see his smiling mouth move as he laughed and teased her in closer with another piece.

What he did next cemented my belief I'd chosen the correct target.

I crossed the street and slipped in the building, donning my latex gloves so I wouldn't leave fingerprints. The girl's screams were muffled, and as I approached the man from behind with the handcuffs in my hand, I felt my gorge rising.

He yelped when I yanked his arms back and cuffed him. I pulled him away from the girl, and with his trousers around his ankles, he stumbled and fell. He rolled onto his side to see what was going on, and I tried not to react to the sight of his erection. No blood, no penetration, but there was no mistaking what he'd been on the verge of doing.

I pointed Mauss's gun at the man.

"What do you think you're doing?" he demanded, wide-eyed.

"G-God's work," I said hoarsely, my gun hand shaking so much I had to steady it with my left hand.

I pulled the trigger, but nothing happened.

The gun's safety was on. And then it wasn't.

I looked the child rapist in the face as I pulled the trigger, sending the round into his right eye.

There. I did it. I killed someone evil face to face.

The sound of the gunshot ringing in my ears, I fumbled around on the floor until my fingers found and closed around the shell casing.

I wanted to tell the girl I was sorry for shooting him near her, sorry I hadn't been sure enough at first to step in before he scared her, but I didn't have the nerve.

Hearing the shouts, I fled out the back of the building, the gun shoved in my jacket pocket. I ran into a couple who shouted in Spanish, and I pushed away from them, pointing at the building.

"Ayudar," I said frantically, wishing the Spanish language had been as easy to pick up as mathematics. The little girl needed help. "La nena. Herido."

Even more alarmed, they rushed in the building, and I ran away.

That had been horrible. And I'd actually used God's name to justify what I did. How arrogant was that? I had acted on what I believed, nothing more.

I hadn't meant to say anything. Finley had almost gotten the drop on me as I'd stood there demanding answers because I was so confident I had the advantage. Lucas had shot Finley before his needle made it to me, but I'd learned my lesson. With Mauss, of course there were answers I'd wanted, information only he could know, but interrogating him had been Domino's job, not mine. As soon as I had an advantage, I'd used it to subdue Mauss, not chat him up. Killing him had been an accident.

That monster in his Sunday best had flustered me with the way he looked at me, talking to me like I was the one who'd broken the rules, not him.

Christ, that poor little girl. If I'd waited a moment longer, he would've penetrated her.

I fell to my knees and vomited.

I pressed on, hiking the path that would take me back to my motorcycle, but I finally had to crawl into some thorny bushes to hide while I sobbed silently until the worst of the emotion was spent.

On the trip back to Austin where I stored my motorcycle, I tried to rationally evaluate the incident for how I could improve. However, my mind kept drifting as I debated whether or not I could pull that trigger over and over again. How many people were in the lab? Dozens, minimum. Perhaps a handful of them would see jail time if outed, if the government even allowed some journalist's story to go public.

No, that wasn't good enough. In fact, that seemed like the most likely way to get myself caged or killed. They had to be stopped, and like Winter, I was willing to do what the law couldn't or wouldn't do to protect the community.

My hands shook, and my trigger finger jerked on its own. I clasped my hands tightly together to make them still.

I didn't want to do this.

But no one else was going to. They voted for each step supporting cloning because they were so seduced by the propaganda. They rallied around it like it was a symbol of hope when it was nothing but selfishness and commerce. Why stop drinking when a battered liver could be replaced by a perfect match? Why would a man adopt a child when one could be grown who was the genetic match for him, his dead kid, or his favorite celebrity? If cloned parts made it so a person could live as long as he wanted, why would he give money to charity? He was going to need those funds himself.

I would've signed petitions and voted against all related legislation if I had the right to vote, but it wasn't enough. I gave as much money as I could to organizations which fought to block it, but that wasn't enough either. It was never going to be enough because the majority of people had no inkling of the consequences of actually getting what they wanted.

I suddenly understood why people wrote manifestos when they were on the verge of huge acts.

Who would I even write mine to? Who would I even want to explain it all to? Who had earned the right to learn my entire history as well as my plans for the future? Someone would have to be strong to get through it without giving up on humanity, moral to see the depravity of the people who were involved, and visionary enough to understand the need and impact of what I would some-day do.

Someday.

Time was passing. It was already almost the end of May. Every day, that lab was doing the devil's work, and every day I was stymied from doing anything about it. I had to find that place. I had to lay all this on Jason's lap and have him find it for me.

He would feel my desperation, though. How would I explain it? That I feared they would come after him? Would he believe he was that special to me now that I was with Winter? And that's even if I got in to see him in the first place.

Tears of frustration and helplessness flooded my eyes, but this time I ignored them. Of course, there were tasks I could perform until I learned where the lab was. I needed to go over what happened in that abandoned building again, learn from my mistakes. Killing in cold blood wasn't merely about technique and a sense of righteousness. It involved killing off parts of myself, too. This wasn't going to come easy at all.

When I got back to the firebase, I found myself under Winter's sharp scrutiny. I hadn't knowingly given him an indication of what I'd gone to do or that I'd actually done it, and he didn't ask me anything or offer a comment. His strange expression eventually faded into a thoughtful smile before he walked away.

I wanted to chase him down and demand to know what he thought he saw in me to make him look like that, but I forced myself to do what I normally did upon returning to the firebase: I checked on my plane and then returned to the barracks to check my gear.

It wasn't until I got into bed that I found that the incident in the outlands wasn't quite done with me yet. When I curled on my side and slid my hand under my pillow, I froze mid-yawn at the feel of a small, cold metal cylinder. My finger traced it to the hollow point tip, and I felt the color drain from my cheeks. I enclosed the bullet in my fist and fled to the bathroom to shut myself in a stall.

The sight of the round confirmed it was a sniper round, likely from Lucas, the government assassin Domino had assigned to hunt down Mauss with me. I'd learned plenty about analyzing my surroundings for threats due to being paired with him. If there had been anything I didn't like about faking my death and escaping, it had been betraying Lucas and Domino.

Lucas had carefully hand-engraved a few words on the round.

DON'T MAKE ME USE THIS

I trembled.

CHAPTER 33

DOPPELGANGER

The next morning, I was about to round the corner of the barracks when I heard Risa say, "Why can't Ty know about this?"

I pressed against the corrugated metal wall.

"Are you serious?" Winter said. "Why would I want her to know that some old pilot looks like her? Just get the whiskey from her if you can and see if she has any history books for Ty, okay? Don't complicate it."

"What should I use for a trade? Sounds like I'm asking a lot of this chick. What was her name again?"

"Bookworm. Everyone calls her Book though. I'll find something to trade before you leave."

When Winter came around the corner and saw me standing there with my arms folded across my chest and a raised eyebrow, he gritted his teeth.

He said without preamble, "It was supposed to be a surprise. Remember when I had an IFE over on FOB One and some pilot fixed my plane? You weren't giving me the time of day because you were married so I gave her the whiskey I'd bought for you. If she still has it, I want it back for you. Seems like a lot of trouble for a bottle of booze, but it's MacArrans, and it was expensive. Even though I don't drink that stuff, I was sorry I sent it her way as soon as I did it, but I haven't had a chance to get over there to get it back."

"This is all deeply fascinating, but you know the part I'm curious about is why you think I would care if some pilot resembles me."

"It's not resembling. She has some of your mannerisms, uses certain phrases the same way you do, and looks exactly like you will when you're older. I didn't tell you because I figured you'd want to go meet her. I didn't want you stuck trying to get rid of the old bitch because she suddenly realized how great you turned out after she gave you up for adoption. And if she still didn't want you, I didn't want you to have to deal with that either."

I had heard some startling things in my life, but for some reason I found myself unable to form words. He was level-headed and detail-oriented, and if he said the woman strongly resembled me, I believed him.

However, I knew the woman he spoke of wasn't my mother, a small, dark woman I only resembled in a few minor features. Anyone who saw the family together had commented how much my dad's Viking blood ran strong in his three tall, fair girls.

I thought of the clones, but this other pilot being one made even less sense than if Winter had seen my actual mother. After Greyson, the lab had been forced to use a 14-year-old clone to repair me because the only other clone had been suffering from a nasty infection. While I'd been living in the lab, Finley had faked her death and smuggled her out. After his termination, I'd seen her in stasis in the lab where I'd killed Mauss. She'd been in her early twenties, not old enough to be mistaken for my mother.

A jolt went through me as another connection fell into place. FOB One, that firebase where Winter had set down his wounded jet, was the same place Cris had gone before his behavior toward me had changed so radically. And his new girlfriend was like who he'd thought I was. He'd thought I was like the woman in Jason's file of Miranda Donovan.

Ergo—

"What the hell?" I said before I could stop it.

"It doesn't concern us," Winter said firmly. "She gave you up, so to hell with her."

Poor Winter. His history as an abandoned child provided him with no other explanation.

"I don't have any intention of going to see her," I assured him.

"Yeah?"

"There's no reason why I should. Like you said, nothing good can come from it."

He pulled me into his arms. "I didn't want to upset you, but I should've told you all this sooner. I'm sorry."

"It's okay," I said, burrowing into his warmth.

"Do you want her details?"

I hesitated. Cris's girlfriend's call sign was Bookworm, for God's sake. Did that slut read Cris's copy of Kierkegaard, too?

The muscles in my fingers contracted, but I forced them to go limp before they finished shaping into fists or the illusion I was choking someone. No, I wasn't ready for a showdown with a doppelganger who'd stolen my husband. I did my cause no good from a jail cell.

"Not yet. I don't think I'm ready for that. I need to do some thinking first."

He brushed his lips across mine. "Just let me know when you're ready. If you decide you want to meet her, I'll go with you if you want."

That night while Winter was in the air, I considered this new player on the field with fear making my trigger finger twitch. I had to learn more about her, hopefully without her learning about me. In fact, it would suit me fine if she didn't know I existed.

I had to admit it could be a coincidence. Sometimes people looked like each other without having any kind of genetic tie whatsoever. And as for our similar mannerisms, that would make sense if Jason was one of her instructors in flight school. I'd noticed that Risa handled her flight gear and equipment the exact same way I did, the way Jason taught us.

There was another possibility, one that truly alarmed me.

That day in the lab, a woman had called me Annalise by mistake. The initials AMF had been carved under one of the lab's library shelves. The woman's call sign was Bookworm, likely after a penchant for reading as much as I did. I easily could've been saddled with a moniker like that if people hadn't seen me yank out a contact lens when a bug stuck in it. My yellow iris had been out there for all to see, and my classmates had christened me Sunshine on the spot.

What did the AMF stand for? Could it truly be her? Was she an older clone of me?

No, there was no way. They would've used her to repair me. The lab never would've let someone so expensive to create be used in such a dangerous job.

That the other pilot looked like an older version of me was nothing more than a coincidence.

I strode to my locker to peruse my books, deciding to find one to give Winter for Risa to use in trade. I didn't want Risa to know I knew about my possible doppel-ganger because she would want to talk about it.

I frowned at my options. I was fond of my current library to the point where I didn't want to let go of any of my books. Most people didn't enjoy the scholarly tomes I favored anyway.

I dug around behind my spare boots to see if any books had fallen off the back of the shelf, and my hand snagged a torn paperback. I saw the slutty, pouty-lipped woman swooning over the bulges of her swarthy pirate on the cover, and I smiled grimly. It was the perfect book for a husband-stealing whore.

Husband-stealing...

My mouth was held so tightly, it was difficult to swallow.

No way could it be her. That slut had to have died more than a hundred years ago. Finley never would've taken her to be part of his collective. He had chosen brilliant, talented people to seed his utopia, and the woman I thought of never would've made the cut.

Never.

But how many absolutes had turned out to be negotiable? What if Finley had decided that having a wanton woman would be useful to have around? It would explain a lot about Cris's defection, too.

On the astronomical chance my doppelganger was indeed more than a stranger with similar features, I taped a tiny disc under the spine before I repaired the rest of the spine and glued in the signature that had come loose. Finding the disc was only my first challenge to her. If she didn't know about Miranda Donovan, hadn't been down in the lab, and didn't know American history, she wouldn't make it through the levels of decryption to get to the first Read Me file with my manifesto. The hard-core material was hidden so deeply that the disc contained three times more encryption files than data files.

I felt better afterward. Lighter. Cleaner. As if the knowledge of my whole ugly backstory was now someone else's burden to carry for a while.

When I met up with Winter after he debriefed from his flight late that night, I handed him the book. "Have Risa trade this."

He glanced at the cover and at me, amused. "Risa's more likely to jack off to this than trade it."

"Oh, she'll hunt for the juicy parts, but the sex scenes are vague and sweet so she'll pass it on," I said, making him laugh. "Look, Risa needs to get this book to that woman's hands whether she has a trade or not. With a name like Bookworm, she's the only person there who's unlikely to toss it into a dumpster. Even terrible books need a home."

CHAPTER 34

GOOD NIGHT

Ears ringing, I couldn't understand what was being said. It didn't matter. By that point, I didn't care.

Strong hands pulled me out of my cockpit, passing me from person to person as splashes of fire suppression foam hit me. At ground level, they carried me to a safe distance.

Looking past Johnny, I caught a glimpse of *Good Night*'s broken wing, and with ice in my veins I shut my eyes before I could see the rest of it. As the event played over and over in my mind, I again felt the sickening crunch after I took the hit meant for Winter.

A Clan Wilson pilot had gone kamikaze. I admired the bastard's determination.

"Stay with us."

I wanted to tell Johnny I was still there, but my throat was so raw that speech deteriorated into nothing but my mouth moving and breath coming out. My lips cracked from the dryness, and I tasted blood. If I'd had the energy, I would've vomited.

"You're all right," he told me. "You're safe."

What a pack of lies.

I passed out.

I regained consciousness before we reached the infirmary, and I sincerely hoped that my doppelganger at FOB One hadn't deciphered my file and come to find me because I was in no condition to deal with her.

Given the rare privilege to refuse medical care thanks to the lab's fear the military bioscanners could detect more than they were meant to, I told the medics I was functional and they had no choice but to believe me.

I stumbled back toward the tarmac. Out past the hangar, I saw Ranger strip my crippled jet with urgent but sure hands, pulling out trickles of the fuel and anything else that might detonate if there was a short or someone sneezed despite the foam that covered her.

Ignoring the other voices clamoring for my attention, I tried several times to get his name out, and my voice was so hoarse and low he didn't hear it until I was all but on top of him.

"It's bad," Ranger told me as he worked. His St. Christopher medal swung free, and he stuffed it back down his collar without the usual kiss to the worn metal. "She already meets two criteria to be blacklisted."

My eyes narrowed at the overreaction. My jet was a sturdy, bad ass piece of hardware, not some paper airplane.

Johnny turned away from the wreckage and nodded. "After your investigation, salvage what you can and haul the carcass off to the junk heap at the other end of the firebase."

Carcass? Junk? How could they refer to her so callously? Pain tightened my chest until I struggled to breathe.

"H-E will want it," Ranger said. "They'll need to know if she outflew her jet, and I haven't got the tools for the analysis here."

"Then tell them to come get it," Johnny said.

My flight chief, Michael, stared at the charges Ranger pulled from the ejection seat. Eyes wild, Michael said to no one in particular, or perhaps to everyone, "Her ejection seat was fine when she left. I always make sure of that. *I checked it.*"

I heard the rapid heel beats of doll boots.

"What happened?" Tomai demanded as she skidded to a stop. Her hair was wild, and the T-shirt stuffed into her pants showed she hadn't wasted the time to put on a bra. The wild rose sleeve tattoo on her left arm had a new branch with sharp thorns and an overblown, petal-dropping bloom. The reminder of the stalker who'd left me flowers made me jerk my gaze away.

Without emotion, Risa said, "*Knuckle Dragger* fire-balled. Winter said *Good Night* intercepted a hit meant for *Spider Monkey*. I have to tell you that even I knew this was a terrible combination of aircrews. Harrison can't make a fast decision when the pressure is on. Well, couldn't. We're lucky we lost only one team."

I wasn't surprised Risa could offer so much. Her gossip network was faster than a lightning strike, so at this point she probably knew more than I did.

Tomai's eyes took in the smashed canopy.

Risa continued in that same flat voice that was so strange to hear from her. "She couldn't eject. The hoses to her flight suit fired like they were supposed to, but the damage to the canopy prevented the computer from deploying her seat charges."

221

"I checked her ejection system," Michael whimpered. "I checked it."

Risa ignored him, but her pallor matched his. "She must fly under a lucky star or be doing the devil's work because she got that bird all the way here. I can't imagine what that must've been like. Wind tearing through the cockpit, no comm, no gunner, no way for her to reconnect to the computer. All she could do was wrestle the stick and ride *Good Night* to the ground one way or the other."

"Lose the drama," Tomai said. "She survived."

She signaled Johnny to force Michael, Risa, and the spectators away.

"Nutshell," she said to me, scooping up the flight recorder. Ranger opened his mouth but shut it when he saw her already reaching for his chain of custody form.

"Plane-to-plane contact," I told her. "I managed to prevent our fuel tanks from kissing, but at the cost of my canopy."

"Injuries?"

"Minimal. My throat feels windblown and raw, but I'm pretty sure that was just from me screaming."

I tried to smile, but it wasn't happening.

"Too pale," she commented, her dark eyes narrowed beneath her overplucked eyebrows. "Way too pale."

"Ma'am, as soon as the umbilicals popped, I lost voice command and my heads up display. That would've made it a challenge to fly even if the rest of *Good Night* was intact."

I swallowed with difficulty, looking at my jet. She resembled a beer can someone had crushed with his fist. If Jason had been with me, he would've been killed. My heart clenched so painfully I staggered, catching myself by grabbing her shoulder. Her bones felt tiny, so fragile under my grasp, but she held me upright without difficulty.

222

"Infirmary."

I said hoarsely, "Ma'am, there's honestly nothing they can do for me. It was hands down the worst experience of my life, and that's saying quite a bit. If my hands are a little chilly to the touch and I'm a little pale for a few hours, so what?"

She studied me, deciding whether or not to believe me. "Forty-eight hours downtime. See a medic if there's no improvement. Promise me."

I nodded dutifully.

After she'd left, I felt Ranger's eyes on me.

"You did a dumb thing, lady," he said, tossing a lozenge at me. It was an atrocious honey-menthol, but I tucked it into my mouth anyway.

"I didn't have time to think it through, Ranger."

"*Good Night*'s safe to approach now."

It must've been my imagination, but it felt like her frenetic heat hadn't fully dissipated yet.

"I'm going to chill here a while," I said.

It looked like he was about to argue with me. He pushed the curls back from his boyish face like he needed me to see how serious his expression was before he voiced his objection.

"Ranger, give me this, okay?"

He reluctantly withdrew.

I couldn't bring myself to get into the cockpit again, so I lay down in the foamy crease where the fuselage met her good wing. She ticked as she cooled, and I tried to give her the heat of my body, but I was cold. Always so cold.

"Ty?"

"I warned you," I growled at Winter without opening my eyes. "I was doing fine, but you were still too focused on trying to protect me instead of showing enough

223

situational awareness to realize you were in trouble. Take a good look at *Good Night*, and then get away from me."

He was silent for a long time, and eventually he left me alone.

After a while, I fell asleep cradled against *Good Night's* fuselage.

With shaking hands, I raised the bottle of water to my lips while my eyes stayed fixed on Risa's jet, *Bastard*. I wore my flight suit and my flight gear, everything but the helmet and my weapon.

"Take a knee," Tomai said.

"No."

I set aside my drink and climbed the fuselage again.

Come on, do this. No emotion is stronger than your will, especially not fear.

Vibrations coming intermittently. Wind sounding like a scream in my ear or is the scream mine?

Let it go, do you hear me? It was nothing more than a horrible dream.

Not a dream. Reality. Vibrations and shudders signaling Good Night's *approaching death. Acid pains in my hands and arms as I tried to guide the stick.*

You think that will happen again? Next time you'll eject or you'll die.

I can't do this.

You will.

I can't do this.

You have in the past and you've survived it, a sure indication you can do it again.

I can't do this.

What choice have you got?

I'll tell them I can't. I'll give them an honest psych eval, and they'll understand I can't do this. I'm the last person they should be trusting with lives anyway. Deaths, sure, but not lives.

You can do this and you will. You're strong and focused and—

No, I—

You can and you will.

No—

You will because you have to. Failure is not an option. Showing a sign of weakness is never an option. You can be pushed to your knees, but you will never drop to them in defeat of your own volition. Now get in that jet. You will not try. You will do. You have complete control over your own actions. If you can't perform this single action, what makes you think you can take on the lab? Logically, there is nothing wrong with this jet and you know it, so get in there.

Vibrations, screaming, fear, suffocation, pain—

Moments later I was dry heaving on the tarmac.

I stumbled back in the bay and with shaking hands reached for my bottle of water to rinse the stomach acid from my mouth.

"Ty."

I ignored Tomai.

This used to be utterly natural to you, and it will be that way again. There's nothing wrong with this plane, and there's nothing wrong with you. Now get in there and—

A brutal grip on my arm stopped me from climbing up.

"Enough."

"I decide when it's enough," I snarled, jerking my arm free with bruising force.

I climbed up the fuselage. I got in the jet. I started fastening my harness.

225

And then I broke.

Lying on my back outside, bile burning my throat, I felt tears of frustration and fear come to my eyes. I didn't even try to hide them, even when they overflowed and ran down into my ears.

Then I got up and strode back inside the hangar.

I pointed at *Bastard*. "I will be getting back in that plane. I will be flying combat again. I will *not* back down," I told Ranger and Johnny and Michael and Tomai and everyone else gathered there, my voice getting louder and colder with each word. "I am a combat pilot for the Republic of Texas and there is not a force on this planet that can make me back down."

My gaze was met with awkward silence and uneasy looks.

"*Nothing is stronger than my will,*" I roared.

Tomai came to a decision. From her expression, I knew what it was before she said, "You're relieved of duty until further notice."

CHAPTER 35

WEAK SPOT

At the flight academy's track, I attacked my laps like they were alive, each step a hard-driving thrust of my shoe against the pavement, each breath sucked in sharp and deep, each swing of my arms like a knife blade slicing the air.

I had failed and in more ways than one. I still couldn't bully away my fear of flying a Battle Axe, but as I tried to think it through, I realized the situation had far wider repercussions than I first realized.

Not that I didn't appreciate being shown a hole in my preparations for the lab assault, but it was so obvious an oversight my fury had no bounds.

I had forgotten about allies.

I had forgotten about the necessity of seeing an ally fall and continuing the mission without them instead of sacrificing myself to help them.

I had forgotten about allies stepping in to stop me, attempts to persuade me to stand down while my gun was pointed at the villain.

I had forgotten about allies being used as shields or hostages.

Christ, I was stupid. I had to be able to let them die. I had to be able to sink a round in them to clear my path, to put them out of their misery, to get the job done.

I needed to get back to the firing range. I needed to imagine their faces, visualize their intentional or unintentional interference, and I had to envision dropping them. I had to guess what they'd say, what their cries of pain would sound like, what their shock, anger, and betrayal would look like. Who would beg and who would be defiant? Who would look at me like they suspected I was capable of it all along?

I tried to imagine shooting Winter and failed miserably. In fact, I apparently cared more for him than I cared for myself and everyone who would be devastated by the lab. If I'd been killed in that dogfight, the lab would go on forever.

With a roar, I launched toward the bleachers, taking the risers by twos. At the top, I wanted to hurl myself over the rail and into space, but there was no pole to catch like I had at the Hernandez flight school. Instead, I grabbed the top rail with both hands and let my body flip over the rail. The second bar hit the back of my arms at elbow level, and my lower back hit the uppermost part of the concrete riser. Pain shot through me like lightning to burn away my weakness.

Once the shockwave died out, I turned, one hand letting go to regrip and then the other, and I pulled myself back over the rail.

Panting, I stood at the top, looking down at the stunned expressions and ignoring the exclamations. I didn't need to explain myself to anyone, and I definitely didn't need their help righting myself and returning to my desired path.

Hands on my hips and jaw set, I stepped down the bleachers and started my cool down laps.

I had to break up with Winter or learn to hate him. Either way, I figured that would cost me a partner at the lab assault. It was fitting because he would've been doing it more for me than for humanity. The motive did matter. If I had the money to hire someone who got off on the idea of killing a ton of people, I would not have accepted them as a teammate.

Okay, so unless I happened to find another lab victim with righteous fury, I was on my own.

But that was the way it was meant to happen. An internal conflict handled internally, like when Finley had been terminated. Mauss, too.

Risa fell into step beside me. Before my controlled plane crash, she'd already arranged to visit her family in Austin for a few days, and I'd been surprised Tomai hadn't canceled her plans now that we were short pilots and planes.

Risa said, "I thought you were going to try to fly off the edge. No idea why you would, though. It's too high to land without damage but not high enough to kill yourself. What would be the point?"

"What do you want?"

"Well, all your crazy is hanging out, so, as your friend, I thought I'd help you tuck that shit back in."

"I don't care what people think."

"I know you don't, but passing for normal will help you stay out of the psych ward, for one, and help you keep your job, for two."

"No one's ever going to put me in that kind of place."

"Only because you're smart enough to play sane. Have you spoken to Cris?"

"Why?" I demanded. "Because it would be so much fun to tell him how pissed I am he trashed my apartment? I won't give him the satisfaction."

"He what?"

"When I got home, all my belongings were thrown on the floor, most of the breakables were broken, and all the cushions and pillows were slashed. The stuffing was all over the place."

"Sounds more like you got robbed."

"I don't have anything to rob."

"They might've thought you hid the expensive stuff."

"And maybe Cris is as big a psycho as Jason is."

She shook her head. "Jason would drain your bank account and give your money to a charity you hate. Cris would sleep with someone younger and prettier than you. Trey's the only one who would trash your apartment, and lucky for us, he has zero interest in you because you're not stupid."

"Your family is a mess."

"Everyone's family is. I've just got more family to be messy than usual," she reminded me. "Was anything missing from your apartment?"

"No," I said, thinking it over anew. "It's likely you're right. Making me buy a new lamp isn't much of a revenge tactic."

She laughed. "It would work on Jason though. He spends a ridiculous amount of time picking out stuff for his house. Even stealing a sock from him would make him have a meltdown."

Seeing the glint in her eye, I said, "Don't do it."

"Oh, he'll burn me to ash," she agreed. "But some-times I can't help myself. And speaking of people who can't help themselves, Winter asked me again if you're willing to talk to him yet."

"I refuse to think about him today."

"Do you think of him at all?"

I shot her a black look.

"You're with Winter because he's easy. When you're not with him, do you even think about him?"

"I'm not discussing him with you."

"You just were," she pointed out. "You are coming to my birthday party tonight, right?"

"Because I'm such a pleasure to be around?"

"Because it would be good for you to lighten up. You're too serious."

I was glad she hadn't been looking at me when she said that. My lab counselor used to use that very line to justify his unwanted changes to my environment.

That was it. I mean, how many signs did it take to remind me of my duty to end that place?

I needed to have a conversation with Cris. It was time for some honesty.

But first, I needed a crash test dummy for the latest date-rape drug, a powder that was reputed to knock people out when they absorbed it through their skin. "Hey, Risa, is there somewhere you have to be?"

CHAPTER 36

WHISPERS OF DEATH

"Well, this is a surprise," Cris said when he took my call a few hours later.

Despite the flat tone, I felt a warm thrum of recognition at the sound of his deep voice, like the clouds had been blown aside to let a shaft of sunlight shine down on me.

"You left a message after you heard about my last flight in *Good Night*," I reminded him as I centered the new table lamp on the new end table.

"That doesn't mean I expected you to grace me with a phone call."

"Will you come over? I made stuffed zucchini."

"One of my favorites," he acknowledged. "Must be some favor you need."

"I made it without thinking. I saw Risa today, and her eyes reminded me of yours. All of the sudden I found myself reading Kierkegaard and making dinner for you. I'm in town all week so if tonight is no good—"

"No," he sighed, "I'm on my way."

He arrived at my flat with a book on British imperialism, Chinese takeout, and a grim smile.

"Well, don't you look pleased to see me," I commented, withstanding the dutiful brush of his lips on my cheek as I took the book.

"Today has already sucked, so what's one more chore?"

"Well, you do look like crap." He did, too, like a parasite had sapped his life force. It was rather startling, honestly. His call sign wasn't Granite for nothing. I wondered what could possibly have ground him down.

"So do you," he said, unpacking the food. "I got you sweet and sour chicken, plain rice, and some spring rolls."

"What about the zucchini?"

"It's my favorite, not yours. I'll take the extras with me. Now that the pleasantries are done with, will you deign to tell me what this is all about?"

"I'm having difficulty recovering from my in-flight emergency. What else would it be?"

He raised an eyebrow at me. "You can't think I try to predict you anymore." Glancing around, his expression turned puzzled. "Is that a new couch? Wait, everything in here is new. What was the matter with the old stuff? Did it remind you of me? No, don't answer. I don't care."

We ate in strained silence. He must've taken a few days off because his beard was coming in thickly. Did I see some gray that hadn't been there before?

"How are you?" I asked.

His gaze was shuttered. "If I thought you cared, I might've answered. What do you want?"

I didn't know what to say, let alone how to say it. I fiddled with the wrapper encasing the fortune cookie but realized it showed a lack of calm. I opened the cookie with a snap and pulled out my fortune: *True gold fears no fire.*

I snorted and showed it to him. The corner of his mouth twitched, and then he laughed.

I crunched half of the cookie between my teeth. "I don't want a repeat of what happened."

"How wonderfully vague."

"I'm referring to the flight. The impulse to take a bullet for someone else."

"So you're looking for my advice on becoming an even bigger bitch by eliminating one of your only admirable traits?"

"What are my other admirable traits?"

He gave me a sarcastic smile. "You're great in bed."

I didn't rise to the bait. "I'm a good person, and I want to help people in trouble, but it scares me to know when a situation gets ugly I place a higher value on others' lives than my own."

"I wouldn't go that far," he said, crossing his arms over his chest and leaning back. "You're just assuming the other person can't take a hit the way you can. Whether you want to consider that faith in your abilities or doubt in the other person's is up to you." With a cool smile, he added, "Perhaps you could label it unmitigated arrogance on your part."

"Anyone who spends time with Jason ends up arrogant."

He was starting to relax, and this time his smile held everything I used to love: warmth, irony, and male heat. "You're probably right. If—"

His expression went queer, and he clamped his mouth shut as he shoved away from the table. I did, too, preparing for a fight, but he shot past me to the bathroom. I heard him vomiting violently.

"So much for dinner," I muttered.

I found him sitting against the bathroom wall, trembling, his eyes closed. Sweat ran down his face and drenched his T-shirt.

"Do you need medical assistance?" I asked.

He didn't seem to hear me.

I crouched beside him and smoothed the hair off his face.

"Cris, look at me," I coaxed. "You know I didn't intentionally give you food poisoning, right?"

His eyelids fluttered open. "I'm okay."

"Like hell," I said kindly.

"Sometimes the cure is as awful as the illness."

"And perhaps you made the situation worse by working too much when your body's telling you something's amiss."

He closed his eyes, and I wet the edge of a towel and wiped his face. His skin felt thin and weak like tissue paper. I strained under his weight as I helped him upright.

"Cris, you need a doctor."

He said, "I saw one."

I froze, but his weight propelled me forward. "Are you terminal?"

"So you can put a bullet in me in the guise of a mercy killing? Fuck you. And stop pretending you care."

I toppled him onto the couch and filled a glass with water, my mouth set. I didn't like seeing him like this, my mountain laid low by some bacteria or virus or whatever. "Do you want me to call someone?"

"No. You summoned me, and I came trotting over like a dog, so let's talk about this."

He drank enough water to rinse his mouth before pushing the glass away and lying down.

I sighed and lifted his head and shoulders so I could sit with his head in my lap. Eyes closed to his fragility, I curled a lock of his thick, sweaty hair around my finger. I wanted nothing more than to wrap around him and give him comfort as much as I took it. God, I wished our relationship had turned out differently.

It's not too late. We could flee. We could leave all of this behind and try again to salvage what's between us. Somewhere quiet. Beyond the clans. I am never going to find the lab, nor am I ever going to be free of it while I live within its reach. It's over. They won. Of course they did. I was a fool to think I could shut down a project no one but me thinks is immoral.

But there's still a chance to save what I've got with you. But would you go far away with me, Cris? Even when we're snarling at each other, we can't deny the bond between us, but is it enough?

"Did you ever wonder what you would do if you came face to face with a clone of yourself?" I asked him. Before I asked him to flee the country with me, it was only fair he know everything.

"Thanks to you, I have."

"Would you find it agreeable?"

"Depends on my mood. If one arrived at this very moment, no, not so much."

But he would still help his clone. That was just who Cris was.

"I met one," I said softly. I felt him jerk under my hand but refused to open my eyes and see his expression. "When I was in that other lab after I killed Mauss, I wriggled through the wall insulation and ended up in the basement."

"They were all dead," he said, letting me know he remembered what I'd told him those nights I'd attempted to tell him about my past. "All of Finley and Mauss's

236

victims had been killed when their stasis tubes were deliberately shut off. One of your clones was among the dead?"

"No, I said I met one, not that I saw the remains of one," I said, annoyed. I focused on his eyes. They were bloodshot, but his gaze was so unflinching it was easy to ignore how weak the rest of him was. "There was the big bay full of the dead villains down there, but there was also a separate room with an empty cryo tube. It had my name engraved on it. It was... waiting for me."

After a long silence while I tried to find words, he said, "That would bother me."

"No, what would bother you was the pair of chairs in front of it that made viewing your naked, frozen self a leisure activity," I said with a ghost of a smile. "I still don't quite know what to make of that setup. Mauss had wanted me dead from the moment he found out I had cloned parts inside me. He'd said he was protecting the human species, so he would not have seated himself in front of my occupied icer with a glass of booze after a long, hard day of being righteous."

Cris snorted, the edges of his mouth lifting.

"I don't know," I sighed. "It's feasible the chair next to Finley's was meant for me so he could persuade me to volunteer for his future utopia, thinking people would be more sensitive to the rights of people no matter how they were created by the time he released me. I did like that about him. His unflagging hope, his faith someday humankind would get its act together."

"Where does the clone come in?"

"Well, my clothes had been so saturated that I dripped blood, which wasn't what a woman trying to escape her handlers would wish for. I opened a little door to what I'd thought would be a bathroom, but instead I found a closet containing a clone of me in perfect cryo suspension."

"Wow," he said thoughtfully. "Finley got it to work. Do you know what this means to the space program?"

I opened my eyes to glare at him. "Nice scientific tangent during my moment of crisis."

His eyes crinkled with rueful humor at the rebuke. "Sorry."

In the silence, I curled the lock of his hair around my first finger, then my second, back and forth, back and forth. My hands were perspiring. So were my legs under his head. He didn't have a fever, but he always generated a lot of heat. The discomfort was growing, but I withstood it.

No, this was the time for honesty. I wanted him—needed him—close like this even if he were on fire.

"You think you know how you'll react when you see one, but you don't," I told him. "Up until you see one, you have the luxury of believing it isn't so. I know I live in what once was a cloned body, I know my original brain is alive only because of her body since mine failed so spectacularly at Greyson, but I promise you that meeting a live clone is entirely different than knowing you're built from one."

"Are you certain she was even alive? The cryo experiment Finley initially put you in was faulty, but if she wasn't in it very long, she could've been dead but wouldn't have started to rot yet."

"No, it looked different than the old ones at the other lab. Plus, Finley told me he got it working. Plus, I just knew."

"Are you okay knowing she's down there in that icer?"

"I said I met her. I don't know how many times I have to say that. I met her. Spoke to her. I hatched her."

"You what?"

"Hatched her," I said helplessly. "I couldn't leave her in there. Lucas and Domino must've been looking for me, so they'd find her. I was Miranda Prime, but they still treated me like biotech property instead of a person. I couldn't bear the idea of her being returned to the lab. I followed the instructions on the icer, and I hatched her. But then there was this big, naked Miranda in front of me. She looked surprised to see me, but she spoke to me like I used to speak. She was curious and intelligent, and she was standing there being me."

He sat up, steadying himself with his hands splayed on the couch cushions.

"There's yet another Miranda out there?" he said in a neutral voice. He must've been excited by the idea, but my expression made it clear I wasn't.

"No," I whispered miserably. "There isn't."

He was very still. "Ty, look at me."

Through the tears, I complied. The alarm on his face made me want to jerk my gaze away, but I didn't.

"What did you do?" he asked in a pained voice.

CHAPTER 37

BLIND EYE

Cris and I sat beside each other on the couch, gazes locked. My chest was so tight, I could barely draw breath.

"What did you do?" he repeated.

Was there any chance he could possibly understand what I was about to tell him?

"I wasn't thinking," I said, hating the desperation in my voice, hating how much I needed his forgiveness. "Thanks to someone trying to kill me, I was bleeding badly, and I'd walked through the valley of dead people only to find out Finley meant to ice me up again. I can try to be calm and rational all the time, but sometimes I can't manage it."

"No," he said. He wiped away my tears, and his lips burned a kiss on my forehead. "I know you. You want the disadvantaged to be free and safe. You wouldn't lay a hand on that poor, victimized clone. I know you wouldn't. You'd stand over her like a mama tiger protecting a cub.

That's what you did in the hospital when they tried to take our baby. You fought and fought for her."

"It happened so fast," I whispered, tears spilling onto my cheeks. "She didn't suffer. She never even saw it coming. My hands shot out, and I broke her neck."

"You're amazing with matching infinitesimal details to find a pattern no one else does, so you must've sensed she had some malignant anomaly. You would never coldly murder someone."

"Cris."

"No, listen to me. A part of you must've seen the icer broke her in a way that meant she was going to die horribly, even if you can't think of what that might be now. I know you. You would never so coldly murder someone."

Again, I thought of Winter's comment that while Cris and I were both good people, we were at opposite ends of that spectrum. I felt horrible about killing the clone, but a part of me did wonder if it was for the best. This world wasn't ready for clones yet. There definitely were no safeguards for keeping me from breeding with the human-born population using my clone's womb.

Seeing my hands go to my abdomen, Cris groaned and embraced me, caging me within his arms.

"I think about the baby, too," he told me. "How old she'd be, what she'd be doing, and what we would be teaching her. The books we'd read her. How different our lives would be."

"And if we'd still be together," I whispered. "It wasn't meant to be like this. We didn't marry out of love, so why are we still so connected?"

His lips were soft and familiar on mine.

"We did marry out of love," he countered. After a moment's hesitation, he muttered, "But now I hate you so much it burns like acid inside me. That burn is the

241

first thing I feel each morning and the last thing I feel each night."

"Why did you hit me? You said it was over a lie, but what did I say?"

"Christ, do we have to go into that?" he said pushing me away. "If you believe something I know is a lie, or if I believe something you know to be a lie, does that make it any less the truth for one of us?"

"I reserve the right to know what charges are being leveled against me."

"What an American way to think of it," he snarled. "Nice world you Americans left us."

"What about what you Texans have done to me? It wasn't the Hernandez down in that lab torturing me, it was the same clansmen I'm supposed to die to protect in that jet. The only reason I never sent all the ordinance I've got into that viper's nest is because I couldn't find it."

"You couldn't find your ordinance?" he said sarcastically.

"The lab," I snapped.

"You can't be serious. We talked about how the people running a secret government lab were likely to react if they thought you were looking for it. You did it anyway? Why?"

"So I could send them a scathing letter by messenger," I snarled. "Was I really supposed to ignore the moral imperative to protect the rights of people who were designed not to have any?"

The stunned silence didn't last long.

"You're talking about an assault on a bunch of doctors," he said, eyes wide. "The same people who repaired you after an experiment some American started? What kind of twisted vigilante morality is that? Is this Winter's idea?"

"No, I never told him anything."

"This is insane," he muttered.

"It has to stop. What they are doing, what they are creating, it has to be stopped. Everything I want to do to them, they have earned, trust me."

He got to his feet, refusing to hear any more. "You need to be careful who you say this in front of."

"Why? I already told you I can't find the damned place. That makes everything hypothetical."

"No, it still sounds psychotic no matter how much you want to gloss over it as some kind of morality discussion. Anybody who doesn't know you would think you're arguing for the cold-blooded murder of a bunch of unarmed people."

I gritted my teeth at his unwillingness to consider the good that would come from those deaths, but my remark died on my lips when I saw his ashen complexion. He was swaying a little, too.

I bit my lip. "You're dying, aren't you?"

"I have no intention of being that accommodating."

"I don't want you dead," I told him. "I—"

"Well, that's something."

"Just stop," I yelled. "For once, will you listen to me? Stop shrugging off anything that doesn't fit your Miranda fantasy and pay attention to what I'm trying to tell you."

"No, you stop," he snapped, sweat beading on his temples. "However awful I look, I promise you I feel worse. I need to take my meds and go lie down. I'll call you in the morning after we've both calmed down."

Crying, I watched him shuffle out the door. I didn't want to let him go. "Do you want me to come with you so you'll get home okay?"

He shook his head before grabbing me and pressing a firm kiss on my lips. "You're so fucking broken."

"Right back at you," I snarled.

He grinned and pulled the door shut.

Less than an hour later, my palmer signaled an incoming call from Jason. I shut off my phone, but he remotely turned it on again. Cursing hackers in general and him in particular, I stuck my palmer under the couch cushions to muffle the sound. The tone got louder and more annoying, ranging from metal screeching to a baby crying, but I refused to respond.

That tattletale Risa had no doubt gone to the family problem-solver to report my behavior at the track. Well, I had drugged her, too, but she'd blamed her sudden sleepiness on exhaustion. Compared to everything else, my snit at the track was meaningless, so whatever he had to say about it could wait until morning.

Eventually, he must've understood I wasn't going to yield, and my palmer fell silent.

Immediately afterward, I heard someone unlock my front door, and I lunged for my gun.

Jason strode in like he owned the place.

Gritting my teeth, I holstered my weapon.

"So what if I can't get in an Axe at the moment?" I snapped, even if it killed me to admit that to my mentor. "If you'd been in the cockpit for that ride, you'd know why."

"I read the report, and I will not sit in an Axe until they make reattachment of the umbilicals possible after a computer-aborted ejection. You shouldn't either. It's unsafe."

I blinked. The whole reason I hadn't contacted him for help after wrecking *Good Night* was suddenly moot. He could hate me all day long about my relationships with Cris and Winter, but he would've helped me get back into the cockpit to defend his clan. Well, unless I had destroyed the plane he'd gone to so much trouble to get for me. Originally, she'd been slated to go to one of the clan's top-ranked teams.

"Why are you here?" I asked, sinking into a chair.

"Cris told me you intend revenge on the place that rebuilt you, although you made it sound far nobler. What was it? That's right. You mean to save us all from human rights violations."

My eyes went wide. My cheeks went cold as the color drained from my face.

"Have I been misinformed, Miranda?"

"He told you that?" I whispered. Why had I trusted Cris?

"He recognized you needed more help than he was able to give at the moment." He handed me a garment bag. "Get dressed. I want to find out more about this lab of yours."

I stared at him. "What? Where are we going?"

"We are going to break into the Ministry of Science and Technology."

CHAPTER 38

MOSTLY

"You hack everything," I told Jason as I pulled the seatbelt across and clicked it into place a few minutes later. I hated his car. It was some low-slung sports car that no doubt handled like a dream, but it would give me a view of nothing but guard rails and truck undercarriages. "Why can't you tap-tap-tap your way through their network?"

"Wow, that never occurred to me," he said with feigned surprise. "Thank you for your insight."

I bit my lip, hoping we were only forcing our way into some unmanned substation to get to an internal server or something. I'd acted questionably in my life—well, okay, some actions were unarguably unethical—but nothing like this.

Not that it mattered. His curiosity was no match for my unshakable need to get the information about the lab. I'd follow him into Hell to get those coordinates.

"The aspects you are most upset about will never be eliminated," he told me as we sat at a traffic light. "Not the cloning, not the human experimentation, and not the agencies operating without proper oversight. Like it or not, major advancements in society are usually accomplished through secrecy and a certain callousness about human rights. No matter what you do there, the ideas will manifest somewhere else if they haven't already."

His eyes bored into mine.

"Do you understand that?" he asked.

"It's green," I said, motioning at the light.

His gaze returned to the road as we accelerated. "Even if you merely wanted to expose it, most people believe any short-term and limited human rights violations are worth it. The concepts of cryo and bioengineering give people hope."

"Only the people who haven't thought it through would think it a sane option."

"Look at your life. Who would even consider you a victim? Not only are you now young, gorgeous, and healthy, but they also provided you a new identity and the means to rebuild your life in aviation, albeit under a different name. The tax payers paid for that, but they are not supposed to receive anything in return?"

"Don't you dare support this, Jason."

"What? I do believe it took them years to fix you, and your immune system must have been reduced to nearly nothing. Now add the political and security issues resulting from you being a Hernandez visa holder supposedly being killed by Texans on Farragut lands. Now imagine the media onslaught. It would have been a catastrophe if they hadn't held you in secret."

I glared at him. "You only ever think about yourself. You wouldn't care what happened to me if I weren't useful to you in the cockpit or as a research assistant. You're overlooking the lab's actions simply because they made it possible for you to get me back as your sidekick."

"Don't downplay your ability to contribute," he chided. "Even as a novice, your grasp of advanced physics and aeronautics was formidable. You have no idea how hungry I was to work with you. I still am."

"Don't stroke me. Not everyone is like you, you know. A lot of people would want that place eliminated if they knew about the rights violations alone."

"Really? It has been my experience that desperation, greed, and selfishness beat morality nine times out of ten. Don't misunderstand me. There are some aspects to what occurred I take issue with, but they are not necessarily the ones you do."

"Your sole annoyance is that they hid my existence from you," I snapped. "I'm surprised you don't blame me for that."

"Who says I don't?"

I ground my teeth, refusing to tell him what lengths I'd gone to for him while under the lab's thumb.

"When your husband Paul was killed, what would you have done to get him back?" he asked me.

"Don't talk about him."

"I have lost people I loved, both slowly to disease and quickly through accidents. They were beautiful human beings by anyone's estimation, and if I'd had new avenues to fight for their continued existence, I would have used them first and suffered the consequences later."

"Cris told me how much you all loved your grandfather, but he had a very full life. There comes a point where you step aside and make room for the next generation."

The muscle in his jaw twitched. "What about a child?"

My heart lurched in my chest. Had Cris told him about the miscarriage, too?

His hands twisting on the steering wheel until his knuckles whitened, he said, "Aren't you going to argue that a child hasn't been around long enough to contribute or that since a person has only had a few years to know the child the love and pain is less?"

"I would not harvest parts from one live child to repair another," I snapped. "There are some lines you don't cross."

"Tell me, have you ever truly loved anyone? It seems like your feelings are easily boxed in by arbitrary rules. Do you even check your loved one's pulse for yourself before the mortuary sends the remains into the fire?"

"Don't you ever doubt my ability to care about someone," I snarled. "I know far more about dealing with love and loss than you ever will."

"I have experienced loss you cannot possibly relate to," he threw back.

The odd hitch to his voice reminded me of when we'd crossed paths outside his tailor's after my escape from the lab. Jason must've lost someone. That was why he'd left aviation for those years. He'd met someone, loved hard, then lost her. Did he honestly think I didn't know what that was like?

A knot formed in my gut. Women had been trying to get close to him for ages, but I was the one who actually had. I hadn't meant to, but I'd formed a strong, unique bond with Jason while he'd been a guest instructor at the Hernandez flight academy. It never occurred to me he'd find that with someone else.

"After I died, you whored it up with some passionate Italian bitch, didn't you? What did she die of?"

His eyes widened, and he burst out laughing. "What? My God, are you jealous?"

"Of course not. You and I weren't together."

"That emotion you refuse to feel when you think about me being with someone else is the same emotion I refuse to feel when I think about you being with Cris or Winter."

"I'm not doing this. I'm especially not doing it with a man who'd carve out the liver of an innocent bystander to give to his hot, alcoholic girlfriend."

"I would never do that."

"There's hope for you after all."

"I said I would never do it, not that I wouldn't pay to have someone else do it for me."

"Pull over."

He laughed again. "Relax. You're the last woman I was with."

"That was years ago. Jason, you need to get laid."

"And risk you going homicidal on the Italian temptress I'm in bed with? I don't think so."

My teeth gnashed.

"But we're off topic," he said. "We were talking about cloning and other pro-life technologies."

"Pro-life?" I spluttered.

"You don't think procreation assistance and longevity extension technologies are conducive to maintaining a healthy population? The miscarriage rate keeps rising. The average age people die at keeps dropping. Before too long, some difficult decisions will have to be made."

"Yes, but this is not the solution. And if the human race overwhelmingly believes this *is* the answer, the species isn't worth saving because they have forgotten what it means to be human."

He raised an eyebrow at me. "You don't mean that. However, I do appreciate that you have yet to resort to the argument about us all being God's children. Since Texas is predominantly Christian and the Bible's stance is anti-cloning—"

"Don't smugly argue an issue you have no working knowledge of. I lived it, Jason. I know what it's like to be regarded as biotech property by one contingent and a

250

threat to the species by another. I live with the knowledge girls were slaughtered to keep me alive."

"Don't interrupt me," he chided.

"Seriously? That's your response? Even if you can't muster any moral outrage, can't you at least care that someone damaged your precious student-pilot-what-ever?"

"Will you calm down? I'm just making conversation. I'll hold off on the real discussion until I've got some facts in front of me. It won't be too much longer."

I looked where he motioned and saw the angular MoST building rise before us.

We were really doing this, really going to felony tres-pass into the headquarters of one of the ministries. I could feel Jason's anticipation, see it in the fine tremble of his hand as the adrenaline flooded his system.

"Could you be any more excited about this?"

Jason laughed.

"You do know I've never done anything like this before, right?" I said.

"Neither have I," he said, pulling his car into one of the reserved parking spaces at the far end of the lot. "I suspect our success will depend on attitude."

I said, "Just for future reference, that was the perfect opportunity for you to lie to me by saying you know what the hell you're doing."

Chuckling, he handed me a slim bar with a funny hook on the end. It was heavy and almost as long as my arm. I hoped he didn't expect me to use it as a weapon. It was utterly incongruous with the stylish skirted suit he'd made me wear.

He tucked several black cases in the pockets of his suit and left the car. He helped me out of the car, his hand firm on my elbow while I got my high heels underneath me. It didn't help that he'd parked almost on top of a nubby manhole cover.

He took the bar from me and inserted the end of it in the catch of the manhole cover to lift it up and swing it aside.

"I needed nice clothes for this?" I commented, plucking the silky blouse away from my body as the August humidity hit me like a wave.

"Yes. You first. Fast and quiet."

I jerked off my shoes, held the edges of them in my teeth, hiked up my skirt, and descended the ladder into the darkness.

I felt around the floor with my foot, checking the surface all the way to the edges of the tunnel. The slabs of metal grating were rougher on the edges but worn smooth in the center so I would be fine in bare feet. Thank God.

Jason pulled the manhole cover across, leaving us in complete blackness.

It's the killing time.

I heard the metallic clink of the tool being set on the ground. I felt him move around me and heard him touch the walls of the tunnel, learning its dimensions. Hands on my waist, he pointed me squarely. He took a moment to align himself beside me before taking my hand and pulling me forward.

Nearly running, we hurried down the service tunnel.

My heart lurched unevenly against my ribs.

The lab had been black like this when Mauss had hunted his victims. It had been quiet like this, too, with muffled sounds and the furtive need not to be caught.

We were too loud. We were going way too fast to pass silently. Jason's hand was hot and dry in mine, and when I tried to pull my hand back so I could slow down to a safer pace, his grip tightened.

Was this a dream? I felt dizzy, unsure. I'd dreamt this, dreamt of escaping the lab with Jason. Over and over I'd dreamt of running through inky corridors, the promise of gunpowder and blood a few steps behind us.

No, it's okay. We're not in the lab. We're simply breaching the Ministry of Science and Technology headquarters.

I realized I was holding my breath and forced myself to breathe normally. I smelled that iron blood rust scent, and my stomach seized up.

Try to smell Jason's clean, subtle cologne. He always smells good.

He slowed, then stopped, and his hands shot out to catch me if I stumbled. He tapped the shoes in my hand, and I braced myself on his arm while I put on the stilettos. The muscles leapt under my touch. Was it adrenaline or was he still that affected by me?

I took a few cautious steps to learn how to move quietly while he retucked his shirt and adjusted his suit. I heard the familiar sound of his hands smoothing over the fine cloth.

He pressed a computer tablet slightly larger than a palmer into my hand.

After a few seconds of stillness to allow our breaths to even out, he opened a door into a hall so bright it hurt my eyes. We stepped out. He quickly closed the door behind us, the sound masked by a piece of plastic hitting the flooring.

"I'll get it," he said in a perfectly normal voice, having created a natural pause to give our eyes a few more seconds to adjust. He retrieved the badge from the floor and handed it to me. I clipped it onto my lapel as he complained about the short-sightedness of the second in line to the MoST throne.

It was at that moment a woman came around the corner and caught us.

CHAPTER 39

SEX GAMES

Confronted by a woman dripping authority in the MoST hallway, Jason and I stopped short, eyes wide.

Her expression showed she knew she had us, too.

No, the smirk was aimed at Jason like she agreed with Jason's assessment of the ADMoST.

Without comment, she stepped around us and continued on her way.

Jason raised an amused eyebrow at me and walked down the hallway. The I-told-you-so was implied by his swagger.

Drawing attention to ourselves like that shouldn't have worked. Yet, who didn't at some point have a boss they thought was a jackass?

There was no end to what I learned from Jason.

Ten minutes later we were three floors up in a large room with banks of computer equipment. Were these the servers? They threw off waves of heat as we passed them while icy air poured in from the ceiling vents, leaving me with the odd sensation of different body parts being hot while others were chilled.

He paused as if reading the blinking lights on the machines and motioned for me to follow him deeper into the maze.

I didn't want to. I wanted to leave. There had to be another way to find the information.

What if we were apprehended? How was I going to explain this to Domino? This was obviously a nefarious plan to collect data on a secret government facility, and since I was involved, the natural assumption would be we were targeting the lab.

I wiped my sweaty hands on my skirt. I needed to calm down.

Using one of his handmade devices, Jason connected one server to the tablet. An immediate flood of gibberish filled the screen. He plugged his other gear to the tablet's remaining ports as I crept away.

Heart pounding, I peered around the edge of the server.

Jesus, what was I doing here? I was obviously no use on any tech-driven mission, and Jason could obviously handle himself. Had I only been invited along in case it came down to violence? I hoped not. I had nothing menacing on me other than a pair of designer stilettos.

Maybe he wanted to be captured. Maybe he would prefer I were behind bars rather than dead. Had he lured me here to get caught while he indulged his curiosity about the lab now that he learned I thought it was worth killing over?

Abruptly he disconnected everything and stole through the room. I followed him out the side door. I expected more servers or workstations, but we were in another hallway. We were almost to the fire escape doors when we heard the crackle of a radio and a security guard's response.

I turned toward the server room but saw no handle on this side of the door.

The heel beats grew louder.

One guard?

I listened closely. No, two walking in step, I decided as I separated the sounds. One was favoring a leg enough to cause a little hesitation. Old injury? Knee?

My arsenal of nasty knee strikes flashed through my mind.

No, no fighting. Not if I could help it.

But how was I going to explain my presence there? All I could think of was to say I was lost, but I seriously doubted that was going to work given the security measures Jason had bypassed in the elevator to access this floor.

Jason.

I whirled, searching for him.

He was halfway down the hall waving frantically at me to join him at the edge of an alcove barely large enough to hold a fake plant. Feeling the strain in my calves, I ran on the balls of my feet, silently cursing Jason for giving me the most useless shoes on earth simply because they completed my outfit.

As soon as I got to him, he yanked me behind the plant and stuck his tongue down my throat.

I bit him, and he bit me back, thrusting his hands up my skirt and yanking down my panties. Belatedly realizing what was going on, I fitted myself to him, devouring his mouth and pulling at his belt like my life depended on it. I wobbled on my shoes and he caught me, lifting me and fitting me against him.

256

The plant was jerked away, and I made a high, startled sound.

Jason looked dazed as he tried to focus on the pair of security guards. I felt more than a little dizzy myself, unable to remember where and who I was for a moment.

One of the security guards muffled a laugh at our disheveled breathlessness.

Jason blushed and scrambled to tuck his erection into his trousers while I pushed down my skirt.

"What are your names?" Jason demanded, but his voice was too deep and too husky to carry the force he likely intended.

"Our names? What are yours?" the unsmiling guard threw back.

Knee strike, I remembered, but for which man? Did it matter? They were big men, too. Strong. Capable.

Armed.

Our chances were dwindling.

"What if I'd had a gun?" Jason barked. "I could have shot you both in the face and traipsed around at my leisure. And what are you two doing patrolling together? The rules for this section are very clear. Or do you not think those servers are worth protecting?"

"We—"

"Every minute you try to justify breaking the rules for your own convenience, the rest of this floor goes unpatrolled," Jason said coldly. "At least one of you needs to get back out there. And the next time I come through here, I expect this plant to be gone. People can hide behind it."

"Obviously."

This time the other man didn't even try to hide his amusement.

Jason's face darkened in anger. "Get your supervisor up here. Now."

"Sir, I don't think you want us exposing your... actions behind that plant. Or is she the wife that goes with that ring?" the man said with a pointed look at the wide, silver ring on Jason's left hand.

Jason stilled.

I sincerely hoped his silence was part of the plan because I still hadn't figured out a way to take down both men without taking a bullet.

The guard who had laughed casually bent down and retrieved my panties. Glaring, Jason snatched them away and shoved them in his pants pocket.

The unsmiling guard said, "I suggest you and your... colleague... return to your assigned area so we can all get back to work."

Dividing his frigid stare between them, Jason straightened his suit and held out his hand for me to precede him. I jerked on my shoes and complied.

They escorted us to the fire doors, which were held slightly ajar by a scrap of wood. With as much dignity as we could, Jason and I stepped through the doorway. The guard shut the door firmly behind us.

Jason grinned at me, obviously having the time of his life.

"There's something very wrong with you," I told him.

Back at his house, behind the veil of his surveillance blockers, I felt like I could stop looking over my shoulder. "Were we successful?"

"Of course," he said, surprised by the question.

"That situation with the guards could've become ugly."

"They've discovered trysting couples there before. It's not the first time someone has propped open that fire door to avoid the hassle of going through the security stations when they have to do a thirty-second job on another floor, either," he said, tossing the fake wedding ring in the box on his desk. "It's all in MoST disciplinary files. We didn't get written up because our clothes and my tone suggested we were executives."

"Why didn't we take the fire stairs in the first place?"

"There's no way to open the doors from the stairwell, and there was no way to know if the door to that floor happened to be propped open when we needed it to be. Thank you for letting me do all the talking."

"It wasn't intentional. I just couldn't come up with an adequate lie," I said. "In fact, I was completely useless. Why did I have to be there with you?"

"I needed a plausible reason to be in a restricted area in case I got stopped. I couldn't very well make out with myself, could I?"

"Are you sure you got it? It took you longer to connect than to dig around in that server."

"Give me a few minutes to clean up the files, and you can see for yourself."

CHAPTER 40

SPACE CADET

While Jason ran the images of the verboten data through his computer programs, I took the folded stack of my clothes in hand and used his hall bathroom to change. My mouth still felt hot and swollen from his kiss, but a glance in the mirror showed it looked tight and prim like usual.

I hung the suit on the hangers, the fancy bra looped inside so it was out of sight. I would've done the same to the panties, but Jason still had them. That bothered me. He'd been a little too involved in that kiss. But since he'd bought the underwear so the pencil skirt wouldn't show panty lines like my cotton underwear would've, it was only fair he keep them. I just would've liked to at least wash them first.

Figuring his hand soap was of better quality than my facial cleanser, I washed my face, scrubbing to remove the pixel-scrambling cream that had confused any digital image of me on the security feeds. He wasn't worried about being described by anyone meeting us face to face, citing how unreliable descriptions usually were, but the security feeds had been worth the extra measures.

Not that he was worried. On the way to his house, he'd assured me he left no trace in the servers.

Examining my fingertips, I saw most of the transparent film obscuring my fingerprints was gone. Jason hadn't been concerned about leaving fingerprints, so I guessed he'd already altered them in the system. Short on trust, I'd used a ridge filler on mine anyway.

I took the tube of lip balm from my pocket and unscrewed the opposite end to reveal a tiny packet containing more of the masking fluid and an envelope of the white powder I'd tried on Risa.

I was about to return to his study when I thought of the way his muscles had jumped when I'd taken his arm. When he'd said he couldn't let women in his bedroom, I doubted he'd meant me. I'd crawled into his bed at Greyson when I'd been so close to dying from my kidney issues that I'd needed his comfort. There'd been no resistance on his part. He'd slept curled around me like I had belonged there. In fact, I wouldn't have been surprised if he told me I was the exception to all his rules.

I padded down the hall toward his bedroom, glancing in the study to ensure he hadn't moved.

Predictably, his bedroom was stylish and orderly like the rest of the house. Why did he need such a large bed? At Greyson, he'd slept quite tidily, not sprawling all over creation. I supposed a smaller bed would've looked out of place in the voluminous room. Idly, I wondered if he slept on the side closest to the bathroom or closest to the door. The nightstands gave no clue. They were similarly outfitted with a lamp, a pair of vintage Italian books, and a framed photograph.

On one nightstand, the photo was of me. Not the current me, but the Hernandez me: pale, I, almost ethereal despite my lack of delicate features. No, I looked fragile. Stubborn and fragile both.

A child dominated the image on the other bedside table. Perhaps it was of Jason when he was four or five years old? Possibly not. I lifted the frame to get a better look. He looked very familiar, but it couldn't have been Jason unless he'd had a little nip and tuck somewhere along the way to refine his features. Was he the fabled Chavez bastard? Jason resembled Alex strongly, but how much of that had been intervention after his mother got pregnant by a lover instead of her MoD-appointed husband?

A preteen gets hit in the face with a baseball and his nose bleeds. A doctor's visit could easily be twisted to indicate a broken nose that required some kind of surgery, creating an opportunity to shape the nose along Chavez lines. The child definitely didn't have the Chavez cheekbones. Even the shape of the ears looked more like mine than Jason's.

A plastic clatter coming from the study prompted me to return the photo to the nightstand.

Jason appeared at the doorway.

"What are you doing?" he asked in a strained voice.

"Seeing if lightning would strike me if I stepped into your bedroom. Who is this?" I asked, indicating the photo. "Let me rephrase that. It's obviously you. Just a different you. How much plastic surgery did it take to make you look like you were Alex Chavez's son?"

His eyes narrowed. "I am Alex Chavez's son. Anyone who looks at us can see that."

"I don't care if you're a bastard. I'm merely curious why you'd bother to lie about it. Your talent is undeniable no matter what your origins, and honestly, this isn't the eighteenth century. No one cares about illegitimacy."

He snatched up the picture and set it on a shelf, turning it so I couldn't see it.

"Are you in the mood to have sex with me?" he demanded.

"Not at all."

"Then get the fuck out of my bedroom."

"There's no need to act like we've never been intimate. If I wanted to have sex, you know we would be wrinkling those sheets."

"Your arrogance knows no bounds."

"No, our singular sexual episode was so hot it's permanently burned into my memory. I feel comfortable believing you remember it, too. It's not like either of us has had so many lovers that the memory is confused and diluted with other experiences."

"I am not a slave to my penis. Your desire to bed me does not guarantee I will put my erection to use."

"Oh, I know that. You'd make me beg for it so you felt we were evenly matched again."

His mouth twitched ominously. "If I wanted a bitch to beg, I would get a dog."

"Bitch? That's harsh."

"You are trespassing."

"I'm not moving in."

"That doesn't mean you have an open invitation."

I pointed at the picture of me. "I don't like that photo. I don't even remember consenting to it being taken."

"So?"

"So it's creepy, stalker-man. Why is it even in here? Are you fixated on me?"

"When I'm having a weak moment and actually consider bringing my date in here, that photo kills the mood because it reminds me that I've been taken in by a lying bitch before."

263

"There's that word again."

"If the collar fits," he said, shrugging. He stepped aside and motioned for me to leave his room. "May we return to my study to converse about a topic that's actually interesting?"

When I returned to his study, I saw he had moved a chair beside his desk.

"While you were invading my privacy, I cleaned up the blueprints," he said, turning one of the screens toward me as I sat. A custom system, his computer probably cost five times my annual salary. He handed me his stylus. "I need you to annotate what is different."

"Why?"

"This file is a proposal, and there's no record this installation was ever built. If you come across an anomaly that makes you realize this is not your lab, I will jettison this data and search for another structure that matches your modified design."

I took the stylus and went through the images, labeling room usages, crossing out blast doors, resketching the rough dimensions of the tanks in the atrium, adding security features, and crossing out fixed equipment here and adding fixed equipment there. I even marked out outlets I knew for a fact were missing despite what the schematic said. When there was an area I'd never been in, I marked it as such.

There was no schematic for the basement where the cryo units were. I held the stylus over the blank area where I knew the elevator actually was, but I couldn't bring myself to add it. Jason would want to know what was on the lower level of the lab. At what point would he stop believing me?

"You must be sure," he murmured when I hesitated. "Nothing *maybe* or *probably*. I must know what we are dealing with."

"I constantly looked for something I could use to get out of there or hide in or behind if someone went on a rampage."

"Like a weapons closet?"

"I wish. I noticed outlets and defib packs that carried a current and high-pressure fire hoses that could knock somebody back with a blast of water. Even well-oiled door hinges meant I could throw the door open in someone's face."

"You paused, though."

"There's something I'm sensing but not seeing," I said. I returned the exquisite stylus to him, wondering if he had a fountain pen, too. Why wave your manicured hand around when you could gesture with yet another symbol of elegant, moneyed style? "The rest of it is unfamiliar."

He shook his head. "You are choosing to misunderstand this blueprint to give yourself a reason to fail because you really don't want to kill anyone, and you *really* don't want to die."

I smiled reluctantly. "Close. I'm choosing to misunderstand because this structure's purpose is so obvious I'm an idiot for not recognizing it until now."

Seen in the original, the blueprints unmistakably showed a space station. One of the lab bosses had said their work benefited space travel, but I hadn't recognized the lab for what it was in its altered state. I'd assumed the lab personnel had adapted some old, pre-existing bunker for their use.

"Long-term isolation experiment?" I asked. "There was no way in or out. It wasn't solely for securing the illegal projects. The isolation is what created a safe, secure environment for those experiments to be created."

"Yes."

"I have to admit that's interesting. Even tiny societies will have a few rotten apples. How do you weigh their worth to the collective against the harm they cause? And when you don't have the option of simply sending them away—like if you're on a space station orbiting a faraway planet—what's left? And if you start a small, remote society with Texan laws, how fast will it deteriorate into a social construct that in no way resembles Texan society? And what will it turn into?"

He made an encouraging noise.

It was brilliant, actually. As far as MoST oversight was concerned, how easy would it be to get bored by the reports of an experiment like that? If the cloning and biotech weren't a part of the agenda and were funded by someone else, then MoST wouldn't be expecting anything from the reports except the usual data-crunching fodder like equipment outages and food tonnage consumption, plus the occasional accident or death.

"I have to admit it's a near perfect setup," I told him. "The lab's self-sustaining as far as food, water, and energy go, so its budgetary needs are minimal. It wouldn't be worth close scrutiny when MoST accountants looked for cash leaks to plug. Be boring, don't ask for anything, don't give anything interesting in return, and be ignored while you do what you want."

"Plus they can use the isolation factor as a reason to deny visitors. That is confirmed by the number of unauthorized modifications they've made to the lab for convenience or aesthetics instead of keeping the original space station design. Some upgrades are to be expected, but most of the ones they made seem to decrease the efficacy of or outright eliminate safety features instead of enhancing them. That means no one is physically checking to see if the integrity of the project is maintained."

"How long is that experiment meant to last?"

"It seems to be open-ended. As you suggested, it does not cost enough to go to the trouble of shutting it down."

"You realize the falsified reports from the lab to MoST mean the experiment is worthless to the space program. Following protocol based on that pack of lies will get a lot of people killed."

"Not all of it. It is understood there are inherent limitations given the power source, gravity, radiation, and so on. The idea is to gauge how people respond to eating the same food, dealing with the same people, and living indoors in the same tin can, not to accurately represent hydroponics limitations in space. What is the point of building space vehicles if your crew goes crazy after a few years in them?"

"I'd also like to think people on a real space station would know better than to remove blast doors and keep all their food stores in one wing. And if they truly are that stupid, they'll reap the penalties of it sooner or later like the theory of natural selection suggests."

He laughed, but none of this was amusing. The discovery of Finley's cryo experiment had actually created a wonderful opportunity for Texas to explore the possibilities of long-term space travel. Worse yet, the cloning had likely started out not as some diabolical plot but as an unexpected, desperate foray into a forbidden technology because they couldn't come up with any other way to save the icer victims. If I'd been a part of the team faced with fifty people dying in a rogue stasis experiment, I might've made a lot of the same decisions they had.

"Miranda," he continued, as if reading my mind, "there really are a lot of non-human experiments there making valid contributions to the goals of both space station life and off-world colonization. I'm actually pleased to see Texas working on some kind of contingency plan for when the Earth becomes too resource-poor and contamination-rich to be inhabitable. Cris would definitely be fascinated by the research. Would you like to read any of it?"

"No, I want to see more about the physical lab, not the projects housed within."

"Are you afraid you'll find some worth in that place?" he teased.

"Nothing's pure evil, Jason. I know that. I'm confident the companies that create nerve gas also give to charity or come up with a few vaccines."

I studied his face while he considered and discarded several options in dealing with me. He didn't expect me to be reasonable or make half of his arguments for him. Dealing in shades of gray, I could easily see the value of leaving the lab alone.

But that didn't mean I was going to.

Jason read my face, and with a few keystrokes, he dissolved all the files into useless garbage.

CHAPTER 41

DON'T LET THE BEDBUGS BITE

I surged forward in my chair with a cry, but there was nothing I could've done to stop the lab files from disappearing from Jason's computer. It would've taken me ten minutes to figure out how to turn his system on.

I'd been so close. Why had I trusted him? How many times did I need him to betray me before I stopped believing in him?

What was I going to do? Jason wasn't going to help me now that I'd confirmed Cris's impression of the situation. I had trusted both men and been betrayed by both. How could they do this to me? If they had ever cared about me, how could they not see what had been done to me? How could they not want to stop it from happening again? Was I ever going to find someone I could trust? Was I ever going to find someone who was willing to do what was right instead of being so goddamned selfish?

I felt like crying, but my well was dry, barren.

In the dark screens of Jason's computer, my stunned expression was reflected as a pale and distorted visage.

"Do not do this, Miranda," he pleaded. "If I cannot convince you any other way, at least recognize that revenge fantasies are nothing compared to what you'll face if you try to act them out."

Fantasies? Was he kidding?

"So I shouldn't try. That's your solution. Let them make more of me, let them use and abuse my clones to try out their medical techniques, and let them prevent me from ever becoming a citizen because I'm classified as their property."

"You know I can get you citizenship."

"The Defense Minister can't, but you can? I don't believe that for a second. That lab won't stop with me. You know that, right? Now that they've proven they can fight off the ministries? They will snatch unregistered people from the outlands."

"For all you know, this is only about your DNA. Your DNA is exceptional. They could not have engineered a better one."

God, I was tired of having the same conversations over and over again.

"Are you serious?" I snapped. "My DNA is only going to get them so far. The war is about a lack of resources. Everything is about the goddamned lack of resources. They change the laws to rob the citizens of more and more, but it's still not enough. Unregistered people in the outlands move farther away from the cities to avoid that, but that leaves them open to be preyed upon by people who want fodder for their human experimentation."

"I refuse to accept paranoid hypotheses or random suspicions as valid reasons," he said firmly, punctuating the words with hard taps of his stylus on the desktop. "I want an example you witnessed directly. Did you ever

270

meet a victim who was in no way connected to the cryo experiment? I will even consider the retelling of an overheard conversation. You've never been sloppy with your research before, and I won't tolerate it now."

"I don't have to humor you about this. I'm not accountable to you. I have a responsibility to end that place."

"Your reply indicates you have no proof whatsoever that challenges the possibility yours was the only DNA strand they ever cloned. If everything points to you being an isolated experiment, can your plan be anything more than a revenge fantasy?"

My rage burst forth before I could stop it. Slapping the desk, I roared, "Biotech is the means to create a class of human beings who can be treated as property. It's slavery."

"My God," he said, rolling his eyes. "Bring on the talk of our future overlord oppressors."

Did I sound that crazy?

I sat down, reconsidering yet again. Christ, I felt like a paper cup being tumbled in the wind sometimes.

My bare wrist made me think of Domino. Legally, he hadn't been able to remove my poison core bracelet, but after the lab authorized it to be removed, his lawyers had managed to find a way to prevent it from being put back on. Maybe I was like that. The law couldn't help me because I was grandfathered in under old biotech laws, but laws were being created to protect anyone else from being trapped in a situation like mine. If I knew for a fact I was the only one this could happen to, would I let it go? But in a world of dwindling resources, could the Texas government be trusted to let the cloning technology, let the *power* fall by the wayside?

"Let me handle it. Please," Jason said. He rubbed his face as if trying to wake himself up, but the clumsiness

271

of his hands warned he was fighting a losing battle. "You know I can punish them."

"These people are beyond your reach. And honestly, I don't want or need your help. You don't know who wields the power down there, so in a split second decision, you wouldn't know who to target if you could only nail one. This is my fight."

"You..."

"You?" I said, smiling.

"You bitch," he said, the words slurring.

"All right, that time I'll accept the moniker. It was on your stylus, by the way. You have a habit of letting the stylus rest in the web between your fingers where the skin is thin. When you get agitated like you've been tonight, you let the stylus slide up and down that web- bing. Granted, I didn't expect it to take this long to work given how fast it worked on Risa, but the important thing is that it was effective."

I held up my fingers and showed him the powder.

He wiped his hands on his trousers, but his moves were sluggish and awkward. His eyelids fluttered, and he went limp.

"Sleep well."

After I raided his closet and bound him to the desk chair with some of his ties, I examined his computer sys- tem, but I couldn't make it past his security measures.

I'd seen the flash of pain on his face when he obliter- ated that data. That move had cost him a bargaining chip he would've preferred to keep, but would he have risked my computer skills improving at the exponential rate I learned everything else? How was he to know the lab had deliberately kept me from getting anywhere near a com- puter because they didn't doubt what carnage I might do if I could get into the mainframe. No, Jason honestly didn't know what I was capable of, so he had chosen to remove that data from the equation, knowing he could break into the MoST mainframe again if necessary.

I'd been in his bedroom long enough for him to secure a copy of that data, but I didn't believe he would've risked that either, not when I was already in his house with an unknown skill set and a powerful need. He must've at least considered the possibility I would turn on him and be in here while he wasn't in a position to stop me.

"Think," I murmured. "Would he really surrender verboten data he could use against me, MoST, or the lab somewhere down the line?"

So what did a tech junkie do when he wanted to hide some information very, very badly? But what if he recognized the assumption his go-to would be some complicated computer wizardry? What was the opposite of high-tech security? Low-tech ingenuity?

I rifled through his pockets and found nothing. He'd probably considered I'd frisk him in the guise of trying to get him into bed. Christ, I hoped he didn't hide anything in any of his books. With his habit of tucking ephemera in his books, it would take hours to find it. He couldn't have known when I would duck back in the room, so it probably wouldn't have been too complicated or too far from his seat at the desk.

I sat beside his unconscious body, but nothing stood out.

Christ, it could be anywhere.

Or nowhere.

I shoved back from the desk with enough force to make it scrape against the floor. The screens wobbled precariously and the plastic training model of a Battle Axe fell off its stand with a clatter.

"Go ahead and fall for all I care," I snarled.

No, I had to be patient, had to think it through. This was Jason, not some stranger. I knew how he operated.

He wouldn't make the assumption the information would be there if he went back to the server room. The information was here somewhere. I was certain of it.

I blew out a sharp breath and rested my elbows on my knees, trying to calm down. The plastic plane model was supported by its wingtip. Unable to handle seeing the plane listing horribly on its side, I replaced it on its stand on the corner of his desk.

Wait. That clatter. I'd heard it while in his bedroom. The training aid was out of the way, unlikely to be knocked over by any normal movement at the desk, even with both of us sitting side by side. Even if he had walked around the other side of the desk, he wouldn't have hit it if he brushed against the edge of the desk.

I picked up the model and examined it. Like the ones at the flight academy, it was a solid piece, drab gray, with a handle coming out the rear. Molded plastic, even the handle was a part of it, not screwed in. There was no way for him to hide a memory chip or anything in it. The base was equally unaccommodating.

So what would've made it fall off its stand, making that distinctive sound when it hit the desktop? On the rare occasion Jason fidgeted, it was with an elegant accessory, not an ugly plastic plane.

I bumped the desktop. The plane wobbled but didn't fall. I hit the desk harder, and again, it didn't fall. I would've heard the desk scrape against the floor if he'd used enough force to knock it off its stand.

I stood at the end of the desk and lifted it up. The edge was a hand's breadth from the floor when the model fell off the stand and hit the floor with a clatter. That was what I'd heard.

I looked down and saw a folded piece of paper where the desk leg had touched the floor.

It couldn't be.

Could it?

Hope flared in my chest.

I kicked aside the paper and set down the desk.

My heart beat so strongly it hurt.

I slowly took the paper, savoring the cold pleasure filling me at the feel of the smooth, bright paper and the whispery sound it made as I lifted it off the wood flooring.

Jason had lied about the facility never being built. The coordinates revealed a location in the desolate west end of what had been the American state of Texas.

Satisfaction flooded me.

Finally.

CHAPTER 42

DATE WITH DESTINY

Well into my trip, a bang was accompanied by the rental truck lurching to one side. Heart racing, I grabbed the steering wheel with both hands to wrench the vehicle back on the road. Scanning my mirrors and the horizon, I wondered if I'd been ambushed. A tire had definitely blown out.

Drive on or pull over? Pulling over to repair the tire left me exposed. I saw cover ahead, but maybe I was expected to retreat there to check the tire. Would they be waiting for me?

To hell with it. I stomped on the brakes and yanked on the steering wheel, coming to a stop with the bulk of the truck between me and the direction of whoever had fired at my tire. Pistol within reach, I quickly changed the tire and then drove off on a tangent course, pushing hard.

I sat on the bench outside the auto repair while the man patched the rental truck's tire. The spare had been a dry-rotted sub-sized piece of crap that I shouldn't have been able to drive on, but luck being a capricious bitch, I made it into the nearest town before losing all the air in it. Lucas never would've had a spare tire fail on him, not with the meticulous way he kept his equipment. If he received the order to terminate me, the bullet penetrating my brain would be as immaculate as the weapon he fired it from.

Was he watching me now? Was anyone? I did feel eyes on me, but if it wasn't paranoia, why wasn't I in custody? If the cops know a bomber is en route to a particular site, they don't wait until he gets there and sets the bomb in place before they nab his ass. After Jason woke up and wriggled free of his bonds, he would try to intercept me. Even if he didn't remember the coordinates for my destination off the top of his head, he definitely knew where to get them.

I glanced at my watch. No, Jason wouldn't even be awake for three or four more hours, not with the additional sedative I'd injected into his vein. Even with the flat tire, I had plenty of time.

The tedium of the road trip from Austin west on the old Interstate 10 had ground away most of my excitement, leaving a hollowness in my belly. I debated what to eat and when to eat. I didn't want to have low blood sugar during the assault, but I didn't want to have a belly so full I was throwing up the first time it clenched, either. How long would the attack take? Less than an hour? I supposed I should eat like I was running a ten or fifteen kilometer race.

I'd packed food, but to kill time I perused the options at the small grocery across the street.

Meandering through the aisles was so ordinary. The pleasantries I exchanged were banal. These people had zero idea the magnitude of what I was about to do for them or the statement I was about to make on the subject of human rights.

With a small bag of candied lemon rind in hand, I returned to the bench and sat down, flushing with happiness.

This was happening. It was finally happening. Soon I would be free of fear. Instead of being crushed under the weight of moral obligation, I would finally have peace.

My smile wouldn't fade.

"Senorita?" The old man smiled in response to my smile and gestured at the truck. The repaired tire was back in place, and the spare tossed in the back. I didn't bother to winch it back under the bed where it belonged. It was time to let go of trivialities.

I drove out to the place I'd chosen to hide the vehicle and hopped out of the truck.

I returned the brown lenses to my eyes to hide the distinctive gold irises and tucked my sun-bleached hair beneath a dark brown wig. I dressed like a lab technician in white and black scrubs with the bold red accent. I'd painted my shoulder harness and pistol to blend in with the uniform so I'd stand up to a casual glance.

Having left my palmer behind so I couldn't be tracked, I checked the terrain against my printed maps and picked up my bag, straining at the weight of the ammo and weaponry. I'd practiced with the extra weight many times, but that didn't make it much easier to carry over terrain so broken and steep.

I found the narrow camouflage door where it was supposed to be, sheltered between two boulders.

Emergency Airlock 1

I rotated the hand wheel until the bars retracted and bit back a grunt as I pushed the heavy door open.

My mouth tightened when I saw the angled, dimly lit chute. The cramped space provided nowhere to hide,

278

but I also didn't see any cameras or windows to give them warning I was coming. Another door with a hand wheel was at the other end.

The flooring was some grippy sort of rubber so my footsteps didn't echo as I stepped in and shut the door behind me. My hair touched the ceiling, and I had to carry the bag in front of me down the narrow corridor, ducking my head every few meters to avoid the lights.

My shoulders bumping the walls, I wondered how Domino made it through such a snug space.

Please, Domino, don't be down here today. I will kill you whether I want to or not.

As Jason had me correct the schematic of the space station in his bid for verboten information, I'd studied the layout of the areas I didn't already know. I'd hoped to see multiple entrances. I doubted anyone would be able to find the entrance that enabled Finley to smuggle people in and out without excavating, and the elevator the administrator had used to show me the basement had buttons for only two floors, 1 and B. I'd practiced my rappelling in case the elevator did actually reach the surface, but once I'd arrived at the coordinates, scouting the area where the elevator should've been had been fruitless.

The lab's original oversized entrance for accommodating the placement of equipment was sealed under tons of dirt, so the chute I traveled was my only way in and out. The few armed people in the lab were likely to be at the security station at the end of the tunnel, so after I made it through there, it would be easy.

At the bottom blast door, I set the bag down, put in my earplugs, and readied the assault rifle. Why hadn't I removed the weapon from its hiding spot in the old house and stashed it somewhere else sooner? Stopping by the house had made me aware of the remains of the life I'd tried to have with Cris that clung to me in ragged shreds.

Cris, I—

I paused, thrusting the thought of him from my mind. I needed to focus.

Be fast. Be calm. Be thorough.

I took a deep breath and reached for the hand wheel.

Chapter 43

Inside, Outside, Upside Down

The door to the lab was well-greased, smooth, and silent on its hinges as I cracked it. The scent of the air pouring through the gap made me pause. Bracing the door so it couldn't be thrust toward me, I sniffed cautiously at the crack.

Burning plastic. The air was smoky but breathable thanks to the air recyclers churning at maximum. There were also the organic smells of freshly turned earth and perforated bowel. There was that blood odor, too, that strange metallic scent that was tasted more than smelled.

I donned my goggles against the smoke. Machine gun ready, I nudged the door open.

The corners of my mouth pulled down at the sight of the evidence someone had used a small explosive device at the security station. The ceiling was peeled back in one section, revealing a slow rain of dirt.

"Idiot," I muttered.

Given my desire not to suffer concussive injuries or get pinned down by tons of dirt in collapsing rooms, I didn't carry pipe bombs. Even if I had carried any, I surely wouldn't have used one at the only way in and out of the place.

The three men at the security office were dead. The aggressor had been thorough, following up the explosive injuries with a bullet through the right eye of each man. I saw with relief none were Domino or Lucas.

I glanced at the security camera feeds, but the computers were dark. I grabbed my bag, stepped over them, and continued forward.

I swept room after room, finding only additional bodies. Each was punctuated with that large-caliber hole through the right eye. My stomach clenched at the sight of them.

The attack done by the former chief of security down here had been carried out under the cover of darkness after he hijacked the security feeds and the lights. It was believed Mauss went after particular people that Finley had preselected.

This attack had no discrimination or subtlety, though, merely the apparent determination that everyone be too dead to be rebuilt.

It was my plan.

I felt the funny tilt in my mind as my brain rebooted, and I expected to come out on the other side of it with the realization I'd already been through the lab, already killed in a fugue state.

But my clip was still full and my trigger finger didn't ache. The dead person at my feet was still dead, though. One of her eyes was brown, and the other was a large hole.

It was my plan, but I hadn't been the one to carry it out.

282

The second explosive had been detonated in a room holding a bank of computers, and I drew out a vial of acid from my bag, affixed it to the nozzle of the nearest fire extinguisher and pulled the pin. I pried off the cover of the remaining tower and directed the spray within, careful not to inhale the resulting smoke.

A burst of muffled gunfire made me jerk back, wide-eyed.

It was still happening.

Stick to the plan. Sweep and clear. Search and destroy. Salt the earth.

But my gun hand shook. I had envisioned every possible scenario but this one. The chances of someone getting here minutes before I did to accomplish the same thing in virtually the same way were so astronomical I couldn't begin to calculate them. It had to be someone I knew, someone who knew I meant to do this.

Jason wouldn't. He had the location and the desire for me to survive to serve his own interests, but violence bothered him to a fault.

Cris could've gotten the location from Jason, and yes, Cris had hit me, but I couldn't see him killing even one person up close and personal unless it was a self-defense situation.

Was it Winter?

But the explosives seemed an odd choice for him. He was careful. Blowing up underground rooms and risking cave-ins wasn't consistent with his survivor mentality. And that was if someone else had told him what I was up to—I definitely had never mentioned the lab to him.

The large atrium was a mess of broken glass, burning plant matter, and murdered animals, fish, and birds. No explosive damage. If a part of the ceiling came down here, it would close off at least some of the radiating corridors, so I guessed that was the reason the assailant hadn't risked it. Closing off an artery that still held live people sort of defeated the purpose.

Barely hearing the staccato bursts of gunfire, I stared helplessly at the crushed skull of the male stoat at my feet. Slinky and agile, he'd been admirably graceful in movement, and when I'd tried to smooth my jerky movements as my muscles had healed, I'd pretended to be like him. I could snarl all day about salting the earth, but I hadn't been referring to the vivariums.

I thought the shots were coming from medical, but sound carried funny down here. The farther into the medical suites I walked, the farther away the gunfire sounded. It looked like his work was done here already, and most of the victims were known to me.

Stunned, I saw the blood splatter on Junie's wedding ring. She must've held her hand up defensively, and the gunman had shot through it into her face. When I'd been held down here, she'd been single, single and yearning for someone with her sense of adventure.

Oh, God, Junie. I'm so sorry.

The room holding Kali, the multi-armed surgical machine, had been treated with another explosive, and her twisted, blackened frame was more menacing than the original polished white. On autopilot, I pried off her console cover and sprayed acid within.

In the recovery room, the bodies of a man and woman were entwined as if they had held each other tightly. Not having an unobstructed shot at their eyes, the gunman had simply fired into their heads repeatedly.

Christ, to feel that helpless that you couldn't protect your mate. It had to be horrible.

There was nowhere to hide down here, not to the casual eye. I'd survived Mauss's assault by climbing on top of the black-topped vivarium tank in the atrium, and Finley taught me there were seams between rooms that someone could force himself through to hide in the insulation. Not that any of these people would know about that. The position of their bodies showed they'd hidden behind desks and equipment or in closets. Junie's was the first defensive wound.

Given the years, if not decades, these people had lived and worked down here, I doubted it occurred to any of them to try to escape. Like a true space station, they had been isolated for so long, conditioned to solve any issues without outside help that it was like the rest of the world didn't exist.

It was a slaughter.

I pushed tears off my face.

The carnage didn't matter. Of course, they were people. Of course, they accomplished good deeds as well as the bad. It didn't matter whether they had worked out of misguided attempts to help humanity or if they hadn't understood the impact and had done what they were told or if they had been afraid not to do what they were told. None of that mattered. They had all played a part, and they all could no longer continue to play a part.

Remember the Nazis.

God, the blood, though.

The smell was so strong it was making me dizzy, and my stomach churned and lurched. Blood pooled on the floors, and as much as I tried not to step in it, sometimes it was inevitable, and I left sticky red footprints in my wake.

I shoved my hand under my shirt to feel the lumpiness of my healed ribs. Not my blood, I assured myself. The sticky footprints were done by me but not made of me. Not this time.

At the end of the medical suite, the locks to a pair of security doors still smoldered from being shot out.

It was the cloning labs. It had to be. More signs of explosions but less thoroughness, so it took me a few minutes to spray acid in what remained. The goggles protected my eyes from the smoke, but my throat felt raw. Why hadn't I thought of a respirator? It wasn't like I hadn't tested the acid on computer memory components to ensure it rendered them unusable. I'd known it would be smoky, but after determining it wasn't poisonous in low to moderate concentrations, I'd moved on with the preparations.

Two more bodies, neither familiar.

Jesus, how many people worked here? There was so much death. I didn't know how much more of this I could stand.

Catching an unexpected scent, I followed it into one of the rooms and froze. The charred remains had been shoved in a glass cabinet out of range of the fire suppression measures.

Mental note: baby human remains can smell like barbecue.

My stomach seized too tightly to allow vomiting. My whole body had seized up too tightly to move.

My poor little clone. She was so little I wasn't sure if she'd even made it from *fetus* to *infant*. The anguish of my miscarriage flooded me, and I found myself ditching my weaponry to go to her.

Snatching up a bottle of saline, I doused her to extinguish the tendrils of smoke, but the stream of water was enough to carve holes in her burnt parts. I grabbed a towel with the intention of wrapping her in it, but as soon as I touched her, she started disintegrating.

Fleeing the sight, I snatched up my gear and ran from the room. A hasty search of the suite didn't reveal anyone else. Finley had wiped out the biologics in the cloning department the last year I'd been in the lab, so the baby likely had been their first viable clone since then.

Prayers left my lips in a litany of grief. For the baby, for that couple, for Junie, for the stoat, for all of them.

Sensing movement behind me, I whirled. It was Isidro, my surgeon. He was disheveled in a wrinkled lab coat and stained tufts of insulation clinging to his wiry black hair. I barely had time for his presence to register before he jammed an injector into my neck.

In the moment between recognizing his face and the numbness starting in, I could've acted. Like with the clone in the basement of the other lab, I could've simply reached out and broken his neck.

He was the one person I sincerely wanted disempowered if no one else. He had been my soulless surgeon, a conscienceless clone terminator, a petty torturer, and alarming innovator. He was there in front of me, and all I did was stare at him as I breathed in the blood smell and smoke.

His shot was already making me numb. He valued me too much for it to be a lethal injection, but the sedative was still a powerful one. Already, I couldn't even speak, couldn't explain to him why I'd let him live.

I hate you, but I won't kill you. I will find another way to take you down, a way that doesn't cost me my soul. The carnage here—I couldn't have done it. Despite it all, I couldn't have, wouldn't have done it. Are you going to learn from this massacre, too? As you stepped over the bodies and slipped in the blood, was this the day you decided cloning wasn't worth the risk?

The Frankenstein to my monster, he caught me as I collapsed, and he held me with the care of someone on the verge of losing someone he loved.

I smelled his fear sweat amid the antiseptic and saw the determination in the set of his jaw and the narrowing of his eyes. He didn't say anything.

The drug finished pulling me under, and I became nothing.

CHAPTER 44

WINK

I surfaced into a nuclear winter. Gasping for air and choking up bitter fluid, I jerked back from the hands holding me, arms flailing to create some space around me.

I couldn't breathe.

"Cough it up already. I don't have all day."

Masculine hands flipped me onto my hands and knees and whacked me painfully on the back. A volley of blue-white fluid burst from my nose and mouth onto the grated walkway that told me I was in the basement of the lab where the cryotubes were.

"There you go," the man said. "That's better, isn't it?"

I collapsed to the floor, riddled with pain. My muscles wouldn't respond but spasmed erratically between the shivers. I was naked.

"You've been in cryo," the man told me. "Looks like a rush job."

I looked at him but had difficulty focusing. I could've sworn I saw my own cold, gold eyes staring back at me. I tried to make sense of it, but my mind kept hiccupping, sending the thoughts flying from my head. "What year?"

"You've only been in cryo for a few hours."

It was the gunman.

"You're one of Finley's victims?" I rasped, trapped between wonder and alarm. "What year? I'm 2014."

His smile came nowhere near to reaching his eyes. "I wondered if you were. They treat you like you are, and you do look sort of familiar."

My vision kept coming and going as I tried to focus on his face again. Was he familiar? Maybe not.

He told me, "You'd better bail unless you want to die. Do you? I guess it would be gentlemanly for me to snuff you."

That last part was delivered with hard mockery.

"I do not want to die," I choked out and spat another mouthful of fluid. My throat and lungs felt like they were lined with broken glass.

His laughter sent a shiver down my spine.

To stop it, I asked, "You gave me a flat tire, didn't you? The guy said I got darted. I thought it was a carjacking attempt."

"Once you packed up your guns and took a straight line out here, I knew you were going after them. The flat tire stalled you long enough for me to break into your truck to see if you had a map that could show me the way in."

"You're the one who trashed my apartment."

"I've gone through your stuff plenty of times, but I'll admit I lost my temper that day."

Stunned, I gaped at him.

He explained, "Look, Finley knew how much I wanted revenge on this place, so he smuggled me out while I was unconscious to make sure I couldn't come back and destroy it. When I wanted to come back to steal some heir-loom seeds from the seed bank, he dosed me again and I woke in that hidden tunnel off the basement. I thought I could sneak out after my business was done, but he got the drop on me and got a syringe in my ass before I could even get a glimpse of topside landmarks."

"How did you find me?"

"I've been tracking you since you emerged from the Oklahoma City lab like you'd found the backdoor out of Hell. I figured if anyone could figure out where the home lab was, it would be you. You found us at Finley's other one, after all. Thanks for the map, by the way. I've been waiting for this a very long time."

He looked around at the carnage. "This is the best day of my life."

His smile was for real this time, and I saw a glimpse of the man he must've been before he woke in this lab. A feeling of recognition stirred in the back of my mind.

"You sent the flowers," I said in wonder, thinking about his reference to heirloom seeds. "You put them in my hair in the lab, you left them at the campsite, and you sent them to my apartment."

"There was a time when I thought about working with you. It wouldn't have worked out though. What did you do with your freedom? Got a boyfriend and played house day after day. Did you think you had forever to change the world? Granted, that was nice work with the child molester—that lone shot into the right eye was simple but effective enough for me to make it my new favorite way to off someone—but why did you stop with him?"

"Did you point the blame for that biotech firm's bombing at me, too?"

"You wouldn't believe the hybrids they were trying to create," he spat.

290

I did know him. I couldn't place him, but I had a distinct memory of him with a pair of my rose shears in his hand.

"You're a botanist, aren't you? What's your name?" I asked. "I'm—"

"Hello? Can anyone hear me?"

Domino's voice boomed through the halls.

The man with me jerked on a mask of Harry Fischer's face, snatched up my bag, and took off without a look back. I lunged after him, but my muscles gave way and I fell on my face, coughing.

My American brother actually left me naked, weaponless, and almost incapacitated in a lab full of bodies while the modern authorities closed in, the bastard.

The sound of his boot heels faded as Domino's grew stronger. When I saw him, I pointed in the direction the man had taken, but he didn't follow. Lucas shot past us with his weapon drawn.

Domino unbuttoned the top of his shirt before yanking it over his head to give it to me. "How many are there?"

"One for sure. Don't know if he was alone. I was. Everywhere I went it was bodies upon bodies until Isidro spiked me in the medical suite. He must've been hiding in the seams in the cloning lab. He might be the sole survivor."

"He's dead. Looks like he was gutted before he was given a wink."

"A what?"

He made a gun with his hand and mimed firing a shot through my right eye.

I shuddered. My stomach clenched, and I pressed my lips together at the surge of regurgitation. Another spasm, and it flew from my mouth.

He pulled me to my feet, and when I couldn't maintain the position, he picked me up and headed for the exit, stepping over the bullet-riddled corpses of other icer victims. Our eyes became red and swollen from the acrid smoke.

I didn't know what to say to him. The whole day had turned out so different than expected I didn't even know whether to lie, tell the truth, or shut my mouth.

CHAPTER 45

OPTION ONE

Domino sucked on a wintergreen mint as he drove, the angry, relentless clicking of the candy against his teeth a sure sign of his mood despite the calmness of his outward appearance.

I sat on the passenger side of his truck with my knees drawn up. Even though the heater blew so hot a thin sheen of perspiration appeared on my skin, I still shivered.

A phone call pierced the tension.

"You're on speaker," Domino said curtly.

"Identity confirmed," Lucas said, his voice breathless and rushed. "Alpha six."

"Romeo."

After the call was terminated, I guessed, "Lucas lost him?" He wouldn't have wasted time calling unless there was a lull from either capture, death, or loss of the target.

"Why should I tell you?"

"Because the gunman and I weren't playing for the same team, and if there's a new threat, I need to know about it."

"He didn't kill you."

"That doesn't make him a friend. That makes him curious about me."

Domino grunted.

I pointed out the hiding spot for my rental truck, and he corrected his course. Lucas was waiting there.

"Six?" Domino asked him, his eyebrow raised.

Lucas nodded. "They covered his escape from the rocks. I got a tag on him and at least one of the others."

"I'll start the track. I want you to sit on her. Overnight, possibly two nights."

Lucas's mouth flattened.

"No one knows her better," Domino said. He dug through my ride, found my clothes, and thrust them at me. "Hurry up."

I'd apparently lost the privacy that came with trust because neither man turned their back.

Domino told Lucas, "Option one is authorized for Tycho Walker Chavez, person present, while she's in your custody."

"Option one authorization confirmed for Tycho Walker Chavez, person present, while she's in my custody," Lucas repeated, and he removed his pistol from his harness. Pale eyes like diamonds, he told me, "You drive."

"Did you tell him he could terminate me?" I asked Domino as I passed him his shirt, knowing damned well that was exactly what had happened. "I didn't kill anyone down there. Neutered a few computers, sure, but since when is that a cardinal offense?"

He ignored me and nodded a farewell to Lucas.

I coughed at the dust his speedy departure stirred up. "The keys are under the bumper. Do you want to reach for them or do you want me to do it?" I asked sarcastically.

It was a painfully awkward, silent ride. When Lucas did answer me, it was monosyllabic. His eyes were on me constantly, but what kept drawing my attention was the black eye of his pistol. It wasn't the first time I'd looked down the barrel of a gun, but I had yet to get used to it. Having a man who was like a friend do it made me angry. I had no intention of doing anything to wound him either with my bare hands or by driving his side of the truck into a concrete column, and he should've known that.

As much as I tried to rid my mind of images of the lab, tremors continued to go through me as I drove, and my stomach felt like a walnut shell with a shriveled kernel inside it.

My icy fingers were light on the steering wheel, but they burned when the warm air from the vents washed over them until I had to shut off the heat.

I'd seen Lucas in a lot of moods but never this frosty, and to be honest, it unsettled me when I truly needed some comfort.

Cris, I wish you were here. Winter would lose respect for me if he knew what I did in the lab. Well, what I didn't do. I didn't even punch Isidro in the nose when he was there in front of me. Maybe I hoped that syringe held a permanent solution so it would finally be over for me. Bullets and needles, bullets and needles. Why can't I die? Why can't—

"Little One," Lucas said sharply, grabbing for the wheel.

"My head," I said thickly, trying to shake the crouching blackness from it. "Something's wrong."

"Pull over."

I couldn't even manage that much. I yanked on the emergency brake and took my foot off the accelerator. The engine stalled as I passed out.

I came to flat on my back on the side of the road with him splashing water on my face. Some of it went up my nose and I rolled over, coughing and blowing snot.

"Gotta love cryo," he said grimly, putting away the portable bioscanner. "It's the gift that keeps on giving. I felt like crap for about a month after my tour."

I pushed up onto all fours, breathing shallowly.

Get up. God won't let you die because you've still got a purpose, so get up and get back into that truck.

Tough talk be damned. I was grateful when Lucas clapped me in restraints and chucked me in the back seat. I wriggled onto my side and closed my eyes, trying to let the hum of the engine lull me to sleep.

God, the blood.

Sticky red footprints, cold eyes, lovers embracing as bullets tore into their heads, cold laughter, a poor, charred baby—

Lucas pulled over and held tissues to my nose so I could blow it instead of getting snot all over the seat, but he left the tears alone, letting them pool in my ear.

Strapping himself back in the driver's seat, he said, "Feeling sorry doesn't mean crap. You know that, right? Domino needs proof before he believes what you went down there to do, but I don't. What gave you the right?"

"This from an assassin?"

"I don't make the call. You know I don't. I execute the command from authorized personnel. You have no authority."

"Evil happens when good people do nothing," I threw back, struggling to get to a sitting position. "You've got a

296

kid. Don't you want to protect her from places like that? Or don't you think it could ever happen to someone you know? Let me tell you something. I couldn't have foreseen or prevented it happening to me. No one was safe."

"It was not your right," he persisted.

"According to any tyrannical government, no one has the right to challenge them."

"How is murdering babies a fight against tyranny?"

"That wasn't me."

"I knew I shouldn't have given you the pass for that kiddie rapist. I should've told Domino what you did, but the world didn't need one more sick asshole who'd bought his way out of a fair trial the only other time he got caught. I didn't want to see you locked up for terminating him. Lesson learned."

"If you—"

"Lie down and shut your mouth. Make any fast moves, and I'll put a round in your brain. Are we crystal clear?"

"That you'll murder the victim? Yes, I understand."

He growled and stomped on the accelerator, only to lift his foot and let the speed drop to the legal limit. He didn't want attention any more than I did.

Option one, indeed. He'd do it, too. He wouldn't like it, but he'd do it. Such was duty.

CHAPTER 46

APOLLO

After marching me through the lobby of a small police station two days later, Domino shut us in an interrogation room. He looked like a conventional cop in his conservative suit, shoulder harness, and hair back to its natural brown color, but it was the eyes that clinched it. No matter what he wore, those eyes gave him away as a lawman.

"You got to me sooner than I expected," I commented, fanning my sweaty face with my ice-cold hand. I looked forward to my internal temperature control sorting itself out.

"I need to wrap up loose ends before someone above me decides to terminate you," he said.

Seven bullets in a box had come with my packet of official documents that day in the outlands, and now I understood each round graphically commemorated a time when some authority had considered killing me. I wondered what Domino would charge to have a new one made with an additional space for the engraved bullet Lucas had left me.

Domino rubbed his jawline and sat down. Arms crossed over his chest, he seemed to be waiting while I processed what he'd said.

I tried to think clearly, but I was light-headed. A fresh sheen of sweat appeared on my skin. My vision faded, and I felt myself toppling.

Domino's bruising grip on my arm kept me from hitting the floor. He sat me in the chair and pressed my head between my knees. The feeling of fainting ebbed, but my stomach was still in turmoil.

"Did you go there to stop that gunman?" Domino demanded, each word like a nail being driven into my brain.

It would've been easy to say yes. He wanted me to, if only to prove to himself he hadn't been mistaken to trust me.

"What does it matter?" I mumbled, rubbing my head.

"I was able to retrieve the security footage. I saw the look on your face when you found that infant," he said.

How could he speak about her in the same blunt way he said everything. Didn't he have a heart?

"Hell, I thought you were going to burst into tears when you saw the dead animals in the atrium."

I wiped the tears off my face with angry swipes. "Your point?"

"I also saw you have a shot at Isidro and not take it, and of anybody, he would've been your prime target. The shooter gutted him, laughing, before killing him. Do you want to see the footage?"

I knew I wouldn't have laughed. I wouldn't have tortured him either.

"Isidro saved you," Domino said. "He had a good hiding place, but he left it to hide you from that guy. He was tortured and killed because he valued you more than himself."

299

I threw up in my mouth again.

He escorted me to the bathroom, and I vomited freely, my hands clenching on the plastic toilet seat.

"But we both know what Isidro did wasn't about you so much as his research," he said, resting his ass on the sink. "It was only ever about your body for him. But still, I don't think you would've done that to him. You're better than that. You're better than all of them."

Was I was meant to affirm I realized I couldn't go through with it? Did it even matter? All those people were still dead because of me.

I thought about the gunman, debated whether to share what I knew of him. Given that he'd left me to the wolves, I wouldn't be surprised if he turned on me in custody and said I was the mastermind and he was following my orders because he was brainwashed, pussy-whipped, or just plain terrified of me.

Back in the interrogation room, I said hesitantly, "The gunman was the one who left me flowers. He thought we would be of like mind given our origins in the stasis experiment. He said he thought I looked familiar. Not a lot, but somewhat. Like from before the experiment. His uncertainty is the only reason I'm still alive. You got there before he could decide to kill me. Or not kill me. I couldn't tell. Who is he?"

"Facial recognition was useless. The salvaged security footage shows him wearing a mask of former ADM Harry Fischer. And as you know, there's no surveillance down in the icer bays."

I didn't react to that name. I'd gone to a lot of trouble to ensure I never would when someone said it. I had to assume Domino had found the ADM's remains in the basement of the abandoned Oklahoma City lab, which meant he had to know about the dead clone on the floor of the next chamber. Did he suspect I killed her? Or did he blame Mauss?

"The gunman's eyes used to be brown," I said suddenly. "He had a plant name, which I thought was funny because he was a botanist. Thorn? Briar? I don't know if it was a nickname. The day we met, he played with my dog and drank coffee and trimmed my rose bushes. That was six months before I was kidnapped for Finley's experiment. It's the only memory I have of him."

Goosebumps broke out across my arms and the hair on the back of my neck lifted. What if that guy had been taken for the experiment because Finley had seen him with me and been curious enough to see if he had use to his collective?

Domino glanced up from his note-taking and indicated the fresh spate of tears wetting my cheeks. "Why are you so upset about what happened down in the lab? You think they earned it, don't you?"

I looked away.

He said, "You want to believe in the system despite it failing you so many times. You must know how long it would take to identify everyone involved in allowing that place to exist, and how impossible it would be to prosecute this without exposing you."

"I don't believe anyone ever tried."

"What do you know of the LC?"

My gaze shot to his, showing my surprise at the change of topic. "The Lieutenant Chieftain is like a vice-president. He doesn't do anything and doesn't have any power unless the Chieftain is incapacitated or killed."

"He's got a unique power most people don't realize. He's in charge of the Texas Rangers."

"Since the fall of the United States, Texas has been a sovereign nation, so wouldn't the Rangers have duties redundant with the national marshals?"

"The marshals fall under the Ministry of Justice. The handful of Rangers under the LC don't, so they can investigate allegations the Ministries can't or won't. It raised a red flag when both the Ministries of Defense and Science and Technology made too many inquiries over the death of a Hernandez flight officer on Farragut lands."

"The Rangers work too slow. I was down there for five years."

"The more it was investigated, the farther it reached. I've managed to get a lot of the people behind bars on other counts, but the LC's been reluctant to make arrests on the Ministry of Defense's senior staff while a war's on."

"You're only trying to nab them on other crimes? What kind of strategy is that?" I said absently, regarding him anew. A Texas Ranger. I had to admit, it impressed me. "Can I see your badge?"

I didn't expect him to humor me, but after a moment, he did. The silver circle held an engraved star in the middle. I lifted it to read his personal identifiers.

"Dominic O. Fischer-Black," I read aloud and then glanced at him. "As in the ruling family Fischers? My, my." I pushed his bifold across the table. "What are you going to do with me?"

"That's up to the LC." He pushed a mint into his mouth. "But I do know he wants you sterilized because the genetic ramifications of clones breeding isn't understood."

"They should've sterilized me as soon as I had my first period," I said, leaning back in my chair. "Tell him not to bother. I already had it done off the books," I lied.

"Who did it?" he said sharply.

My eyes narrowed at his reaction to the biotech property making her own decision. "Relax, it was a tubal ligation, a mostly effective, reversible mechanical barrier to conception. My miscarriage was a dangerous one, and I didn't want to put Cris through another. Whose side are you on, anyway?"

302

"Texas's," he said without hesitation.

I snorted. "I'm on humanity's. Think we'll ever agree on anything?"

"I hope so," he said. "Why did you leave the outlands? You were free."

"I was bored," I said with a ghost of a smile. "Given my dealings with the Hernandez Ministry of Defense, I figured Texas's would give me plenty to work with, and it has. You should see the patterns I see forming over there. It's not very often I get to use the word diabolical, but Defense Minister Juliana Fischer is one diabolical bitch. Her original plan hasn't worked as planned, but she's adjusting masterfully. Even Jason doesn't realize what's happening."

"Yeah, don't bother with the cryptic tease. I have my hands full pulling the plug on the lab."

"How difficult is it to police some bodies, scrap some equipment, and..."

His expression hadn't changed, but I realized the lab wasn't done. Maybe that facility was done, but the lab was eternal like Jason had said.

"You could spend the rest of your life trying to stop it," I said hoarsely, tears stinging my eyes. "But it can't be stopped. It's like illicit drug labs, isn't it? More and more of the tech is out there, more of the clans are developing it, more of the senior staff are encouraging it for their own reasons."

"The LC is debating how much of the lab's work is going to be revealed to the Ministries when he uses the murders as a warning about human trials. The lab was worried about the clones rising up, not the icer victims, who were considered too educated, too moral, and too understanding of the necessity of what was being done."

"We were Americans, remember? Land of the free, home of the brave."

"Being Americans from before the fall meant you all were considered too complacent and too lazy to revolt. Your nation deteriorated for a long time without the masses doing anything more than complain about it."

"I'm not going to sit here and listen to you bash my motherland."

"Even if it's true?"

"Especially because it's true," I snarled.

"Look, the way you feel about the failures of America is the way I feel about the failures of Texas."

"I consider everything in the way I've been handled a failure of Texas," I snapped. "This is all ridiculously easy. I am either a person or I'm not. If I'm not a person, I belong in a contained environment without any trappings that suggest I'm anything other than a laboratory animal. No books, no clothes, nothing more than any simian test subject would get. But if I'm a person, then treat me like one. Let me go or arrest me and put me on trial in front of a jury of my peers. Those are the only choices and you know it. Now am I under arrest or am I walking through that door?"

"You know your position is not that simple. You can't just—"

"Watch me," I snarled. "I have a contractual obligation to return to my firebase, so I'm going back there to fly a plane like only I can fly it to protect the borders of your clan."

"Your clan, too."

"So Texas says, but they sure as hell don't give me any incentive to stay. I mean seriously, Domino, what are the chances I'll ever be treated like a citizen? Zero, right? Why? Because I was born in the wrong century, kidnapped, and stuck in Finley's stupid stasis project while America came tumbling down. How was any of that in my control? Yet I have to pay for it like I'm a felon."

"You fight for Texas. You must value this clan at least a little."

"All that means is that I hated the lab more than I hated the Texas government. I mean, would you ever feel love and loyalty for anyone who finds it inconvenient to recognize your fundamental human rights?"

Pressing his lips together, he picked up his ringing palmer. He listened briefly, the line of his mouth getting even tighter. After he terminated the connection, he nodded at the door. "You've been authorized to return to your firebase."

"Thank you," I said sarcastically to the nearest camera.

CHAPTER 47

GUARDRAIL

As I strode through my hangar, I considered what to tell Tomai. I still didn't know if I could fly. I supposed I could. The whole lab experience seemed to have burned away both my fear and the horrible fury.

Good Night was gone, and another plane crouched in her bay.

Michael watched me approach, wide-eyed. Did he seriously think I'd been gone for good? I was immortal.

"Is that for me?" I asked him, gesturing to the older plane. Harbinger-Ellis no longer had the capacity for building new ones at this point, even if I had earned one.

He nodded. "*Berserker.*"

What a stupid name for a plane. What had the previous pilot been trying to prove? I had a bounty on me because of the way I flew, not because the enemy had been so intimidated by what Jason had christened our jet. "Her name is *Engine Number 9.*"

He smiled, pushing the ball cap so far back his ginger hair showed. "I like that."

I felt Winter's presence behind me, and I turned to face him.

He was stiff. Cold. Confused, too. I was not the same as before. I wasn't calm and controlled anymore. My insides were ashes and embers in a hollow shell.

I embraced him, and his arms eventually lifted to surround me.

"Are you all right?" he murmured.

"Yes."

He left it at that. Like Risa said, he was easy to be with.

We went outside, and he brought me up to speed about the changes in the bay, but I couldn't bring myself to care about new rules and regulations. On a cosmic scale, they were meaningless.

"I was about ready to leave and go back to the outlands," he told me. "You're the only reason I stayed this long."

"Don't say that."

"Why not? This war is crap. We kill people whose only mistake is to show up for duty that day. The guys on the other side of that border are just like you and me."

I raised an eyebrow, and he smiled.

"Well, not like you," he acknowledged. "But good guys anyway, and I'm tired of killing them just because someone told me to. If I have to kill, I want it to be to save the world from some evil madman."

"What on earth have you been reading? Comic books?"

"It's a legitimate medium," he said, brushing a kiss across my mouth so lightly it was sensed more than felt. "You're just a snob."

"That better be an acronym for Svelte Nymph of Beauty."

"I want to spell my name in your freckles."

I snorted, but I was smiling.

Tomai called my name and jerked her chin toward her office. After we were ensconced on either side of her desk, she showed me the screen indicating I had missed a week's worth of mandatory check-ins at the Austin flight academy. A flick of her finger and the screen revealed that I hadn't taken my mandatory flight check, let alone passed it.

"So?" I said, my smile for her cool and amused. "We both know I can get the job done."

"I don't. I do know you went AWOL down there. You showing up here doesn't negate the fact you don't have current orders to be here."

Her rare verbosity told me I'd pissed her off, but the situation didn't call for such emphasis on the technicalities. What did it matter that I'd missed a few roll calls? I was here now, wasn't I?

"Let me get this straight," I said. "You want me to go back down to the flight academy in Austin, check in, and do a simulator flight to prove I can fly when you actually flew with me less than a month ago? All that to get the orders to bring me back to this exact spot?"

"No, I'm requesting a psych eval, too," she said without apology, her shrewd gaze resting on me like she knew an event even more significant than *Good Night*'s demise had occurred since the last time she'd seen me.

"I'm sorry, I thought there was a war on. I checked the schedule on the way in and saw how thin we're stretched. I wasn't aware you had the luxury of sidelining a pilot like me."

Was it my arrogance that made her eyes narrow, or was it the reminder of how much she needed me no matter what condition I was in?

"You're going to get someone killed."

"Definitely," I said with a feral smile.

"Enough with the bullshit bravado. I meant one of us, and you know it. There's no shame in admitting you've lost a step or two."

"Of course there is," I snapped.

"Ty."

"Don't use that Cris tone on me."

"He's worried about you. He and Jason have been calling here constantly to see if we've seen you."

Irritated, I picked at the seam on the thigh of my flight suit. "So what if I took a few days for myself? I need fresh air and open skies to recharge."

"You don't look recharged. In fact, you look worse than ever. How much leave do you have?"

"I don't know," I snarled. "I came here to work, not count my vacation days. Look, let me go back to work. I need a reason to get up in the morning."

"I'm slating you for five days of leave. If you don't have that much time left, I'll give you some of mine. At the end of the week, you will report to the academy for a flight check. I'm authorizing them to pull you for counseling if they feel your performance calls for it."

"What should I do, huh? Sit in a hotel room or the academy barracks waiting for my appointment?"

"You need open air and a great vista? Go down to Big Bend and camp out for a few days. Get this shit out of your system. I need you, but I won't take you like this."

I gritted my teeth. "Five days? Flight check and return to duty on the sixth?"

"If they approve you," she clarified.

"Fine. Whatever. Make sure Michael's got *Engine Number 9* ready for me when I get back."

From there, I went outside and called Cris. "You're an ex. Be an ex and stop checking on me."

"Are you kidding? You knocked Jason out and went on the run."

"Don't be so dramatic. I obviously did not go after the lab because I'm not in a jail or a grave. I was pissed and needed to clear my head. What do I always do when I need to clear my head? I go for a hike. This one was just a little on the long side."

"You drugged my brother."

"Of course I did. He would've had me locked up to save me from myself, and I can't think when I feel caged in. Whether you believe it or not, I did listen to what both of you had to say. I needed to reassess my plan."

I realized I was clutching my wedding ring in my hand. I couldn't bring myself to get rid of the reminder of my tie to him.

"Do you need me to admit I was wrong, Cris? Well, I was."

"What's that supposed to mean?"

"I need to stop dwelling on the past and work toward the future."

"Just like that? A few panicked words from my brother and me and you're suddenly docile and agreeable? Someone threatened you, right?"

"No one had to. I want to be reunited with my child after I die. That wasn't going to happen if I went straight to Hell, even if my motives were pure."

He snorted. "Protecting human rights is the right thing to do, but be honest and admit you were going there for revenge."

310

"I'm not that petty. I already didn't like who I was becoming, but I reached a point where I realized the cost of succeeding was far too high. Why is that so impossible to comprehend?"

"Hang on. Jason just got here. He'll want to speak to you."

"Hello?" Jason said breathlessly. "Who is this?"

I grimaced. "Hi, Jason."

"Fuck you."

I laughed before I could stop it. "I love you, too. Save your breath, okay? I was telling Cris you were right. When push came to shove, I backed down."

"You do not back down."

My grin faded.

He took me off the speaker. "Miranda?"

I flinched. How much had I changed from the first time he'd called me that?

"Jason," I said, and my voice was so hoarse I wasn't sure he could understand it. "The cost was too high."

"Did they threaten one of us?"

"No," I whispered. When I shut my eyes, tears fell onto my cheeks. "They didn't have to. I was corrupted from within."

"I prefer to think you were saved instead."

I clung to the palmer. "Don't be nice. I wasn't."

"Hell, sugar, I know that. I'm taking an Italian temptress out to dinner tonight. I came over to consult Cris about what condom to use."

I disconnected the call and shoved the palmer in my pocket.

Dodging Tomai, I hid out in Winter's bay even after *Spider Monkey* was towed out for a flight.

Winter's words came back to me. How were we making the world a better place by eliminating the men and women in those planes? So what if they were Wilson's people? What possible good could come from the systemic destruction of the best parts of a society? They fought to protect the masses. They were smart, strong, and dutiful, and we killed them off while pardoning vicious criminals due to overcrowding. Why on earth was I being a party to that erosion of civilization?

I waited for Winter, barely able to sit still while his jet was towed into its bay that night.

"I'm done with robbing a weak future of good people," I told him when I couldn't be overheard. "I mean to leave."

"Even if you wanted to, there are a passel of Chavezes that would hunt you down and cuddle you back into submission."

Damn, he was right. There was no walking away. The truth was, if I wanted out of my enlistment, I was confident Jason could manage that, but that wouldn't actually give me the freedom to pursue my own agenda.

"I'd have to have an accident," I said thoughtfully.

Christ, had I really spoken aloud?

Winter regarded me solemnly. When he put his arms around me, I expected his murmur to remind me the repercussions for deserting in a time of war would be severe, but instead he said, "I'm going with you."

"You can meet me. I need to die, and you need to see if it took. If they believe it, you join me when you're ready. I'll be waiting for you. We can disappear in the outlands, can't we?"

"Completely."

"Winter, I'm serious. I'm taking leave, staging my demise, and turning my back on all this senseless death. I mean to make the world a better place."

He withdrew enough to look me in the eye. "What can I do to help, and where do you want to meet afterward?"

But the following morning when he escorted me to the bus that would take me off the firebase for the final time, he said, "It's not too late to change your mind."

"You have doubts?"

"Me? God, no. But you're a lot more attached to these people and this crap than I am."

"No, I'm doing it."

But his words echoed in my mind as I picked up my motorcycle in Austin, and again on the drive south when the torrents of rain came, reminding me I was turning my back on a world of pristine landscaping and climate control.

The motorcycle idled between my legs as I waited for the traffic light to change. It was the last turn. Turning right instead of going straight would put me on a path back toward my firebase. If I turned around, it would take me back to the academy and the Chavez family.

It's not too late.

Winter would be disappointed, but he would appreciate my unease at having so much riding on the actions of others. I could stage an accident all I wanted, but the locals had to be the ones investigating it, and they had to do it in a way that stood up to Jason's scrutiny.

Still, when the red arrow extinguished and the green one was illuminated, I was eager to risk it. I gave my head a sharp shake to clear the rain from the visor of my helmet, and I shot forward toward the entrance to Big Bend Park.

Thank you for recommending this site, Tomai.

After half an hour studying the layout of the park along with the weather forecast, I had to agree this was the perfect place for me to go.

The park ranger at the gate gave me a dubious look when I said I wanted a campsite.

"Lady, it's going to piss rain all night. Don't want a cabin instead?"

"When I called earlier, I was told there were no cabins available."

"We had a cancelation."

"Then, hell, yes, I want a cabin," I retorted, softening my tone with a grin.

After I paid, he showed me where to go on the big wall map, pausing only when the boom of thunder made conversation impossible. "Better hurry," he told me.

"I can't get any wetter," I said with a wry smile, indicating my soaked clothes. "Thanks for your help."

I rode deeper into the park, expecting to see some signs I wasn't the only person out there, but I didn't pass a single vehicle. The boundaries of a sharp turn ahead were marked with a dented guard rail. I checked my odometer, and my heart leapt when I realized it was the right one.

Just like I had envisioned, when I shifted my weight to go through the turn, the rear tire slid on the rain-slick road. I made the expected attempt to correct, but it was too late. The bike went down. My hip, then shoulder hit the pavement. I was dragged off the bike and sent rolling. The momentum drove me along the same path as my bike.

God, I'm good.

The accident file would report I died from a broken neck. Unusual, but not impossible. It was perfect.

My bike hit the guard rail, and two of the old, thick wooden guard rail posts unexpectedly gave way.

Rotted?

No, it was okay. The guard rail sagged but held.

I collided with my bike, and more posts gave way. With a flash of gut-wrenching fear, I tumbled over the side along with my motorcycle.

CHAPTER 48

SHERIFF HIGGINS

It was rumored Sheriff Higgins had a problem.

He was not treated with the same respect as the sheriffs in more populated counties, and since he was a modest man, this was supposedly not an issue. But the locals did cite it as the reason his requests for resources to track down a particularly loathsome man who had taken up residence in the sheriff's beloved Brewster County had been ignored.

When the people who voted him into office asked him how long it would be before their children would be safe, when day after day he must've felt the helplessness and despair grow, well, that's when a lawman might do something he normally wouldn't.

In fact, I was counting on it.

The first man to reach me must've been used to scrambling over broken ground because he reached me while the medic was still fighting with the rappelling harness.

"Found her," the man with the sheriff's badge called out. "The motorcycle, too."

I was sore and bloody, but I hadn't moved a muscle from where I had come to a shuddering stop against a boulder because it took only a few words to turn an accident into a death.

"I'm fine, but if I'm dead, I can kill him," I said, looking up at Sherriff Higgins.

He looked down at me in surprise.

"Stager," I said. "I can kill him and disappear, but only if you let me die first."

"Get the gurney rig," the sheriff called over his shoulder.

"How bad is she?"

The sheriff's dark eyes held mine for a long time, and I could see the conflicted emotions swirling.

"I'm sorry," I said sincerely. "I want the system to work the way it's meant to, too, but sometimes it doesn't. If you're sure about him, absolutely certain he's guilty, I can deal with him. But you have to be able to look me in the eye and tell me it's for the greater good. It's the only way I'll be able to do it."

"Starting CPR. You better hurry," the sheriff told the medic. He eased off my helmet and rolled me onto my back before knotting his hands over my heart and pretending to start compressions. When he switched to pretend mouth-to-mouth, his coffee-scented breath carried a soft question.

"Who are you?"

"My name is Tycho Walker Chavez, and I was a combat pilot. I told them I'd lost my nerve, but they sent me back up anyway. I got two people killed."

Damn, I'd debated that last part while I had lain there and thought I'd decided against it before it fell from my mouth. Would he buy it?

I continued. "I'm on leave, trying to get my head on straight, but there's no going back after a mistake like that. Let me balance the scales by offing your murderer. Please. All you have to do is let me die. I'll never come back to your county again, I promise. I thought a broken neck would do. For me, not Stager."

He yelled back up to the medic, his tone flat. "Take your time. She's gone."

When the medic arrived, I felt his hand like fire on my chilled skin, but he wasn't checking my pulse, just moving my arm out of his way.

"Where's the bioscanner?" the sheriff asked, and I barely caught myself before I reacted. I couldn't fool a machine. If he had changed his mind, all he had to do was say he thought he saw a pulse.

"Broken, same as the last time you asked me."

"Well, are you even going to take a look at the body? You need to be sure she's dead," the sheriff said, making me want to smack him. "Your name's on the paperwork."

"I don't need the bioscanner to determine she's cold, paper white, and unresponsive," the medic said. "Stop pestering me."

"I'd feel better if you checked."

"She went off the road, what, thirty-six hours ago? It stopped raining early yesterday, so when we got down here, was there any sign she tried to drag herself toward shelter or fight off a scavenger? Any sign she moved?"

"Remind me to get a new medic," the sheriff complained.

"You get what you pay for," the medic retorted. "Get my portable bioscanner fixed."

"Your hands aren't broken. Check for pulse and respiration."

"Because you suddenly don't know how? Why are we even fighting about this? If you say she's gone, she's gone."

"It's not enough to me to say she's dead. You have to say it, too."

"All right, I'm saying it. She's dead."

Soon, I felt the sheriff's bony hand on my shoulder, steadying my corpse as the medic tightened the final strap so the gurney could be winched out of the ravine.

"What're we going to do, sheriff? The morgue fridge is still on backorder. I got a bunch of meds in so there's no room for a body to go in my fridge again."

"Well, I don't like folding stiffs in half to get them in there anyway. I'll have Jenny take it to the city morgue."

"After she got fined for illegal transport last time? Good luck."

"The old plant's incinerator probably still works if nothing else. She's going to be ashes in a few days anyway."

"What're you going to tell her family?"

"If she wanted a proper service she should've died in the city."

The medic chuckled.

An hour later, the sheriff opened the trunk of his car and unzipped the body bag enough to open the flap and regard me.

I sat up and saw we were out of sight of the road. He opened a tarp on the ground and helped me out when he realized how stiff and sore I was.

He handed me a set of dry clothes. I quickly donned the tight pants and shirt and yanked on the coat as I scuffed into the old tennis shoes.

"Sorry about the size," he muttered. "You're bigger than I thought."

"It's all right," I said. I wouldn't be wearing them long.

I handed him my clothes, palmer, ID, money, everything. My clothes went back into the body bag, and everything else went into evidence envelopes. I saw my date of death on there: September 3, 2129.

"There won't be enough ashes if you just burn the bag," I felt compelled to point out.

"Oh, I can scrape up enough ashes," he said blandly. "Not everyone here is in the system, but everybody dies. I can think of a girl your size who would've been happy to know I'm going to use her ashes to screw the government."

"Tell me about Stager."

He held out a printed photo with the man's height, weight, eye color, and identifying marks on the back. While I'd been investigating the outlands sheriffs, I'd heard a few rumors about Stager's hatred but not how he'd expressed it other than there had been a body count. Higgins reportedly had a genuine desire to serve and protect the people in his jurisdiction, so if he was sure this man needed to die, that was enough reason for me.

"Do you need him to suffer first?" I asked, studying the photo, holding it with the edge of my T-shirt so I didn't leave fingerprints on it.

"I need him dead," he said painfully.

"No, you need your people to feel safe again. I'm the one who needs him dead," I told him, returning the picture.

"He was last seen in the northeast corner of the county."

"I'll find him."

"You've done this before, haven't you?"

"Sir, I promised I wouldn't come back to your jurisdiction after the deed is done. You don't need to know anything else."

I wrapped the plastic bags around my shoes to obscure my footprints until the next rain. With the black clouds building on the horizon, I was hoping it would be only a few hours away.

I stepped off the tarp and he added it to the body bag to be burned.

After he shut the trunk, he looked at me without saying anything. I wondered if he was thinking about the line he was crossing, the step in the direction away from the man he wanted to believe he was.

"It's time for you to leave," I said gently.

He spun on his heel and got in his car.

I watched him drive off, murmuring, "What a sad world."

When he was out of sight, I spent a considerable amount of time obscuring his tire tracks along the length of the turn-off.

Satisfied, I turned my back to the site and started hiking. I found I was smiling despite the pains and the discomfort.

Hell, I was laughing.

It took me only a day to get to the cache where I had stashed Mauss's gun along with first aid supplies, food and water, and a change of clothes.

I ended up needing four days to find Stager and another three to catch him alone. I used two bullets, one for each eye. I left his body where the sheriff was sure to hear about it, and as promised, I left his county.

I still had another three weeks before I was due to meet up with Winter, but I found myself rushing to get to our rendezvous point. The sheriff's face haunted me, and I needed Winter to reassure me the sheriff and I weren't evil people.

Another question was bothering me that I doubted he'd be able to help me with, though. I was starting to wonder what the difference was between freedom and anarchy.

Unfortunately, I was able to ask him a lot sooner than expected.

"What the hell are you doing here?" I asked bluntly, avoiding his embrace. "We agreed you would wait a month to make sure there were no complications."

"I knew you were going to be fine."

"There's a time for faith and there's a time for sticking to the goddamned plan. Did you take leave like you were supposed to?"

"Tomai wouldn't give it to me. We were short with you out."

"You went AWOL? You were supposed to get as much leave as you could so they wouldn't be looking for you immediately."

"It's fine. We're fine."

"When?" I demanded icily. "When did you go AWOL?"

"Right after you left."

"What?" I said, the color draining from my face. "You left before I was even pronounced dead? If the plan had failed or I had changed my mind, I would've returned to the firebase, and you would've been gone. What were you thinking?"

"I wanted to be with my girlfriend," he snapped.

"Are you kidding me? I trusted you."

"I'm here, aren't I? If you couldn't trust me, there would've been a military police contingent meeting you here instead of me."

"You—"

"Stop," he told me. "It's fine. We're safe. I wouldn't have moved up the timetable if I didn't think so."

"It wasn't your call," I said bluntly.

"I'm the one who's going to make us disappear, remember? You could show some gratitude for everything I do for you. I even got a solid headshot of the chick who looks like you on Firebase One in case you ever want to find out if she is your mom."

I jerked at the mention of her. "Let me see it."

"Nice manners."

"I'm still super pissed at you, Winter. Show me the pic of her."

He had abandoned his palmer along with the rest of his electronics, so what he showed me was a hand-sized hard copy photo of Bookworm, the woman I was sure Cris had left me for. It was a quality image, making it so much worse because there was absolutely no mistaking she and I were from the same genetic line.

Trembling, I sat down on the nearest rock.

"Ty?"

"Not my mother," I said hoarsely. "But I do have to go see her, the sooner the better."

"She's on a firebase," Winter reminded me. "We're free and clear. We're not going back."

"I am," I said. "Not this moment, but I am definitely heading east and waiting for the moment she steps off the firebase."

"Who is she?"

"It doesn't concern you. Not yet, anyway. She may be joining us later on down the line."

"Like hell," he said firmly. "I'm not risking you for some stranger, and I'm not fighting about her here. We need to table all this emotion until we get to our next stop."

"You're right. We need to keep moving."

He held out his hand for the photo, but I stuck it in my jacket pocket instead.

"We don't even hold hands now?"

"I thought you wanted the picture to destroy it so I forget about going after her."

He stared stonily at me. "That's what you think of me?"

"The way you deviated from the plan makes me wary," I snapped. I held out my hand, but this time he was the one who wouldn't take it.

In angry silence, we left the rendezvous point.

No, this wasn't the reunion I'd had in mind at all. The fatal flaw involving any plan that had more than one person in it was that there was more than one person in it. It sure as hell didn't help that Winter now had damaging information against me. I had far more to lose than he did if we were captured and charged with desertion in a time of war.

Christ, I'd really wanted to be able to trust him.

CHAPTER 49

FREEDOM

My back against a pine near the ridgeline of the Guadalupe Mountains, I opened the neck of my coat with my left hand to let the wind wash over my skin as I watched the November sun set over West Texas. I had little love for the government, and frankly, I'd seen prettier places, but the way Texas herself endured through the centuries compelled me to stay within the borders instead of chasing foreign horizons.

When I shifted, I felt my wedding ring from Cris on the chain around my neck. I hadn't forgotten about the woman on FOB One. Cris had hit me over a lie he believed I'd given him, but I suspected the lie was on her side. Maybe she had even tried to pass herself off as the real Miranda. She looked the right age for it. Whether she wanted to call herself Bookworm, AMF, or another name, she was in for one hell of a surprise if she thought I'd tolerate her looking like me, acting like me, and stealing my husband. I just hoped I could keep from breaking her neck like a twig before I got some answers.

It felt good to be able to think without self-censoring again. As delighted as I'd been when Winter had gotten me pregnant, I'd still felt the burden of the obligation of keeping my thoughts pure in order to maintain her innocence and cultivate a natural excitement and curiosity about life.

Winter. What an apt name in the end. The strain in our relationship had eased with our eagerness to show the child the world, but his harsh pragmatism returned with the force of a Siberian wind as soon as we learned the fetus had fallen prey to a developmental issue like the one that had cost my first child her life. I hadn't been able to control my reaction to his announcement he had arranged for an abortion, so I'd gone through the miscarriage alone.

I felt the last of her ashes on my right hand and caught myself before I wiped my fingers on my jeans. As I continued to climb east over the mountains, the last of her would rub off on bark and rock to nourish Texas.

As more and more of my adopted homeland fell under the velvety colors of nightfall, I felt myself smile. I loved that I had the capacity to make Texas a better place for people to live in and love in and even raise a family in if God so blessed them that way. Cris had been correct that one person could make a difference. I finally understood that I already had been personally responsible for some positive changes to society, and I meant to continue to improve the lives of the good, honest, hard-working people of Texas.

After all, I still had Mauss's gun, and I had five bullets left.

EPILOGUE

"This has to be because she destroyed her lab, right?"

"You need to stop asking me that," Jason said, rubbing his temples. Why had he agreed to his brother's visit to his house? He should have known what the conversation would revolve around. "We know she returned to the firebase. Why would they let her anywhere near a fully armed warbird if she had succeeded in her nihilistic plan?"

"But the timing," Cris insisted. "It can't be a coincidence."

"She is dead. It no longer matters what her involvement was."

Cris glared over the edge of his coffee mug, his jaw tensing at the explicit reference to Miranda's death.

"Doesn't matter? The Texas legislature passed a law expanding the government's right to human biologics. If someone classified as a vital clan asset is dying, they could harvest any organ from anyone who's a close enough match to repair him. You won't let us use a clone's tissues to fix him? Fine, we'll use you instead."

"I know what it means."

"She did this," Cris said, his mug hitting the table with so much force the coffee slopped over the sides to puddle on the dining table.

Jason watched the spread of the coffee, but the need to wipe it up and chastise his brother was absent. He found it a challenge to care about anything now that Miranda had slipped through his fingers yet again. How many times had he played his game, pushing her away even as he tried to draw her back to his side where she belonged? Why did he always assume he had all the time in the world to be with her?

Feeling the familiar clench of loss, he pressed his hand over his heart. First Miranda had died at Greyson, then their son in Italy, and now Miranda had died again. Perhaps God didn't mean for him to have a family. But without a family to share his life with, what was the point?

Cris's voice rose. "She destroyed the lab's capacity to clone, so they had to do this. She did this by shoving the issue right in their faces."

Jason wondered if it had occurred to Cris yet that if that were true, it was then likely her death was the result of a MoST termination order.

His beautiful, clever Miranda. So much talent wasted on her obsession with that laboratory.

Dully, he said, "The law will get overturned."

"Of course it will," Cris said, his voice shrill. "They'll use the repeal to pave the way."

Jason knew the MoD had DNA from both of them on file. Hell, most of his family had been sampled as the usual precaution for identifying military remains. How soon would it be before he walked into his classroom and saw a young version of his own face staring back at him?

328

His son was dead and the other Chavez siblings had not reproduced, and as they aged, the chances of them doing so decreased. And the Defense Minister did love their bloodline.

"Jason, did you hear me?"

"I heard you," Jason whispered, head in his hands. "They are going to use the backlash from this law to get the anti-cloning laws repealed."

Now, enjoy a bonus short from Jordana Wells

SWITCH

October 1, 2014, 5:14 AM
Chicago, Illinois, USA

Rion flipped the switch and was half-surprised when the workshop came awash with light. Working as a contractor for a single individual often left him feeling like he was standing on the precipice of a cliff. One word too far in the wrong direction and he could find himself cut off from the lab and out in the street again, trying to hawk his hypothesis to an academic world run by conservative white-haired men who were so afraid of publishing something later proven false that all they did was approve projects that couldn't be proven at all or had been proven already. He had so much more to lose than publishing rights, though. This was his life's work.

Too bad the man he worked for was so sensitive about security. They were Rion's ideas, after all. Why was he the one searched at the beginning and end of every trip to the lab to prove he wasn't smuggling out his own research data? If anything, Rion should be frisking *him*.

With a shudder at the snap of latex gloves, Rion said, "Could we skip the proctology exam today?"

"Do you want to work today?" his employer asked.

Rion sighed again and stripped out of his Ramones T-shirt, jeans, and tighty-whities. And people wondered why he worked three-day shifts. He didn't think his ass could take a daily body cavity search for smuggled memory sticks.

Why was he putting up with this? He could find another way to get the money and equipment he needed to—

Well, no, he couldn't. This was a singular opportunity.

He bent over.

Lupe crouched to pick up the stack of gift cards she'd accidentally knocked off the coffee shop counter with her purse. No one helped her, but they did take the time to groan and comment about the delay.

A man with refined features appeared and asked what she was having. She recognized his voice from the phone calls, and he placed their order.

Juggling her drink while watching the swing of her oversized purse, she wriggled through the crowd to claim a newly emptied table before someone else could. Normally she was fine with standing, but the man had bought her coffee so she wanted to show her appreciation.

When she thought about money, she thought of designer clothes, a great watch, and an air of entitlement that announces the guy thinks you're his bitch just because you're working class. This man didn't have any of that. All he had were cultured speech patterns and a comfort with pulling an envelope fat with twenties and fifties out of his suit coat pocket and sliding it across the table.

"What am I looking for?" she asked him, laying her hand on the envelope and pulling it straight back. The edge caught the water ring left from the previous patron, but soggy bills spent just as well as dry ones.

The man—he had introduced himself as Adam—looked up and away as he appeared to choose his words.

Was he suspicious of his lover? Her new client did seem on the effete side and showed a disinterest in her rack, which other men assured her was stare-worthy. But he showed no interest in other men either, so who knew? All that mattered was he thought he had a problem that some high-priced, selectively scrupulous lawyer couldn't handle.

"I'm concerned with signs of anything unusual," Adam said finally.

"Everyone's different. Some a lot, and some a little. Can you narrow it down?"

"Well, he has an affinity for engineering and physics, so that would be normal. He smokes and likely does drugs. His diet is poor. He's tattooed and pierced, too. I'm looking for anything unusual for *him*."

The man looked thoughtful again, and she waited patiently. For what he paid, she would hang around for a month to let him find the words.

He said, "Perhaps his finances might be revealing. You'll see payments from me—"

"So he works for you?"

He nodded. "I think that's enough to go on." He gave her the target's name, description, and address. "We'll meet back here next week, same time, same place."

"I'll have something for you a lot sooner than that."

"I'm sure. However, I enjoy the cranberry scones here, and they only serve them on Tuesdays."

She watched him leave to see which way he would go, what he drove, or if he put the phone to his ear as if speaking to a partner. He simply crossed the street with the rest of the traffic, and his navy pinstriped suit disappeared with the other suits in the financial district at this time of day.

She sipped her mocha latte. Since Adam had picked up the tab, she'd eagerly ordered one. It wasn't as good as she remembered. The chocolate tasted powdery. She kept drinking it though, unwilling to waste such an expensive luxury.

Automatically, she scanned the other patrons looking for that sign of someone caught in a dilemma or a slow-building rage or anything else that might make a person need the services of a person like her. People did glance at her in return: her thirty extra pounds and cheap clothes stood out in this district. Most of the time, it let her slip around unnoticed, especially if she wore a worn wedding ring and a giant mom purse. Adam had changed the meeting location at the last minute like he suspected her to bug their scheduled meeting place before he got there.

Yeah, she knew Adam was a clever one. But he paid well, too. Very well. If he was trying to buy her love and loyalty, well, mission accomplished.

Yet she scanned the coffee shop's customers for her next client anyway.

Adam left far earlier than strictly necessary to make it to his meeting with Lupe the following week. He took taxis and trains and walked, always changing direction, doubling back, and otherwise making it nearly impossible for someone to follow him.

Not seeing her in the diner, he felt a hint of irritation. Granted, he had changed the location, but that wasn't enough reason for her to be late.

"Hi."

He turned to see her fold her umbrella in the entryway. Her appearance was conservative and polished to better blend into the business district, so she looked overdressed for the diner. She showed no discomfort over that.

2

She ordered a Cobb salad and water with a slice of lemon with an elegant gesture of her hand. She was quite the chameleon, he realized in disgust. A practiced liar.

She detailed discrepancies in Rion's life, but Adam didn't react until she said, "He stopped all automatic payments out of his checking account."

"Are you certain? Perhaps he is closing the account and opening another."

Lupe nodded. "It's possible."

"Find out what's going on there. See if Rion closed out his bank accounts or stopped his internet service. Go to his apartment, too. Look for signs he means to go away for a while."

"Like suitcases?"

"Like signs he's been shredding paperwork or downsizing the amount of personal stuff. What would you do if you couldn't take it with you, but you don't want strangers going through it?"

"You think he's going to run out on you."

Adam smiled at that. "Yes," he lied. "That's exactly what I think."

After the mercenary private investigator had left the diner, Adam felt sick to his stomach from the exchange. He hated lies and secret agendas. Everywhere he looked he saw malice, greed, and corruption on such a massive scale that good people were losing ground faster and faster. Society was a festering cesspool. He couldn't wait to leave it all behind.

God, the world sucked.

Rion had been mugged on his way to the lab. They got younger and meaner every year, but when a kid's got cold eyes and a gun in his hand, his age doesn't matter. You give up your wallet. Lucky for Rion, there was nothing in there worth taking anymore.

Adam was waiting. Rion knew he was late, but he wasn't about to explain why.

He blew cigarette smoke in Adam's face and grinned when the other man coughed. Adam had that whole rich bitch feel to him, and Rion loved thinking up new ways to throw shit on the elegant, cultured man. He'd had a friend buy some really disgusting porn to unsettle Adam, but Rion was actually so repulsed by it that he couldn't bring himself to touch those magazines. God, the crap people got all sexed up about. The world was a truly messed-up place.

"I'm happy to see you back at work," Adam said. "How was your weekend?"

"I met this little whore who looked like you. I made her suck my dick."

Adam's gaze was patient.

Rion ground out his cigarette. The truth was he'd gone to see his grandmother, not that she'd recognized him. The last person on earth who cared about him had succumbed to mental disease. She didn't even smell like vanilla and face powder anymore, just of age and death. That wasn't happening to him.

He threw a pair of latex gloves at the man. "Well, stick your finger up my ass so we can get started, will you?"

He quickly settled in, and fingers flew over the keyboard, bringing up four screens of data. Adam did spend some serious coin to give Rion everything he needed, so everything he had was state of the art. He never would've been able to come close to finishing his research without the other man's help, but that didn't make Rion any more grateful. It irritated him that he lost grant money to theoretical scientists when his work had practical, real-world applications. But it pissed him off that Adam had no intention of letting Rion publish and share his ideas

4

for people to build on. Adam just wanted the golden ticket for himself and to hell with everyone else.

Rion said, "I had a bad acid trip that ended up doing me a favor by giving me an idea how to combat the toxicity of the antifreeze."

It was only to clarify his thoughts that he spoke aloud, launching into a detailed description of how he intended to solve the problem and test it. If alone, he would've said it to the spider plant Adam had brought in to purify the air.

Adam's expression never changed, and he nodded from time to time. Rion doubted that asshole understood any of it, but at least when he heard big words and saw graphs, he kept the money coming.

Not that Rion would need it much longer. This had been the last hurdle. Human trials would come next.

Well, one human's trial. Rion built it, and he would be the first to use it.

He couldn't help himself. He traded his usual snarl for a smile.

Adam saw the tattooed freak's stained teeth and was again amazed that such wonderful intelligence should be wasted on such a worthless human being.

"That's amazing," Adam said, meaning it. Between his M.D. and his extensive reading, he had a firm grasp of what Rion meant to do. Adam understood the ideas. He just couldn't come up with or execute them. "What kind of food would you like delivered today?"

Rion ignored the question, fingers flying over the keyboard.

Adam unlocked the double doors to the other end of the workshop to admire—worship—their creation. The pod stood eight feet tall and three feet wide. The center was a large, clear tube with a hinged lid, and it was framed by such an array of wires, hoses, pumps, and computers that it left him speechless with awe. Behind it was another three feet of equipment, already encased in its metal alloy housing. He rested his hand on it, feeling the faint hum beneath.

They were so close now. So close.

Four days after his lightning bolt about the toxicity issue, Rion was one person away from getting one of Sal's legendary Reuben sandwiches. It was worth the hour-long line. Plus it gave him the time to talk himself out of stopping by the liquor store afterward for a malty, yeasty microbrew. He didn't want to celebrate the completion of his project with an icon of his alcoholism. He liked believing he was strong enough to have an ice water even if he knew the next meal would be his last.

From Lupe's expression the next morning, Adam knew this was the final meeting. He ordered a croissant and a macchiato, but what he was truly savoring was the idea of what she had to tell him.

"He didn't close out anything," she told him as she sat down with her caramel latte. "He just stopped payments and cleaned out the accounts. He also did cash advances on all his credit cards, pulling as much money as they would let him."

"And his apartment?"

"It's empty except for some clothes and furniture. There's some fresh food in the refrigerator, so I think you may have at least a couple of days before he runs. Oh, and the money's not there."

He knew Rion must've converted his American cash into something timeless and tangible, like gold, silver, or gems.

6

Could she see the leap of his pulse? She must've. Like him, she knew things were coming to a head. Could she sense the excitement he tried to hide? He saw the flickers of canny intelligence in her eyes and knew she had an inkling of the importance of what was going on. That was unfortunate.

She said, "What do you want me to do now?"

"Nothing." He handed her an envelope with enough money that she would feel pleasantly compensated, but not so much she would think him a fool to milk for more. "I can handle it from here."

She tucked the envelope into her purse without counting it. Delicately, she said, "I can provide other services. Stop him from leaving. Even if you want me to stop him permanently."

She meant it, he saw.

"The kind of porn he had in there makes me sick," she said grimly. "No one will miss this guy, I promise you. Just something to keep in mind."

"I expect this woman to be well taken care of," Rion said, stabbing his cigarette into his plate. God, why did he start smoking again? It tasted like shit. Blowing the smoke in Adam's face hadn't been worth it. "I just spent a ton of money on this. I've got a great lawyer who will come after you if her hair is greasy like you haven't been washing it or anything like that. And if I hear of even the tiniest bed sore, I will personally cut you a new one with a razor blade."

"Your grandmother will be well taken care of, sir."

"She better be. She's a good woman."

He terminated the connection and threw the phone into the trash along with his pack of cigarettes and his lighter. He gripped the brown paper bag in his hands, knowing the cylinder looked like he was hiding a bottle of booze. At the post office, he opened the bag and unrolled the large envelope filled with handwritten notes and schematics. Adam could frisk him all day long, but he couldn't stop him from writing out his notes from memory.

There was no way he wasn't sharing what he'd created, but it had taken a while to figure out who to send it to. There weren't many people who wouldn't turn around and hand it over to some corporation for a few bucks or commercialize it for their own gain. Other people he knew would hand it over to the government, which was even worse. No, this tech was for the scientific visionaries to build on.

Once the package was mailed, he stepped out onto the sidewalk, feeling better than he ever had before. It was done. Everything on his list was done, so it was time to leave.

He felt light, his lips stretching into a smile.

He laughed outright when he thought of Adam. He thought he was buying a cryopreservation unit that would safely preserve a living person in stasis. Rion had no intention of saving rich assholes like Adam until medicine had caught up with whatever illness they had. After Rion had built it to work perfectly, he'd worked in a little gift that guaranteed it would fail well before the alarms signaled the inhabitant was in trouble. The sedative would wear off before that, too. Rion hoped Adam would regain enough consciousness to know who had screwed him before he died.

But first, it was Rion's turn in the unit.

His hand curled around the bottle of pills in his pocket. His plan was simple. Just before he showed up at the workshop like usual, he would take the entire bottle of prescription sedatives. After being let in, he was going to knock Adam out cold, take his keys, and lock him out of the lab.

8

Then Rion would initiate the automatic start on his cryotube and step in without any of the prep work. No antifreeze meant that when the water in his body froze, the tiny ice spears would puncture his cells. He wouldn't feel it. He wanted his cryotube to be the mechanism of his suicide, but that didn't mean he wanted it to hurt. He'd been hurting for years, drugs and booze failing to put a dent in the depression and helplessness of living in a world where nobody gave a shit about each other. Even his bitch of a mother had stolen everything from her own mother before abandoning them both. He'd never forgotten that look on his grandmother's face.

When Adam first approached him, Rion thought maybe they could do some good, maybe help people explore other worlds. It had given him hope for a time, and he'd prayed his grandmother would stay lucid long enough for him to make her proud.

He'd been a fool. Adam was only in it for himself.

He hoped that after Adam read the suicide note and thawed him, Rion would make a giant mess on the rich man's polished shoes.

A bounce in his step, he went down the alley to his workshop.

A lost, corn-fed tourist whirled. She giggled nervously, her hand gripping her enormous purse underneath her plentiful breasts. "Can you point me towards the subway station?"

"Sure, lady," he sighed, wondering if she knew how lucky she was she'd run into him and not some dreg of society. "You're only a block off. I'll show you."

As soon as he got close to her, she straightened, her expression transforming into something hard and cold. Before his surprise fully registered, she shot him in the face.

Adam flipped on the light and was blinded with a shaft of bright light. His mood was too good for that to annoy him. In fact, he laughed and ducked around the harsh beam. Seeing spots in front of his eyes, he climbed down into the underground lab in Texas. The smell of stone and secrets filled him with an aching pleasure. His heart throbbed wildly when he saw the fiftieth cryogenics unit had finished its diagnostics and was green across the board. The unit had been subject to a rushed dismantling at the workshop followed by transport over many miles of rough ground. He'd been afraid that might create a few faults to be worked out, but it was a sturdy unit intended for space travel, so it had survived the trip.

The last unit. As far as Rion had believed, it was the only one. Adam saw no reason to tell Rion that over the past four years as soon as he perfected a section of the unit, Adam produced forty-nine more. The few setbacks had been minor, and Adam had been fine with the cost of fine-tuning multiple units.

Rion was dead. The presumption of the man to think he would be a part of the future with cryo was insulting. No matter his intellect, who would want him in their community?

Lupe was dead, too. Adam liked things nice and neat.

Like the number fifty. Forty-nine amazing people unappreciated in their time were already in stasis. His goal had been to take one from each of the fifty states, but he'd had to quickly regroup after the tragic death of his Pennsylvania representative in a mugging. He'd decided to take the man's wife, Ms. Illinois, as planned, but in acquiring her, he'd been delighted to come across an equally gifted woman. What did it matter if all the states weren't represented? There probably wouldn't be any states left by the time they woke. Thanks to that last-minute change, he now had an equal number of men and women, and he so did love balance.

It showed the spectrum of specialties reflected in his collective, too. He had engineers, biologists, poets, philosophers, and more. Brilliant, young, and moral, they were the best in America, perfect for preserving for a future beyond this pathetic travesty of a society. That broken nation would collapse, and the bright new world would welcome Adam's gifts. The people he kidnapped would eventually forgive him, too, once their gifts were embraced instead of corporations and government twisting them for profit. It would be utopia on Earth.

The cryotube in front of him was for himself. Number fifty. He was a neurosurgeon. He knew a mind worth saving.

With a burning yearning for a better world, he stripped down and injected the cocktails in the proper sequence. He'd already had several injections of the bio-antifreeze to make sure it permeated his whole system.

"God protect us," he whispered as he looked down at the clusters of cryo units. "God protect us all."

He stepped into his unit, his racing heart thumping erratically as the sedative started dragging him under. He reached around and flipped the switch for the auto-start sequence.

Visit author Jordana Wells at:

JordanaWells.com

Be on the lookout for
Phase Shift: DNA Strand 4

The war between the Republic of Texas and the Clan Wilson is taking its toll on aging pilot Book, who wants nothing more than to keep passing her medical exams so she can keep flying her jet next to her best friend, Hemi. But when the Chavez brothers reveal there is another combat pilot with her face, her name, and her DNA, she realizes that staying in the air may be the least of her problems. As proof mounts that the other woman's claims are legitimate, Book fights to regain her missing memories and recover the secret to who—or what—she truly is.

Coming soon!

www.ingramcontent.com/pod-product-compliance
Lightning Source LLC
Chambersburg PA
CBHW020826180626
46814CB00001B/117